SPECIAL MESSAGE TO READERS

This book is published under the auspices of

THE ULVERSCROFT FOUNDATION

(registered charity No. 264873 UK)

Established in 1972 to provide funds for research, diagnosis and treatment of eye diseases. Examples of contributions made are: —

A Children's Assessment Unit at Moorfield's Hospital, London.

•

Twin operating theatres at the Western Ophthalmic Hospital, London.

•

A Chair of Ophthalmology at the Royal Australian College of Ophthalmologists.

•

The Ulverscroft Children's Eye Unit at the Great Ormond Street Hospital For Sick Children, London.

You can help further the work of the Foundation by making a donation or leaving a legacy. Every contribution, no matter how small, is received with gratitude. Please write for details to:

THE ULVERSCROFT FOUNDATION,
The Green, Bradgate Road, Anstey,
Leicester LE7 7FU, England.
Telephone: (0116) 236 4325

In Australia write to:
THE ULVERSCROFT FOUNDATION,
c/o The Royal Australian and New Zealand
College of Ophthalmologists,
94-98 Chalmers Street, Surry Hills,
N.S.W. 2010, Australia

Emily Hendrickson lives in Reno, Nevada, with her husband. In addition to her many Regency romances, she has also written a Regency reference book.

THE WICKED PROPOSAL

Beautiful Lady Penelope Winthrop wants a husband — but in name only. With her wealth she can purchase the ideal mate — the disappearing kind. And when she helps the Earl of Harford, her distant cousin, to win a wager, he agrees to assist Penelope in her quest. But he finds fault with every candidate for her hand. Over time Penny realizes that she loves the handsome lord. However, when she finds a love letter written to Jonathan by another woman, a wounded Penny returns home. He dashes after her . . . and a race for love begins!

Books by Emily Hendrickson
Published by The House of Ulverscroft:

A PERILOUS ENGAGEMENT
HIDDEN INHERITANCE
LADY SARA'S SCHEME
THE GALLANT LORD IVES
QUEEN OF THE MAY
DOUBLE DECEIT

EMILY HENDRICKSON

THE WICKED PROPOSAL

Complete and Unabridged

ULVERSCROFT
Leicester

First published in Great Britain in 2008 by
Robert Hale Limited
London

First Large Print Edition
published 2009
by arrangement with
Robert Hale Limited
London

British Library CIP Data

Hendrickson, Emily
The wicked proposal.—Large print ed.—
Ulverscroft large print series: historical romance
1. Aristocracy (Social class)—Fiction 2. Love stories
3. Large type books
I. Title
813.5′4 [F]

ISBN 978–1–84782–553–7

Published by
F. A. Thorpe (Publishing)
Anstey, Leicestershire

Set by Words & Graphics Ltd.
Anstey, Leicestershire
Printed and bound in Great Britain by
T. J. International Ltd., Padstow, Cornwall

This book is printed on acid-free paper

1

The young woman garbed in a soft blue pelisse to reflect her sensible blue eyes resolutely entered the attractive town house situated on Upper Brook Street. 'Lady Penelope Winthrop to see Miss Winthrop, if you please,' she intoned in her best manner and with the regal air of one born to command.

Giving a significant look at her companion and former governess, Miss Nilsson, Penelope waited with not a few trepidations while the stout woman in black bombazine — the housekeeper, most likely — trotted off toward the rear of the house, mumbling something about hunting for her mistress. Clearly this was an unusual household.

Penelope glanced about with curious eyes. Although the place appeared respectable enough, peculiar touches could be seen here and there, like the Grecian bust with a paisley shawl draped over his head and a clutch of peacock feathers stuck at a crazy angle in the umbrella stand. She wondered if her cousin possessed a pianoforte, for Penelope dearly loved to play. She did rather well, finding music company.

'I do hope she received my letter,' she muttered to Nilsson in a soft aside.

'I warned you against coming ahead without a clear understanding, my dear,' Nilsson replied in a similarly quiet tone. The basket at her feet gave a lurch, and an inquisitive nose poked from beneath the lid, whiskers quivering, followed by the tip of an orange striped tail and a questing paw. 'It is to be hoped that she will tolerate your pet. Not everyone appreciates a cat, you know.'

An offended 'Meow' followed this comment.

'I shall pay for any damages.'

'How many times must I remind you that you cannot always buy your way through life?' Miss Nilsson said with a touch of asperity in her usually mild voice.

Penelope gave Miss Nilsson a wry look. 'So far it has proved to be remarkably effective. I have yet to see a person who will turn down money.'

'One day you shall discover the truth of the matter. I only hope it does not turn out to be a painful experience.'

An end to this familiar lecture came with the rustle of skirts. A short, plump young woman with untidy brown hair and gold spectacles perched on her little nose peered at the callers with obvious puzzlement as she hurried toward where they waited. She halted directly before Penelope, studying her with a disconcerting gaze. 'Your face is familiar, but I fear I cannot recall where we met,' Miss Winthrop declared with disarming frankness. Tilting her head, she extended her hand in greeting. 'At any rate, welcome.' A paisley shawl similar to the one on the Greek head was draped across her shoulders at a perilous angle, looking about to slide off.

'I am your cousin. You stayed at our home, Fountains, in Kent a few years ago while you painted butterflies and flowers. And this is my companion, Miss Nilsson,' Penelope explained patiently. 'You urged me to visit you sometime.'

'Penelope!' Lettice exclaimed in recognition. 'I believe I had a letter from you not long ago. At least, I think I did. I could not find my spectacles at the moment, and it was put aside.' Turning to the housekeeper, hovering in the background, she added, 'Where did I put that letter?'

The older woman sighed, then shuffled off down the hall, muttering softly to herself as she went. She disappeared through a door near the end of the hall.

Suddenly recalling her manners, Lettice nodded her head toward the hall, then led them along into the haphazardly furnished morning room. 'She ought to have brought you in here, but one does never know.'

At Penelope's silence, Lettice went on, 'But of course you do not know, for how could you? You see,' she confided, 'I am dreadfully absentminded and nearly everyone knows about my difficulty. Ladies sometimes seek my advice, although why they should is totally beyond me. I doubt I would be of help to anyone.'

Hoping the dismay she felt was not revealed on her face, Penelope glanced at Miss Nilsson, then back at her cousin. 'I see. In that case, perhaps I had best leave you.'

'Nonsense! I declare, I am vastly diverted. Why have you suddenly turned up on my doorstep? You have changed a great deal, you know. I say that in defense of my not recognizing you at first. The alteration into womanhood can be most striking in some girls. You certainly have become a beauty,' she concluded without a trace of envy in her voice.

Clearing a restricted throat, Penelope replied, 'I wrote you all about it.' Deciding she might as well plunge to the heart of the problem, now recalling how her cousin could take it into her head to wander off in the middle of a conversation, Penelope continued, 'I need to find a husband, a not-too-unusual dilemma, I fancy. However, I do not wish Cousin Ernest or his mother to know about my decision to wed. One of these days Aunt Winthrop is sure to remember my age and get the idea in her head that she will marry me to Ernest. I assure you that would not be the least to my liking.'

'I fail to see how I may help you, although I can see why you'd not wish to marry our toad of a cousin.' Lettice turned as the housekeeper bustled into the room with a piece of stiff cream paper in her hand. 'Is this it? Wherever did you find it?'

'Stuck in the potted fern, Miss Letty.'

'Fancy that,' Lettice mused as she broke the seal and began reading the letter that had been sent off two weeks before. 'Yes, I see, it is just as you say.'

'Will that be all?' the housekeeper prompted.

'You had best prepare rooms for my cousin and her companion.'

The housekeeper eyed the basket at Penelope's feet with a suspicious look. 'And what's that?'

'That is Muffin, my cat. I could not spend time away from her, for she would never forgive me,' Penelope replied.

Lettice nodded as though the statement made perfect sense. Miss Nilsson exchanged resigned looks with the housekeeper, then stepped forward. 'I'm Miss Nilsson, Mrs . . . ?'

'Flint, ma'am.' She edged toward the door, a harried expression settling on her face.

'Perhaps I may lend a hand, Mrs Flint? I know how it can be when unexpected guests arrive on the scene.' Actually, Miss Nilsson had had little to do with guests, but she sensed the poor housekeeper would be grateful for any help she might get. Nilsson picked up Muffin's basket and followed Mrs Flint from the room.

As the door closed behind the older women, Lettice frowned again. 'I have never heard that accent before. Is it Swedish? I believe it rather charming. I am surprised you have not caught it from her.'

'I doubt you can catch an accent, Lettice, even a Swedish one,' Penelope said, a smile lighting her eyes.

'I suppose not,' Lettice replied with obvious regret in her voice. 'Now,' she went on, 'I should like to know all the details not in your letter and omitted to this point. Like, what sort of husband do you seek? I suppose he must be wildly handsome and sinfully rich.'

'Not at all,' Penelope said with a hint of laughter lurking in her words. 'All I require is a man who will marry me, then take himself off to wherever it is that men enjoy spending their days. As long as he does not bother me, I shall be glad.'

'Goodness! What a peculiar way of looking at marriage. Not very romantic, I must say. It offends the poet in my soul.' Lettice gave Penelope a thoughtful stare, then nodded for her cousin to continue.

'If you must know, I have never believed in love,' Penelope confessed. 'I suppose my parents were examples of such. However, since I rarely saw them, I had little chance to judge for myself. I think it to be simpler and far less trouble to find a gentleman — for I must marry someone equal to my station, I suppose — and make it clear he is free to go as he pleases. I hope he will take himself off to the Continent, as my parents did, and never be seen again.'

'Pity, that,' Lettice murmured. 'You might feel differently had your parents been home instead of forever traipsing about the world. But I still do not understand why you wish to select a husband in such a cold-blooded manner. No poetry in the least.'

'No interference, either. I like my life as it is. Herbs and medicine fascinate me. I enjoy cooking as well. Can you imagine a gentleman permitting me to indulge my fancy in the kitchen?' She gave a toss of her head, revealing the pure line of her cheek, an errant blond curl.

'Take off that bonnet, please.' When

Penelope complied, Lettice rubbed the end of her nose while she studied her cousin, then said, 'I should think your husband would indulge your fancy anywhere you took a notion to indulge, if you catch my meaning.'

'I am not certain I do, but let it pass. What I need is someone to take me about, help me with a mantua-maker, and point out the man most likely to agree to my proposal.'

'Sounds wicked to me, tricking a man into marriage not intended to be a real one.'

'Even in the wilds of Kent, tales reach my ears of the London gentlemen. They gamble, wench, and generally enjoy their life of debauchery. I suspect that somewhere there is a man of acceptable birth who is in need of money, enough so he will not quibble at my proposal.'

At these firm words from her cousin, Lettice placed a hand on her heart, a dismayed gasp revealing her reaction all too well. 'I can see you are determined to find such a man. I daresay there are enough of them around.' Giving her cousin a thoughtful stare, Lettice rose. 'Come, you must be longing for a rest and change. I truly do not know what help I may be in your quest. However, we shall muddle along the best we can.'

Misgivings fluttering about Penelope like

butterflies around a flowerbed, she followed her cousin from the room and up the stairs. At the door to a pretty little bedroom, they paused.

'This is a nice place in which to think. I believe you are in need of some serious thinking, Penelope. And call me Letty. It would be ever so much easier.' Taking Penelope's silence as agreement, she continued, 'I shall go out in the garden and commune with nature. Do you like to take walks? I hope so. I do *not* have enough nature in the garden here.'

With those strange words, Letty turned away, bustled along the hall, then marched down the stairs with a firm tread.

Left alone, Penelope tested the bed, and finding it to be quite comfortable, leaned back against her pillow. Her plans had definitely taken a twist for the worse. Her memories of Cousin Letty had been those of a vague but sweet woman some five years her senior who liked to pen poems and paint watercolors. It seemed a lot had happened in the intervening years to change Letty into a rather eccentric person. What help she might be was clearly debatable.

A gentle rap at the door brought Miss Nilsson.

'A fine pickle this is!' Penelope declared,

sitting up. 'My cousin is a sweet person, but slightly birdwitted, if you ask me.' Penelope rose from the bed, then crossed to assist in unpacking a trunk that had been carried up from the coach in which they had traveled from Kent to London.

'Now, do not get yourself in a pucker, my dear,' Nilsson urged. 'Perhaps she will be more help than you expect. Have a little patience. I feel certain it will all work out in the end.'

Penelope gave her closest friend and mentor a fond smile. 'Dear Miss Nilsson, what would I do without you, I wonder.'

'Become a savage, what else?' came the immediate reply in the familiar accent.

Chuckling, they both set to, and in short order had the articles of clothing and all the other things considered necessary stowed neatly away.

Over the dinner table, Penelope had an opportunity to further assess her cousin. Since Letty had insisted upon Miss Nilsson joining them, Penelope was able to exchange a knowing glance with her from time to time.

A discreetly attired maid brought the food to the table and served with the help of the housekeeper. Penelope could not refrain from a curious glance at this departure from the customary.

'You have noticed this is a feminine household, I suppose,' Letty said after the maid had left the room. 'I have heard horrid stories of nasty footmen who seduce the women of the house, and I'll have none of it.'

'I doubt if they are *very* nasty if they are able to seduce the ladies in question,' Penelope replied thoughtfully. 'However, I quite see your point, and it certainly is something to consider. How fortunate that my chef, Henri, is of an age to be my father. One scarcely thinks of an older man in a romantic light.'

Miss Nilsson was given to a fit of coughing, and the subject was immediately changed to one of health. Letty appeared quite fascinated with the work Penelope had done with herbs and potions, plying her with questions all through the meal until the apple torte was served.

'I can see we have much to learn from each other. I do hope your quest is not immediately successful. There are a great many things I wish to know,' Letty informed her as they strolled up to the small drawing room on the first floor.

'This is a charming house. I do not recall its being in the family. Is it a recent purchase, then?' Penelope ran a finger along the back of a damask-covered chair as she slowly crossed the pleasant room. Like the morning room off the entry, it was furnished in a bizarre, haphazard manner, with a character rather like that of its eccentric mistress.

'My elder brother was only too anxious to get me off his hands when he brought home his bride. I chose this house as being near the activities I enjoy and in a respectable part of town. I may be lost in poetry much of the time, but I do know what is proper.'

'That is indeed a comfort, Cousin.' Penelope's smile took away any sting that might have gone with her words.

'It was partly furnished. The rest of what I needed came from the attics of the family house.'

'If the ones in town are like those out at Everton Hall, I can see you had a wide choice.'

'How did your parents leave you situated?' Letty inquired with a tilt of her head. 'I'd not ask, but since you are here to find a husband, it is best to know. Sometimes one can drop a hint in the proper ear and do wonders, you know.' Letty picked up Muffin, who had wandered into the drawing room to hunt for a comfortable spot. In minutes Letty had reduced the cat to a purring, blissful lump of fur.

Glad that her pet found favor, yet mildly annoyed she had sought another, Penelope replied in a slightly abrupt way, 'Very well, I should say. Everything that was not entailed was placed in my name. That includes twenty thousand pounds per year in income, as well as the charming estate you saw in Kent. My guardian and the lawyer shall handle the settlement and the like.' Penelope gave her cousin a wistful smile. 'My guardian spends most of his time climbing mountains in Austria. I last heard from him following the death of my parents years ago.' She took a deep breath, then concluded, 'I suspect I am considered an heiress, sufficiently so that I ought not have the least trouble finding someone who will do just as I wish.'

'Ah, that again.' Letty frowned, exchanging a guarded look with Miss Nilsson.

'Mind you, I can only judge from what I have heard, but I rather believe it to be the case in regards to the desirability of money,' Penelope said with all due modesty. She looked to her cousin to see if she might refute the matter.

'I see,' Letty replied, her eyes behind her spectacles assessing her cousin in a most thorough manner. 'I rather think we shall have to ward off the fortune seekers instead of hunting for a husband, should word get about that you are so well-to-do.'

Disconcerted by her cousin's scrutiny, and

feeling that somehow her search for a husband was out of the ordinary, when she was quite certain it was not, Penelope rose to drift across to the fireplace. What a peculiar room. How her cousin could tolerate this conglomeration was more than she could imagine. 'Hodgepodge' was the kindest description one might make of it. Or perhaps 'late attic.'

'I believe an invitation came in the mail that might be of interest to us. At least, I think I still have it.' Letty pushed her spectacles up on her nose, frowning in concern as she did. 'As I recall, it is the Collison ball for their eldest daughter. Ought to be a splash that will draw the crowd you seek. Not that I am an adequate judge, but you could get an idea. Perhaps you might even see a gentleman who would suit your purpose while there? Young Collison is accounted quite a catch, or so someone told me . . . I think.' She gave a sad sigh and shook her head at Penelope. 'I shall warn you right now that you will most likely fare better with Miss Nilsson than to depend on me for guidance. I fear I am totally at sea when it comes to fashion and the doings of the *haut ton*.'

'Oh, dear,' Penelope replied softly. She strongly suspected her cousin was more inclined to forget the necessary, rather than not know what was what.

The following morning Penelope was prevailed upon to produce a few of her herbal potions for Letty. A cream for dry skin, a light pomade to tame her unruly hair, and a lip salve with a ladylike hint of color to it began the list of things Letty desired.

'Not that I am at all vain, mind you, but I forget to take care of myself. I hope, once completed, these will prompt me when I see them on the dressing table.' Letty beamed a happy, if absent-minded, smile on Penelope, then bustled off in the direction of her little study at the rear of the ground floor, where she usually retired to write her poetry.

Penelope was extremely curious to see what her cousin had composed, but so far her hints had brought about no offers to share the work from Letty's pen.

Muffin wound herself about Penelope's skirts, complaining of neglect, which Penelope knew to be a gross exaggeration. The cat had curled up on the bed during the night, seeking warmth and a comforting hand.

Penelope measured the prepared ox marrow for the lip salve, then added white pomatum, also ready for use. After properly blending, she stirred in the remaining ingredients, dropping in a hint of alcanet to color the salve a delicate red. When completed, she put the salve into a pretty jar with a nice tight lid. It was precisely the sort of thing a lady would enjoy having on her dressing table for very discreet use.

When Miss Nilsson peeked into the stillroom to see how Penelope fared, she was met with a frowning face. 'What is it, my dear?'

'I do not have sufficient jars and bottles with me. I wonder if we might not find some attractive ones on Bond Street? Perhaps my cousin will take us there. I saw some lovely things in the last issue of the *Lady's Monthly Museum.*' Penelope gave a final pat to the jar of lip salve, then turned to inspect the ingredients for the fine-quality pomade her cousin wished.

'Most likely we shall have to go on our own,' Miss Nilsson replied with a rueful smile. 'Mrs Flint tells me that once Miss Letty is into her poetry, she will not be bothered for anything. I suspect a shopping expedition to be at the bottom of her priority list.'

'Whatever shall I do, Nilsson?' Penelope asked, her concern clear in her voice. 'It seems to me that I have made a mistake in seeking the help of my cousin, no matter that she seems a dear sort.'

‘A trifle wanting in a few ways, perhaps, but you are correct to say she seems a good person. I do not know what manner of poetry she writes. I trust it reflects her heart. For now, we shall manage the best we can. Something will turn up,’ Nilsson added in her pretty, lilting voice.

‘We shall make a hasty trip to Bond Street, where I am persuaded the proper containers should be found,’ Penelope declared. ‘Perhaps we can obtain a glance at London gentlemen as well while we are out and about.’ She tossed a twinkling glance at her companion.

Miss Nilsson shot her employer a shrewd look, then nodded. ‘I trust it will do you no harm.’

They left word with Mrs Flint that Lady Penelope required a number of items, and they set off for Bond Street with expectant hearts.

Purchase of the jars and bottles was amazingly simple. Of course, it helped that cost was no object and that all Penelope had to do was decide which of the lovely items presented for view she wished to buy. Once they left the little shop, the two women strolled along the street, admiring the contents of the various windows.

‘This is rather exciting, Nilsson. Fancy seeing such lovely things, and not on the pages of magazines!' Penelope gazed at each window with the rapt attention of a child.

They were passing Mitchell's, the bookseller's and stationer's shop, when a young buck came tearing out the door, colliding with the bemused Penelope. He was followed by another gentleman, who hurried to catch Penelope, who looked about to fall.

'Oh, I say, miss, dashed sorry. Didn't look where I was going, y'see. Hope no damage has been done?' The more slender of the men, the one who had crashed into her, peered anxiously at the lovely young woman now held lightly in the protection of his friend's arms.

'You clunch, 'tis a wonder she's not swooned away at your thoughtless sprint.' The second man inspected Penelope's pelisse and bonnet for damage, then stepped back, giving a proper bow. 'Stephen Collison at your service, ma'am. Sorry to disturb you. This young fellow is inclined to rush about without a thought for the mayhem he causes.'

'I apologized, Collison,' the dasher snapped in a low aside to his friend. Then he turned his charm on Penelope with a smile. 'Fair beauty, I count myself devastated if I so much as injured a feather of your bonnet. Allow me to atone? I shall escort you to safety.'

'Ha!' Collison declared in an amused voice.

'She would be far safer with me, Willowby.'

'If you didn't pause to bet on her chances of returning home in one piece, that is,' gibed the dashing Willowby.

It was far too much for Penelope to resist. Laughter gurgled up from within in a captivating way, enchanting both men, who had expected her to issue a scold at the very least.

'What scamps you are, to be sure,' she managed to say at last. 'I am quite all right, though Mr Collison is correct. You, Mr Willowby, ought to look where you are going. To so madly dash about is to invite disaster.'

Willowby opened his mouth to say something, but was stopped by a discreet jab in his ribs.

'The fair lady supports my opinion,' Collison said. 'We shall not delay you further, ladies. I hope we shall meet again soon. A proper meeting, when we may learn the identity of the newest charmer in London. My parents are giving a ball for my sister soon. Dare I hope that you will attend?'

The flicker of acknowledgment in her eyes and the faint nod of recognition brought a handsome grin to Mr Collison's face. His blue eyes danced as he again bowed. 'Until then.'

Penelope watched the two gentlemen stroll

down the street, the one named Collison swinging an elegant cane. The tilt of his beaver hat was precisely so, and that coat was cut by a master hand, she could tell.

'Vastly different from the provincials, would you not say, Nilsson?' She glanced at her companion, then gently urged her along the street again.

'I had heard London manners were better, but this is scarcely the case.'

'Perhaps they are better under proper circumstances,' Penelope replied while eyeing the retreating figures. 'I wonder if either of them is in need of money,' she mused as they disappeared from sight. 'Mr Collison appears to enjoy a bet, from what was hinted at. Maybe . . . '

A repressive look from Miss Nilsson ended that line of speculation.

When they returned to the house on Upper Brook Street, Penelope was greeted by an indignant Muffin. Nothing would do but that she take her up and soothe wounded sensibilities with much stroking and gentle words.

'How you do spoil that cat,' Nilsson declared, a fond look in her eyes contrary to the asperity of her words.

'Other than you and Henri, she is the only one who gives me affection without expecting something in return.' And then Penelope acknowledged to herself that the two adults were both on her staff and well-paid for their devotion. 'Most likely she would desert me if I failed to reward her with a kipper or two now and again.'

She turned away to remove her pelisse and thus missed the look of pity on her companion's face.

'I found it!' a jubilant Letty cried as she sailed down the hall to greet them. 'The Collison ball is tomorrow evening.'

'We met a Collison while on Bond Street. Young Mr Collison saved me from a nasty fall.'

'Mister? Hardly, my girl. The only *young* Collison male is Lord Stephen. His elder brother is Viscount Bremerton. Nonetheless, Lord Stephen is possessed of a sizable income, as his father has settled a handsome estate on him, provided he can manage not to gamble it away. If you wish, you may be properly introduced tomorrow evening.'

'What did I tell you, Nilsson? One of them *is* most likely in need of money,' Penelope murmured to her companion.

Her cousin's sharp ears caught the remark and she rounded upon Penelope with a narrow look. 'You are a fool if you think to take on a gamester for a husband. Your fortune will be gone like a thistledown if you do. Have you forgotten that your husband will have complete control over your money once you wed?'

Penelope cradled her cat in her arms, absently scratching her under the chin while meeting the steady gaze from Miss Nilsson. 'It seems that finding a husband will not be quite as simple as I had hoped.' It would be ideal if she could find someone else to advise her on the matter. But who might serve? What a pity she didn't have another cousin in town, one more up to snuff.

2

The Collison ball was far more grand than Penelope had expected. Flambeaux blazed from their holders to either side of the canopied entrance as the carriage drew up before the house. Linkboys dashed about with additional flares, and an ornately dressed footman assisted them from the carriage with a flourish.

Once inside, the decorations surpassed anything she had thought would be done for a coming-out ball. Masses of spring flowers were everywhere, with pink silk draping the walls. The hundreds of candles were tinted a matching pink and the honored Lady Anne was dressed in the same hue. Her gown was a confection of silk and lace that made Penelope think of everything that was sweet and feminine.

Lord and Lady Collison appeared delighted to see the reclusive Miss Lettice Winthrop attend their little affair, as Lady Collison so quaintly called it.

'Your cousin?' she queried as Letty presented Penelope.

'I suspect I am related to a quarter of

Society, ma'am,' Penelope replied by way of reply as she curtsied in a graceful manner, one to make Miss Nilsson proud.

Behind her, Miss Nilsson drifted along in her quietly regal custom, nodding as befitted a companion of some small distinction. After all, she was a relative — albeit a rather distant one — of the King of Sweden. It had quite suited her to leave the cold Swedish winters for the milder English climate and more agreeable surroundings. For Fountains had been a marvelous place to reside, with duties that were light and pleasurable. Standing mother to an heiress who was also a delightful girl was not an odious task in the least.

Letty nudged Penelope along to the far side of the room, away from where a cluster of very pretty girls stood gossiping and laughing. Their chaperons and mothers gathered on dainty gilt chairs to exchange the latest news, which was likely very little, seeing that they met nearly every day at the various entertainments.

'For whom are you searching?' Penelope inquired in an undertone, wishing that she had taken the effort to seek out a fashionable mantua-maker who had more skill at translating the designs in *La Belle Assemblée*. Her rural mantua-maker had tried, but had clearly not quite managed the task.

'No one,' Letty replied as her gaze scanned the throng of people.

'I see,' Penelope replied, greatly puzzled and wondering if her cousin had forgotten where they were. 'By the bye, I'd as soon that you did not mention my financial status to anyone here, at least for the moment. I wish to do a bit of looking about for myself at first.'

Letty pushed her spectacles up on her nose as she turned to survey her cousin. 'I thought your entire reason for being here was to find a husband as quickly as possible. You do understand that if one of Aunt Winthrop's friends writes her that you are attending the parties in London, the fat will be in the fire?'

'No,' a startled Penelope replied in a faint voice. 'I had not considered that possibility.'

'Besides, a number of the tabbies are bound to remember your parents and the wealth they left.' Just then a gangly ginger-haired young man, perhaps a year or two older than Letty, came strolling across the polished wood floor to where the two young women stood. Letty ignored him.

'I say, Letty, I had no idea you meant to attend this do. Glad to see you here. Ought to get out more often. Better than secluding yourself in that moldy old room.'

‘I write there, Mr Oglethorpe,’ Letty replied in freezing accents.

He, in turn, ignored her outburst and bowed to Penelope. ‘May I present myself, since Letty is in a miff? Andrew Oglethorpe, at your service, ma’am.’

Letty gave an outraged sniff, then said in a strained voice, ‘My cousin, Lady Penelope Winthrop. She is immune to you, Andrew. I doubt a poet is to her liking in the least. Especially one who hasn’t the taste he was born with. She has come to Town for a nice visit.’

‘Shall I compose an ode to the dimples in your cheeks, my dear?’ replied the unoffended Mr Oglethorpe.

Since he was looking at Letty, Penelope prudently sidled up to Miss Nilsson. ‘What strange people,’ Penelope murmured.

‘I believe poets tend to be that way,’ Nilsson answered in a similar undertone.

‘I had hoped my cousin might be of help in my quest. She seems absorbed in another direction, to the exclusion of all else.’

‘So it would appear, but whether it is poetry or the poet who most fascinates her is hard to say.’

They exchanged amused glances, then watched as Lady Anne and her father stepped out on the floor to begin the ball.

Lord Stephen Collison was also there, partnering his youngest sister. He was even more handsome than the morning they had met, Penelope decided. Biscuit pantaloons fitted snugly on well-muscled legs, and that corbeaeu coat over a waistcoat of cream satin was positively elegant. He danced well too. She wondered how prone he was to gambling. A little she could tolerate. Excessive gaming was something else. Unless . . . she might be able to have her trustees stipulate that her money was to remain in their control? It might be possible. Her guardian offered little help far off in Austria.

Once the initial dance concluded, she was surprised to find Lord Stephen coming her way.

'Ah, fair unknown, you came!' He bowed over her hand, then noticed Letty and Andrew Oglethorpe. 'Miss Winthrop, Oglethorpe. Nice to see you again.' He glanced pointedly at Penelope.

'Lady Penelope Winthrop, allow me to present Lord Stephen Collison. My cousin is from Kent and has come to enjoy the delights of London for a time.'

Penelope curtsied low to the attractive gentleman. 'I am charmed to see you again, sir. Such a gallant rescuer is always a welcome sight.'

Lord Stephen explained the circumstances under which they had met with an amused, offhand manner, then requested Penelope's hand for the following dance.

Miss Nilsson nodded, then seated herself on one of those dainty gilt chairs which usually range the walls of ballrooms.

'I suppose I cannot have the next waltz. You most likely have not had time to obtain permission to waltz as yet.' Lord Stephen smiled down at her, his blue eyes alight with charm.

'I am distantly related to Mrs Drummond-Burrell, so perhaps that will not be too difficult.' She looked about the room, searching for a neutral topic. 'Your sister looks to be a charming girl. She ought not have the least trouble finding a husband of good standing.'

He gave her a surprised look, then frowned. 'That is what these things are all about, aren't they? Usually everyone pretends otherwise.'

'I am too outspoken.' Penelope blushed a delicate rose. 'It is my country manners, sir. I shall have to learn to guard my tongue.'

'And I suppose I must share your beauty with every beau and dandy in the room. I can see meaningful looks coming my way with every turn we make.'

'Fie, sir, what flummery,' Penelope chuckled in that endearing way she had, and Lord Stephen appeared enchanted.

His attention was not unnoticed by his mother, who promptly sought out Miss Nilsson. She learned precisely what she desired to know: that the companion was of the highest respectability and that the Winthrop girl apparently had a sizable inheritance. Stories about the earl and his countess returned to her mind. Yes, indeed, there was a fortune there, unless the estate had been mismanaged or the next earl had acquired everything. Somehow, she doubted that, as rumor had it that the previous Earl of Everton had provided well for his only child.

When the country dance drew to an end, Penelope discovered Lord Stephen had been correct. At least to the extent that Mr Willowby waited to request a proper introduction and the next dance. Again Letty absently did her duty, leaving Penelope to cope as best she might with the impressed Mr Willowby.

Yet it was not long before Penelope began to detect a subtle alteration in the attentions paid to her. Young men did seek her side, but they seemed not the cream of the group, nor were they the sort she wished to attract. They were apparently all under the hatches, definitely possessing not a feather to fly with, judging from the whispers that reached her ears. It seemed each of them was eager to let her know the poor financial standing of the other hopefuls.

She was about to beg Letty, who did not appear to be enjoying the ball in the least, to depart, when a faint stir occurred at the entrance to the ballroom. Penelope was standing with Miss Nilsson, merely watching the glittering scene, and wishing she had someone more knowledgeable to assist her, when a man strolled in, bowed to his hostess, making her blush and laugh with his words.

Penelope forgot her manners and stared. He wasn't the most handsome man in the room, but he possessed an air about him, an intangible aura of power and grace that attracted the eye. Glancing about, Penelope observed that a good many other eyes were drawn to him as well, mostly feminine ones.

His brown hair was arranged in the latest casual style. If she had thought Lord Stephen did well by his biscuit pantaloons, he was completely put in the shade by the stunning ensemble of black pantaloons and tailcoat with a white quilted satin waistcoat that had to be the supreme elegance of fashion. Penelope glanced down at her dress, one that had pleased her when she put it on. It was a delicate blue jaconet trimmed with knots of white ribbon. Now it looked insipid and too girlish by far, certainly nothing that would catch the eye of this dashing gentleman. The thought crossed her mind that it was unlikely that he needed money.

'Very smart, would you not say?' Miss Nilsson commented.

'Most assuredly,' Penelope said in awed tones.

'I see you have caught sight of our relative,' Letty snapped, although softly. 'Impertinent man.'

Before Penelope could request an explanation, Lord Stephen appeared to claim his second dance, a cotillion.

'My cousin just informed me that I am related to the man who just entered the room — the one in black. She neglected to say who he is, however. Living in the country without an elderly aunt around to keep me up-to-date, I have not a clue to his identity.'

'Harford? Fancy you being related to him. He, I beg to inform you — for you must be the only woman in all of London who doesn't know — is the Earl of Harford. Jonathan to his closest friends. The Trent men are all a lot of handsome devils. Is he a close relation?'

The figure of the dance swung her away from Lord Stephen's side, so she was spared an answer for the moment.

Penelope gave the new arrival an appraising glance; then, when she drew close to Lord Stephen once again, she queried, 'Does he gamble?'

'That's like asking if a man breathes. Every gentleman does a flutter at the tables or has a go at the odds now and again. Some more than others.'

As an answer it was less than she wished, but she dared not reveal greater interest in the newcomer. However, the reply had brought intriguing thoughts. Lord Stephen, Mr Willowby, and probably most of the other men in the room gambled. Would any of them be agreeable to her proposal? The proposal Letty deemed so wicked? Would they consider it such? Or merely a pragmatic solution to her problem? And possibly theirs?

While at Fountains, she had approached her dilemma with an analytical eye, totally forgetting that there would be a flesh-and-blood man involved as well. Now, looking about her, allowing her gaze to return to the dashing Lord Harford, she became uncomfortably aware that she might be getting more than she bargained for, should she pursue her original intent. If only she had a brother, an uncle, some man whose advice she might seek.

She endured another dance with one of the suspected pockets-to-let gentlemen, then retired behind a convenient screen. It was draped in a swath of pink and concealed the door to the terrace, a place Lady Collison evidently wished left unfrequented.

From what Penelope had observed so far, her trip to London was doomed to failure. Unless she yielded to one of those dandies in need of funds, or found a lady of standing to assist her, she was sunk. Her claim to be related to Mrs Drummond-Burrell was quite true, but it was a distant kinship. It could never be sufficient for her to hope a sponsorship might be forthcoming.

'I say, old chap, did you hear the latest?'

Penelope stiffened at hearing a voice from the other side. Mr Willowby was there, sounding like he planned a gossip. She moved to tiptoe away, when his next words stopped her in her steps.

'It seems Harford succumbed at last, bet on a sure thing, only this time Collison won!'

The laughter was general, and seemed without malice. 'How deep?'

'A plummy thing, my friends.'

The voices of the others were amused, and sought details which, owing to the sudden increase of the sound of the music, Penelope could not hear.

But she well knew that in the cant of the day, a plum was one hundred thousand pounds! Unless Mr Willowby merely intended to imply his friend had bet a horrendous sum of money? Possibly. Either way, here was a most plausible person, a distant relative — although she had never heard of him before — now in dire need of money.

And money was the one thing she had in abundance. Pity he did not look the type to settle down with marriage. From all she had read and heard from the gossips in the country, those handsome sorts spent their time chasing after women, most definitely in the plural and certainly not a green girl like herself. However, she might be able to utilize him in some manner.

Her head awhirl with ideas, she slipped from behind the screen, then wove her way through the throng of guests to where Letty and Miss Nilsson sat discussing poetry with Mr Oglethorpe. Letty did not look pleased about something.

'Well, what do you think of your first London affair?' Letty said in her abrupt manner.

Seizing her opportunity, Penelope smiled in what she hoped to be a wan, interesting fashion. 'I fear it has fatigued me more than I expected.'

'Good. We can leave at once. Miss Nilsson, shall we?' Letty jumped up, dismissing Mr Oglethorpe's polite protestations with an impatient wave of her hand.

Miss Nilsson soothed his feelings with her kind words. 'I very much enjoyed your explanations of that work by Lord Byron. If it is not too much trouble, I would very much like to learn a little about that new poet, Keats.'

'Delighted, ma'am. So nice to know there are ladies interested in worthwhile things.' He bestowed a narrow look on Letty, who missed it because she was fussing with her shawl.

At last they made their farewells and hurried out to their waiting carriage.

Once in Upper Brook Street, Letty insisted they all have a soothing cup of herbal tea before going to their rooms. Penelope was rather absentminded for once.

'Hmm?' she responded to a question from Letty.

'I said, what did you think of our relative, Lord Harford?'

'What is the kinship there? I cannot recall hearing of him before.' Penelope toyed with her dainty cup, sipping the chamomile tea with little enthusiasm.

'Let me see, I suppose he is your third cousin, once removed.' Letty adjusted her shawl, then pushed her spectacles up on her little nose. She then explained that their great-great-grandmother was a Trent, thus the connection.

'Close, but not too close.' At the look of inquiry, Penelope politely smiled, then said, 'One cannot help but be curious, you know.'

Miss Nilsson raised a brow at that nonsensical remark.

Later, when they reached Penelope's room, Miss Nilsson nudged her inside, then assisted her with the pins and tapes to her gown. 'What are you thinking, my dear? I know that expression far too well to let it slip past me.'

Stepping out of her pretty but insipid gown, Penelope said in a firm voice, 'In the morning I intend to seek out my third cousin, once removed, and make a bargain with him.'

Miss Nilsson knew better than to reveal her shock at this outrageous proposal. It was all of a piece with coming to London to hunt for a husband who would then disappear.

'And what do you intend to offer him in return?'

'Money. What else is there?'

'Indeed,' came the thoughtful reply. Miss Nilsson quietly went about assisting Penelope, then walked to her room in a pensive mood.

The following morning, while Letty sequestered herself in her little study, Penelope set out with Miss Nilsson at her side. Only when the carriage deposited them before an austere, elegant house did her qualms surface to give her pause.

'I believe the house suits him well, Nilsson.'

'Lady Penelope, are you certain you do the correct thing?' Miss Nilsson, looking almost Quakerish in dove gray, placed a restraining hand on Penelope's arm.

'I am aware it is not proper to call upon a gentleman at his home. But he is my relative and you are with me. Surely that makes a slight difference? Besides, I am not all that known.' This last remark seemed to set the cap on her intent, and she marched forth to the rather imposing front door.

The man who answered was not at all what she expected. He was a portly person with round cheeks and jolly blue eyes. Such a kindly soul made it much easier for Penelope to state her outrageous request.

'Would you be so kind as to inform Lord Harford that his cousin Lady Penelope Winthrop wishes to speak with him?'

No brow was raised, but Penelope received the distinct impression that the butler was most astonished at her presence. He ushered the two women into an attractive morning room furnished in the latest stare of fashion, then left. Penelope watched his retreating back while the tiny flutters in her stomach grew to definite quaking. A glance at Nilsson was no help. That good lady held a look of reproof in her eyes that told Penelope she would have been better off staying in bed that morning. Unable to sit, she looked about her at the beautiful chairs and paintings.

Penelope was studying the lushly figured Turkish carpet when a stir at the door brought her gaze up. Her cousin, albeit her very distant cousin, walked toward her, examining her with a narrow, skeptical gaze.

'*Cousin* Penelope?'

She fought the desire to cringe at the tone in his voice. The man quite obviously did not believe their connection. 'My great-great-grandmother was Sophronia Trent. I believe that makes us third cousins, once removed.'

He looked thoughtful. 'Quite so. And to what do I owe the pleasure of this morning call?' He drew closer, the deep blue velvet of his casually open banyan seeming to reflect the black color of his eyes. His attire was immaculate: gray breeches, spotless stockings, a white shirt with crisp ruffles concealing the buttons at the neck. Penelope felt like a frump. A country frump.

She ignored his stress of the word 'morning.' 'I have need of your help, sir.'

'I would not have suspected you had been

in Town long enough to get into trouble.' His brows rose fractionally.

'I am not in trouble. Precisely. But, you see, I have come to London for the reason so many other young ladies come — to find myself a husband. Last evening made it plain that I need someone more up to snuff than Letty to assist me. She is a dear, but not terribly aware of what is going on in Society. And if she does find out, most likely she forgets it, if you know what I mean.'

'I fail to see how I may be of assistance to you.' He languidly crossed the room, reclining in an elegant rosewood chair after courteously seating his new cousin.

'I had best speak quite plainly to save time. I need a sponsor.' She raised a hand at his protesting stir. 'I am aware you can scarcely do such a thing. I am not *that* green. However, I believe you might help in other ways. I need advice on how to go on . . . a good mantua-maker, for example.' She cast a derogatory glance at her simple sprigged muslin. While pretty, it was scarcely *à la mode*.

'Granted,' he conceded in an utterly odious manner.

'And, since I am an heiress, I need someone who knows the *ton* well enough to tell me which gentleman I may accept, and which one to avoid. I have no desire to be saddled with a gamester, sir, or a man with an upper story to let.' She gave him a worried glare, for the interview had become fraught with anxiety. He did not welcome her. She could understand that. But could he not have mercy on a young, helpless relative?

'Let me see, all you require is a decent sort of husband after getting properly rigged out? Nothing more than that?'

His sarcasm was not lost on her. She chose to ignore it, for she could hardly pull caps with him when she wished his help. She wryly smiled, then added, 'I should like a husband who would take himself off somewhere — possibly the Continent — so I might be left in peace to attend to my interests.' She tilted her face, giving him a considering look. 'What a pity you are not in the line for marriage. I should think you would be only too happy to part ways with me,' she concluded in her frequently outspoken way.

His eyes narrowed again as he considered her words. 'You do not see me as husband material, then?'

'Goodness me, no,' she declared fervently. He intimidated her to the point of alarm, although she would never let on so to him.

He made no reply, so Penelope plunged ahead with what she hoped would be her winning argument. 'I should be happy to pay you, you know. Merely name your fee.'

In the silence that followed that statement, Penelope could hear the ticking of the mantel clock, the faint rumble of the carriages that passed the house, and somewhere in the distance — belowstairs perhaps — an altercation between distinctly angry people.

'My *fee*?'

'Forgive me, I inadvertently overheard that you had lost a vast sum in a wager with Lord Stephen Collison. I thought perhaps you might be in need of help, and we could mutually assist one another. I am generous, I promise. I believe a person ought to be properly rewarded.'

Penelope dropped her gaze to her lap to study her pretty blue limerick gloves, thus she missed the amused gleam that briefly entered his lordship's eyes.

'Is that so? Well, well.' He ought to say no, as he fully intended to do eventually, and shoo this impossible child on her way. Why he persisted in leading her on, he didn't know. She entertained him, with her serious blue eyes and outrageous request. Fee, indeed. She thought him to be as penniless as those bucks who had clustered about her last evening. The wager that had been lost had not been a monetary one — at least not yet. He had lost to Collison, and as a result this evening was required to produce a fine dinner designed for the taste of gentlemen. He knew his French chef could manage it with a flick of his hand. However, if the dinner failed to come off for some reason, the damage would be considerable.

Jonathan had no intention of losing that wager. It was a matter of principle with him, as it was to most gentlemen of the *ton*. He had been contemplating the menu he had composed and had been about to hand it to his chef when his new 'cousin' had presented herself at his door.

Jonathan rubbed his jaw as he considered the problem, thus concealing much of his inner reflections. She was certainly a diverting creature, with those remarkable blue eyes, enchanting face, and, if he was any judge of it, a rather trim form. 'Take off your bonnet, please.'

Startled at his words, she withdrew slightly, then reached up to remove her chip bonnet tied with the same blue as the sprigs on her gown. Silvery-gold hair, neatly drawn into a simple chignon, was more than pleasing, in spite of the rather dowdy style she affected. He had noticed her hair last night from across the room. He hadn't believed it real, thinking it either a wig or a trick of the lighting. Now he could see that it was undeniably genuine.

'Hmm. Are you willing to cut it?' Why did he persist? He couldn't actually partake in this wild scheme.

She swallowed with care, then nodded. 'I could see that the way I wear it is not the fashion.'

He shook his head, ashamed of himself for raising her hopes even a trifle. 'I realize your need for sound advice: the sea of matrimony is fraught with dangers. However, what you suggest is out of the question. You must see that. It is wicked just to contemplate such a plan.'

'Oh, please, Lord Harford, I would not be any trouble.'

He couldn't repress the smile that tilted his mouth. Trouble? He'd wager that she inspired the word. In spite of her meek attitude, he'd caught her glance of defiance, the hint of impertinence in her voice. The mere circumstance of her being here was sufficient to warrant caution on his part. His life did not need any complications at the moment.

He shook his head, ignoring the woeful look on that exquisite little face, the pleading in those beautiful eyes. She would melt the heart of a lesser man. 'It is not seemly.'

'I daresay you do quite a number of things I might consider unseemly, sir. I cannot believe that helping out an orphaned cousin in dire need of your assistance to be unseemly.' Scorn flashed from her eyes.

'Orphaned? That, I did not know.' What was in his head? He couldn't help her out. Unthinkable. He was about to deny her once and for all, when his butler entered the room, standing just inside the door, a look of extreme agitation on his face.

'Sir? If I could have a word with you? Immediately?'

Glancing at his newly discovered cousin, Jonathan had an idea. If she thought him beset by other troubles, perhaps she would depart and leave him alone. 'Speak up, Darling.'

Penelope blinked at the name, thinking it most unusual.

''Tis the chef, René. He decamped. Just like that, sir.' Darling wrung his hands in dismay.

Jonathan sprang from his chair, striding across the room. 'Left? No reason? The cook or kitchen maids not giving him a problem?'

'Lord Stephen's man was outside. I suspect a bit of hugger-mugger, if you don't mind my saying so, sir.' The butler gave an emphatic nod of his graying head as he concluded this observation. 'What shall you do, sir? Ought I search for a new chef?'

'Damn the man!' Jonathan slammed his fist against the wall. 'Collison lured him away just when I most needed him, with that dinner on this evening. What a rotten thing to do! Even if it is a wager, I expected better from Collison, *and* the chef. Where am I to find a superb French chef in so short a time, I ask you?'

'You seem quite desperate,' inserted Penelope, her eyes sparkling with sudden hope.

'Do you happen to know a French chef who could take over this menu on a moment's notice?' He picked up the card upon which he had jotted his proposed dinner and waved it in her direction. 'I think not!'

'Oh, but I do.' She gave him a demure yet confident smile and settled on her chair a bit more comfortably.

Startled, he paused in his pacing and stared at her. 'Do you, by Jove? Where may I find this man? And who is he? What is his experience?'

'Not he, but she. That is to say, *I* am the chef. I have been carefully trained by our own French chef, Henri. I assure you, I can cook anything, and splendidly, too.'

'Nonsense! Utterly absurd!' He looked at the companion and noted that she sat with a serene smile on her face. Could it be true?

His spirits leapt up.

'I shall make a bargain with you.' Penelope rose from her chair, then crossed to take the menu card from his hand. She looked it over, nodded. 'I will cook your dinner, and do a better job, or, at the very least, as good a job of it as your former chef.'

'And in exchange I will . . . ?' he replied with a sinking heart. Something told him the price she would exact.

'You will do as I proposed.'

3

'I feared you would ask that of me,' Lord Harford replied in his most distant manner. 'But what can I do? I have been placed in a damnable spot.' He recalled the presence of ladies, and apologized. 'Forgive me, my anger outruns my tongue.'

Miss Nilsson nodded with gracious forbearance while Penelope stood, her head tilted in consideration. She tapped the menu card against her chin; then, looking at Lord Harford with determined eyes, she stated her argument.

'I should say that you have little choice in the matter at this point, my lord.' Penelope waved the card beneath his nose. 'Agree to the terms now, for there is no time to waste if I am to have that dinner ready when your guests arrive.'

He glared at the sparkling eyes that defied him to say no to her proposal. How could he have thought her pretty? She was a gamine in a lady's clothes. It was wicked, positively wicked, to even think of an earl's daughter descending to the kitchens to cook! 'Oh, for pity's sake! I concede. I'll do as you wish. But you must be discreet, mind you.'

'No one shall know that I have prepared your dinner unless *you* tell them, my lord,' Penelope teased, her humor restored now that she was to have a bit of fun in the kitchen and get her adviser, just as she had wished.

'Nor shall they know that I am responsible for your clothes, coiffure, or demeanor.' He ran his hand through his carefully arranged hair, totally destroying the effect his valet had worked so diligently to achieve. 'Much less the approval of your suitors. Egad, what a coil.'

Penelope merely smiled, then turned to the butler. 'Please show me to the kitchen, Darling.' She had observed that Lord Harford pronounced the name as though it was spelled Dareling, and she followed suit. To Miss Nilsson she added, 'I imagine you had best smooth things over with Letty, should she realize I am gone. If you wish, you may return here, but I shan't require you.' Her bonnet dangling from the ribbons in her hand, Penelope paused by the door to cast a reassuring look at her companion and dear friend.

The Swedish lady merely nodded and coolly replied, 'I believe it best to say as little as possible to Miss Letty. Leave her to me. I shall see you later, for I intend to assure myself that your lessons from Henri were not in vain.'

Jonathan watched them all leave. Darling escorted Lady Penelope off through the green baize door, while the quiet Miss Nilsson let herself out the front.

Jonathan paced the floor of his elegant morning room. Had he gone mad? To permit a lady of rank to cook the dinner for his guests just to win a wager? While it seemed an unthinkable proposition, he was up against the wall. It was also inconceivable that he permit Collison to win that blasted bet. Then he recalled those twinkling blue eyes, that exquisite silvery-blond hair, and groaned. How on earth could that exquisite little thing, for she couldn't have stood above five feet and perhaps five inches, cook a dinner? He wondered how she would feel in his arms, or that perfect little mouth beneath his, then shook himself, irate with his musings.

He marched up the stairs to his room, calling for his valet, Perkins. Once impeccably dressed in his usual style, his hair restored to casual perfection, he took himself off to White's. If he could forget for a few hours the total disaster that surely awaited him when his guests arrived for dinner this evening, he might just survive the day.

The thought crossed his mind that should

she fail her task, he would be free of his promise. Even that prospect didn't cheer him. He confessed that he devoutly hoped that Lady Penelope Winthrop, third cousin once removed, actually knew how to cook.

⋆ ⋆ ⋆

At White's he established himself in the morning room with a group of friends. Willowby entered the room shortly after Jonathan arrived, looking as though he was vastly amused about something. Jonathan strongly suspected he knew what it was.

'Surprised to see you here this morning, Harford,' Willowby said in a sly manner.

'I suppose I could be elsewhere, such as riding, I fancy. But why are you so confounded? Am I not frequently seen in this room?' Jonathan hoped his smile was sufficiently confident. Oh, if only Lady Penelope did well. Why Collison wished to see him so ignominiously defeated, he didn't know. But he did know he would do what he could to see that the dinner got served, and served successfully.

Willowby shrugged his narrow, though well-padded, shoulders. 'Oh, I don't know. Thought perhaps you might be concerned about your dinner this evening. You haven't forgotten? Your chef will turn out his usual excellence?' There was a subtle inflection in his voice, snickering, perhaps.

'Forget? Never. I have left my chosen menu in capable hands. You are in for a treat, Willowby. The dinner served you this evening will be the likes of which you have never eaten before.' With those words Jonathan smiled, then turned to the others, deliberately changing the topic of conversation.

His good friends, sensing something was amiss, followed his lead, and soon they were deep in the merits of the leading contenders for the upcoming race at Newmarket.

Willowby remained for a few minutes, then drifted away to join several others on the far side of the room.

* * *

Penelope examined the kitchen as she shed her pelisse, absently handed it to Darling along with her bonnet, then walked to the pantry to inspect the provisions. It was well-stocked, but she would need a number of things to prepare the dishes on the menu. She turned to the cook Darling had introduced as Mrs Barker.

'I shall take the place of the worthless creature who so callously left his employer in the lurch. I have been trained by the finest chef in England, or so I feel. Have no fears that I shall fail Lord Harford.' She beamed a confident smile at Mrs Barker, thus winning her support, if not her loyalty.

'But I will need your assistance. I fear I cannot shop for the remaining items needed for these dishes. Normally I would choose them myself, for the fish must be the finest and just out of the water, the beef ought to be a most tender cut, and the other things must be of equal quality. If one is to serve the best dishes possible, one must have the finest ingredients. Could I impose upon you to search out what is required? I know you must be capable, else my cousin would not employ you.'

'Your cousin, my lady?' said the astonished cook. She hadn't believed Mr Darling when he had carried that tale to her ears.

'If you please?' Penelope flashed a smile at her.

The slightly reserved cook melted under that beguiling smile. The knowledge that this young woman was cousin to her master, and wished to help him in his dilemma completed the persuasion. 'Just tell me what to buy, and I'll see to it you get the best.'

The two women put their heads together, softly discussing the number of guests and the amounts of food required. Darling, seeing how well they were getting along, permitted himself a small smile of hope, then stepped inside his pantry to check the silver and crystal before fetching the wines for the dinner. It just might be possible that the evening could be saved after all.

In short order Penelope had spread out a hastily scribbled plan of sorts on the well-scrubbed center table. Off to one side, serving dishes from the side dressers were taken down, to be freshly washed by the kitchen maid. The skullery maid was set to scrubbing the chopping block, for Penelope firmly believed in cleanliness in the kitchen. The haster, the large racked cupboard used to keep dishes of meat warm, was inspected and approved, then set in readiness to be placed by the oven to be used later.

'You are to be complimented on your kitchen. It is clean and well-stocked. Lord Harford is fortunate to have so capable a cook.' Penelope crossed her fingers beneath the enormous holland-cloth apron she had donned to cover her muslin round gown. The starched white fabric crackled as she leaned over the table again. She had no way of knowing the cook was capable. She merely sensed that her newly discovered cousin would not suffer fools about him, nor incompetence, for that matter.

The cook glowed with pride at this accolade, deciding that she would do everything in her power to assist this nice young lady. Hanging her apron on a peg, she said, 'I'll be off to the markets, then.' She took the list from Penelope, gathered her cloak from the back hall, and was gone.

The hours that followed were busy ones for the kitchen staff. Penelope began the meats that required roasting, then turned to produce elegant sweets and puddings. When she discovered a day-old sponge cake, she set about making a tipsy cake, pouring sufficient sherry over it to soak in nicely. Once she had added the custard and the almond slivers, she surveyed the results before placing it aside. There was enough sherry in that cake to bring a smile to any one of those gentlemen's faces, should he consume a sizable piece.

Cook returned with the needed items, and then the two women quietly began the real work of the dinner.

Penelope attacked tartlets, fancy cream sauces, and elegant dishes of vegetables. The cook made the dainty meringues that Lord Harford enjoyed, then prepared the stock for the soup.

It was a good many hours later that a very hesitant Lord Harford peered into the kitchen, expecting he knew not what. He saw two roasts sputtering by the fire behind the meat screen. Savory aromas drifted across to tease his nose and entice his palate. Various dishes now completed and ready for serving sat in the warming oven.

The room was hot, and the crisp white apron Penelope had donned that morning now looked wilted, with interesting smudges of brown, pink, and cream here and there. She had a dash of flour on her pert nose. That entrancing smile seemed a trifle weary.

That a lovely woman should go to this length just to obtain his help suddenly unnerved him. What if he failed her? It seemed that she had spoken the truth, she did know how to cook, and judging by the appearance and aroma, quite well.

'We shall do you proud, my lord,' Penelope said in a quiet voice. 'I believe your friends will enjoy this dinner.'

'From the looks of things, I'd say it will be a dinner to remember.' He wanted to reassure her, offer her support.

'I hope so,' she replied, her gaze seeking his for a moment before she returned to her task.

He entered the room, strolling across the spotless floor, wondering how it managed to stay so clean while in the midst of all the hubbub. 'I am impressed.'

She took note of his inspection, then replied, 'It was Hippocrates who insisted on boiled water and clean hands while attending patients. I believe that spotless surroundings add to the quality of the end results in a kitchen, Lord Harford.' She gestured to a wooden bucket with mop leaning against it. 'We see to it that the floor is frequently mopped and the table is often scrubbed.' She smoothed her hand over the yellowish-white sycamore wood of the kitchen table as she spoke.

He leaned against the corner of that table, folding his arms as he continued to watch, not a little curious about this newly acquired cousin.

'How is it that Lady Penelope Winthrop is so at home in the kitchen? I would have expected you to scarcely know of its existence. Few women I am acquainted with are so informed.' He recalled one Society matron who had declared she had no idea where her kitchen was located.

Penelope shrugged, deftly shaping the dough for crisp little French-style rolls she intended to serve with the soup now simmering on the back of the stove. Rather than bake them this morning, she had waited until late, desiring them fresh from the oven. 'I wanted company and became bored with the school-room. Henri was pleased to have me as a student, and I quite liked my lessons. If I did well, I enjoyed the results. He made me taste the failures as well, which proved to be a wondrous spur to improvement.' Her eyes lit up with remembered happy times.

'Surely your parents did not approve of such?' He noted the fading of her delightful smile and his curiosity grew.

'I have no idea as to what they might have thought. You see, they never knew about it. My parents appeared for possibly two weeks a year — around Christmas — provided there was not a marvelous Christmas party to attend. In which case,' she added with a trace of bitterness in her voice, 'they whirled into the house with an armload of gifts, then disappeared again. I do not believe they were at all interested in me or my doings, other than to receive the written reports of my progress.' She placed the last of the shaped dough on the pan, then handed it to the cook, adding some softly spoken instructions.

'I often thought,' she continued, 'Miss Nilsson ought to include some entirely silly account just to see if they actually looked at those reports.' Penelope sighed, then gave her cousin a tired smile. 'Of course, someone might have seen them and wondered a bit about this strange girl in the country.'

'But that is monstrous! You mean to tell me that you have been sequestered in the country all your life?'

' 'Twas hardly a prison, my lord.' Her eyes sparkled with returned humor. 'I had jaunts to the village, visits with the vicar and his wife, and I always attended church, for it was lovely to see so many people. Miss Nilsson and I explored the estate. I discovered a great interest in plants, especially healing herbs. Many Swedes are herbalists, you know.'

He found he couldn't utter a word. This beautiful young woman had spent her life secluded on a great estate, with no one her age, no pleasures such as girls must enjoy. Small wonder she took to what she might find — cooking and hunting about for herbs. He sniffed the air, noting the fragrance lingering in the room.

'And do you cook with herbs as well?' His chef had been superb in his way, but some of his dishes were lacking.

'But, of course,' she answered with a hint of accent coloring her voice.

'Is there anything I might do?' he offered, although he hadn't the faintest notion of how he might help.

Penelope giggled, her eyes crinkling up in a charming way. 'I very much doubt it. You could look in on Darling and tell him how impressed you are with his table setting. I expect he has outdone himself.'

Suddenly aware that he was very much in the way, Jonathan left the kitchen, a place he had heretofore ignored, and wandered up to the ground floor, where he found Darling putting the finishing touches on the dining room. Chairs were in place before a table set with crisp linen. The plate was polished to an eye-blinking shine, candles stood ready for lighting, and a low bowl of hothouse fruit was arranged in the center so that his friends might converse with ease. When alone, gentlemen did not observe the proprieties of conversation with the person to either side, but enjoyed easy chatting back and forth.

'Well done, Darling. I have just been to the kitchen. Do you know, I believe we might actually pull this thing off?'

'Yes, indeed, sir.' The butler beamed at his lordship. Then he glanced at the long-case clock just visible in the hall. 'I fancy you'll be wanting to dress, sir. It won't be long now.'

Jonathan whirled around to look at the time. Nodding, he ran lightly up the stairs after greeting Miss Nilsson, who had entered while he was in discussion with Darling. The footman stood at her side, uncertain what to do with this peculiar female who seemed proper, but had presented herself at the front door and entered the house as though she had a right

'I shall see you later, Miss Nilsson,' Jonathan called over the banister. 'Lady Penelope is in the kitchen; go see what she has done.'

Darling escorted Miss Nilsson through the baize door and into the kitchen. He wasn't quite certain how to behave to a lady who was also a chef, even if only for a day. 'Your ladyship, Miss Nilsson has come.' He escaped into his pantry to check the wines once again.

'I see you have everything under control.' Nilsson surveyed the area, taking note of the prepared foods, the air of expectancy that hung over the room.

Penelope brushed a strand of hair from her cheek, then walked over to drop down on the chair off to one side. 'Oh, Nilsson, I hope it is not a disaster.' She glanced at the small clock atop the dresser, checking the hour.

'May I?' Miss Nilsson queried, not waiting for an answer she knew would be affirmative. They had undergone too many similar situations for permission to be denied. At least, Nilsson had performed this sort of check before.

She picked up the by-now-stained and smudged menu card, then quickly hunted out the various dishes, sniffing, tasting with a quickly provided spoon from the kitchen maid. When Nilsson had finished her round of inspection, she returned to where Penelope sat in quiet exhaustion.

'Well?' Penelope asked, expecting nothing but bare truth.

'Superb. They do not in the least deserve such a meal. I ought to put in a pot of pepper, just to give them their just deserts.'

'Nilsson, what would I do without you!' Penelope declared with a watery chuckle. Her fatigue faded away with a sip of wine, followed by renewed determination from the praise of one who was a stickler for perfection. Penelope popped up to check the soup.

'I am relieved he chose a simple menu suitable for gentlemen and not at all pretentious. I fear I would have been lost had I to perform the wizardry Henri can do at a moment's notice.'

'You did well, my dear. Now to the service.'

From the hall, sounds of the entering guests could be faintly heard. Darling had disappeared not long ago to answer the door and keep things under his unobtrusive control.

'They are all eager to have their meal. Ha!' Darling sniffed as he returned to the kitchen, his disdain for some of the guests quite clear. 'Just wait until they get a sip of that soup. I do hope you made a great deal of it, for it has been making my mouth water for hours,' he said daringly.

'There is ample, never fear,' Penelope replied as she watched the massive tureen carried from the kitchen.

* * *

In the cozy morning room, into which the gentlemen had wandered after entering the house, Willowby and Collison approached Jonathan, the gleam in their eyes most self-congratulatory.

'Everything going well, old fellow?' Collison purred. 'No problems?' added Willowby.

'Well, I was concerned when my chef decamped this morning, but after seeing the results of the new one I discovered, I am confident you will enjoy your meal.'

'Discovered a chef the same day as your dinner? Impossible!' Collison declared with a lofty disdain.

Jonathan gave a slight shrug, smiled confidently, then motioned to his butler, who had appeared-at the doorway. 'Darling?'

The butler gave a stately bow of his head. 'Dinner is served, my lord.'

There was no set order this evening, and they immediately rambled toward the dining room. Everyone was eager to discover who was to win the wager. Word had seeped out about the missing chef. They all knew it was utterly impossible to find another chef of the same caliber, especially on a moment's notice. They very much feared poor old Harford was going to lose this one. His friends were sorry, but his two perennial opponents sat with pleased anticipation on their faces.

Then Darling entered with the soup course. The footman followed with the French-style rolls, bringing a wonderful fresh-baked aroma into the room. Jaded appetites picked up, mouths began to water at the sight of the soup being ladled into bowls.

Jonathan picked up his spoon, and the others eagerly followed. A hint of wine and herbs, with vegetables, rabbit, and pheasant superbly blended together. Crisp rolls with fresh country butter. He began to relax. It was incredibly simple, but outstanding.

Silence reigned at the dinner table instead of the usual chatter. Intent upon delectable food, the men ignored each other and concentrated on the meal for a time.

Once finished, the soup was removed by

fish, then came the roasted meats. The hearty vegetable dishes and salads, with the interesting flavors and seasonings, finally prompted several of the men to comment to one another. Theirs was an unusual group, one who appreciated fine food superbly prepared, although none of them would have declared themselves to be gourmets. They customarily dined at each other's tables, enjoyed a good conversation and a bit of gossip, but tonight was quite special. As good a fellow as Collison might be, few were sorry to see that it appeared he would lose his bet if it meant they enjoyed this meal.

Collison sat with a fixed smile on his face. In an undertone he said to Willowby, 'How the devil do you suppose he managed to find a Frenchie at the last minute? These sauces are most definitely not English.'

'Dashed if I know,' Willowby muttered in reply, stuffing his mouth with a forkful of succulent roast. 'Whoever he is, he's a good cook,' he added in an understatement, not wanting to give offense to the friend who would undoubtedly lose his wager. He wondered how much Collison had paid to lure René away from Harford. Stood to reason it was a packet, for everyone knew Harford to be a generous employer.

The remove was set before them, and when

that was cleared away, the sweets and puddings were brought in upon tray after tray. Like little boys presented with an entire Christmas pudding they all stared at the results of Penelope's afternoon. The tipsy cake stood to one side with the meringues, the other sweets and puddings surrounding them in profusion.

'Just where does one start, old boy?' Sir Aubrey Preston inquired with a laugh.

That remark broke the silence, and the various offerings were soon tried. The tipsy cake disappeared completely, being a favorite of nearly every gentleman present.

At last the meal concluded and Jonathan waited with an expectant air. He had won the bet! No one could deny that he had served a superb meal that appealed to the gentlemen. Hearty fare, well-presented, and plenty of excellent wine with each course.

'I wish I could lure your chef away, but I suppose you'd not part with him?' Sir Aubrey inquired in the lazy voice of one who is happily replete.

Jonathan lowered his gaze to the table, concealing his inner mirth at that request. His chef? The lovely blond who now graced his kitchen? How could he get around her identity? He wouldn't put it past someone to demand the chef appear so he might receive their praise. 'Never,' Jonathan finally answered, hoping he would have to say no more on that score.

Collison pushed back his chair, rising to toast his host. 'I thought I had you at a loss, old friend. I see I vastly underestimated you. Here's to the host of the hour. You have won fair and square.' After tossing off his wine, he reached in his pocket to extract the sum of money he'd not thought to pay. It hurt a bit, but he always paid his debts, and Harford had won with a splendid meal. He just wished he knew where he had managed to find that chef. He could have sworn there was not a one to be found in the entire city.

'It was nasty of you to abscond with René just when I needed him. However, the replacement I found more than surpassed him.' Jonathan repressed a chuckle. If they only knew in how many ways she surpassed the dour Frenchman. The man might have been an excellent chef, but he had a face that could stop a clock.

Conversation turned to other topics and the men sat for perhaps an hour over their port, chatting away about everything and anything of interest to men of the city.

* * *

In the kitchen, Penelope took off her apron, tossing it aside with the numerous cloths to be laundered.

Mrs Barker shook her head, nudging Penelope to a chair. 'Now, my lady, you just rest. We're used to cleaning up after a dinner. That Frenchie never lifted a finger once the cooking was done. The girls are good at their work, and we'll have the kitchen to order in no time.'

Penelope believed her. She had admired the efficient way Mrs Barker had handled the returning plates, scraping them clean, then immersing them in hot soapy water before rinsing them to place on the drying rack. The kitchen maid scurried about, helping with this and that, smoothing the path for food going out and dishes coming back. It had been a well-ordered drill.

'I can see that. I expect I could leave now, but I intend to have a word with Lord Harford before I go.'

'Gracious, ma'am! That might be hours, if they get to playing at cards an' the like.'

'I shall wait,' Penelope declared, brooking no argument.

Miss Nilsson nodded her agreement, for she knew quite well what Penelope was about. 'We shall wait in your parlor, if we may, Mrs Barker?'

Overwhelmed that a fine lady — even if she did know how to cook — would be seated in her parlor, Mrs Barker ushered the ladies into her neat room, then left to supervise the cleaning up.

Hours later a flushed and triumphant Lord Harford entered the kitchen to seek his cousin. Upon being told where she was, he hurried to the cook's parlor. There he found Penelope curled up on Cook's comfortable armchair — asleep.

She stirred, then opened her eyes to stare up at him, her long lashes fluttering until she became fully awake, 'You won,' she stated.

'We won, my dear.' He pulled her from the chair and gave her a hearty kiss, before it sank in on his fuzzy brain that she was a lady as well as his cousin, and deserved to be treated with greater respect. But he had quite enjoyed that kiss. With a bit of tutoring it could meet all his expectations.

Flustered but determined, in spite of that exuberant kiss, Penelope stood her ground. 'Then, when do we begin, my lord?'

4

Not one to put off the inevitable, Lord Harford gave Lady Penelope a lopsided smile and bowed. 'Tomorrow, or ought I say today? I shall present myself at our cousin's house at your earliest convenience, my dear third cousin, once removed.'

Miss Nilsson rose from her quiet corner. 'That had best be after noon. Shall we say one of the clock, my lord?'

Suddenly remembering that the Swedish lady was present and much the chaperon, Lord Harford nodded his agreement, then offered his arm to Penelope. 'I am much indebted to you, Cousin.'

She gave him an amused, albeit tired, smile. 'Just do not forget, if you please.'

As he escorted them to the carriage he had ordered, Lord Harford very much doubted that he would be allowed such liberty.

* * *

In spite of the lateness of the previous evening, Jonathan awoke early, taking himself off for a morning ride in the park to rid his brain of lingering cobwebs. He did not get very far before he was stopped by one of those present at his dinner of last evening.

'Dashed fine meal, Harford,' declared Sir Aubrey Preston once again. 'Don't suppose you'd care to part with the name of your new chef, or better yet, where you managed to find such a wonder at the last minute?'

'You have the right of it, Preston. I wouldn't.'

'I feared as much.' Sir Aubrey sighed, then joined Jonathan on a silent ride through the morning mists. 'I do like tipsy cake,' he said eventually, breaking the silence. 'And that was a fine one. Just the right amount of sherry, don't y'know?'

'I know,' Jonathan confirmed, thinking of the excellent food that had been placed on the table. His thoughts also strayed to the young woman who had created that sweet. The years she must have spent alone, her entire life with naught but a hired companion, never mind that Nilsson looked to be a kind and intelligent woman. Hired was hired.

Jonathan was a bit spoiled, as he'd be the first to admit. His mother and sisters doted on him, and his younger brother was a good lad, always ready for a lark. Although Jonathan felt the need to supervise him, he did so with a light hand, earning him the affection of the boy. He had always been well-served by those in his employ. Yes, he was a most fortunate man.

Poor Cousin Penelope. He tried to imagine what it must have been like to have parents who made brief and exceedingly rare appearances, and couldn't.

⋆ ⋆ ⋆

Penelope stood at the door to the breakfast parlor, staring at the sideboard. There were no gently steaming dishes of food in the bain-marie, no eggs or ham. A meager stack of toast with a pot of marmalade took pride of place.

'Mrs Flint,' Penelope said to the approaching house-keeper, 'I fear I slept overlong this morning and have totally missed my breakfast.'

The housekeeper raised her gaze to the ceiling and gave a long-suffering sigh. 'No, what's in there is what was ordered by Miss Letty. It seems she's taken up with some heathen notion. Declares she will eat nothing but vegetables, perhaps a bit of grains. No fish, no fowl, and no meat. She allows that we may have a bit of cheese and milk, and once a week an egg. Now, I ask you, my lady! How can one go on with no more than porridge and turnips?' It was a measure of Mrs Flint's distress that she so forgot herself as to speak plainly to Penelope, something she would never have done otherwise.

'I cannot credit that she expects the rest of us to do so as well.' Penelope gave an indignant look down the hall at the door to the little study where Letty secreted herself each day.

'I only know my orders, my lady.' Mrs Flint recalled herself, and her cheeks reddened as she realized her forwardness.

'Hm,' Penelope replied. She tactfully ignored the housekeeper's embarrassment and followed her to the kitchen. Once in familiar surroundings, Penelope quickly whipped up a buttered egg, carved a thin slice of country ham, then seated herself at the center table to eat her breakfast before Letty found out about her heresy.

'What did she order for dinner, pray tell?' Penelope inquired after wiping her mouth following the final bite of her tasty breakfast.

Still shaken by the sight of a guest who had efficiently created a meal for herself, the cook handed a small card to Penelope. 'Potato-and-leek soup with fresh bread and cheese, my lady.'

Mrs Flint popped into the kitchen from her stillroom, to offer a comment. 'She wants no meat! Mind you, we aren't likely to have company save yourselves, but I would like to know what she thinks will keep body and soul together. Turnips and parsnips, carrots and the like. What rubbish! Beggin' your pardon, my lady.'

'Perhaps she is merely on a slimming program,' Penelope said with hope in her voice.

'Aye, and pigs will fly,' Mrs Flint muttered before she whisked herself back into the stillroom, where she was in the process of preparing a delicate nut torte.

Penelope soon discovered that the entire household, with the lone exception of Letty, was in a grumpish state. Even Miss Nilsson's usually calm temper was badly frayed. The maids frowned as they went about their work, things were dropped, and hasty words were snapped.

'I see you are tiffed this morning,' Penelope whispered as her companion grimaced following a view of the breakfast parlor and its insignificant contents.

'Mr Oglethorpe has come to call, and my stomach growls so that I dare not present myself. You shall have to entertain him until Letty can be persuaded to come out.'

Torn between preparing something for her companion to eat, an act which Penelope knew would horrify Nilsson, and doing the courteous with Mr Oglethorpe, Penelope wavered.

'This way, Miss Nilsson,' Mrs Flint whispered with a conspiratorial smile.

Satisfied that the servants were rebelling in a discreet but necessary way, Penelope slipped off to the morning room, where Mr Oglethorpe paced before the empty hearth.

'Good day, sir.'

'I was hoping to see you first.' He paused, coloring fiercely as he searched for words in an embarrassed manner. 'You must help me, Lady Penelope,' he declared with a frustrated thrust of his hand into his ginger-colored hair. His nice gray eyes beseeched with desperate appeal. 'I have been courting Letty Winthrop for what seems like an age. She cares for me, I know she does. Yet she raises one obstacle after another.'

'I can imagine,' Penelope murmured, thinking of the latest start her cousin had embarked upon. 'Perhaps she feels unsure of herself.'

'I would do anything for her, she must know that,' he declared awkwardly.

Penelope shook her head, sinking down on the nearest chair to ponder the problem of her peculiar cousin.

'Do you know the latest, Mr Oglethorpe? Miss Letty has become what she calls a natural diet follower. Once the present supply of meat is consumed, there is to be no more purchased for this household. We are to subsist mostly on vegetables.'

'Egad! She must have heard about Shelley. He has written a thing called *Vindication of a Natural Diet* and I fancy she must have read it.' Andrew Oglethorpe also sank down upon a chair to contemplate his beloved's latest notion.

'Percy Shelley, the poet? What does he know about diet? Does he practice medicine and cook when he isn't penning odes?' Penelope rubbed her chin in speculation, staring out the window as though to find the solution.

'Lady Penelope, have you ever *read* any of Letty's poetry?' Mr Oglethorpe said in a hesitant voice.

'I cannot say that I have. Why?' Her gaze flew to his face, taking note of his highly embarrassed flush.

Whatever Mr Oglethorpe was about to confide had to be postponed when Letty sailed into the room, her face bearing a self-satisfied look.

'You look well, Cousin Penelope. I fancy my program of improvement is going to do you good. Mr Oglethorpe, what brings *you* to my hearth?'

He gave her a narrow look. 'I begin to wonder.'

His hint of possible disenchantment fazed Letty not the least. She plumped herself down on the sofa to regale them of her latest efforts, and how she simply knew that her new natural diet would improve her poetry.

Penelope looked at Mr Oglethorpe. He leaned against the mantelpiece, somewhat behind Letty, and was shaking his head in the most gloomy manner possible.

'Letty, I fear that your household is not best pleased with the notion of forsaking meat,' he offered.

'A natural diet from the bounty of the earth will have them cheerful in a trice,' Letty declared, quite obviously unwilling to see any point but her own.

A stir at the door brought Penelope to her feet. 'Lord Harford, what a surprise.' Her voice did not betray the fact she had been waiting for him.

Harford looked about the room, observing that there would be no quiet spot where he might discuss plans with Lady Penelope. He had best offer his alternative plan.

'Good afternoon, cousins, Oglethorpe. I trust I find you all well?'

'As well as can be,' murmured Penelope, thinking of the meatless meals to come.

Harford seized the opportunity. 'I believe you could use a bit of pink in your cheeks, Lady Penelope. Would you like to take a drive in my carriage? Now?'

Penelope floated across the room with deceptive speed. 'Just what I longed for — a bit of fresh air. I feel sure that Miss Nilsson would adore to join us.'

'By all means.' Harford nodded with resignation. Why he would rather be alone with his impossible cousin, he couldn't have said. Of course, that kiss lingered in the back of his mind. One did not go about kissing a near-stranger, even if she were your cousin, yet it had been rather delightful, even if he had been a trifle elevated at the time. Not foxed, mind you, just a touch bosky.

Penelope surveyed the tastefully rigged-out landau with approving eyes. Black leather gleamed with the soft patina of diligent polishing. Four chestnuts awaited the office to start with commendable patience. The coachman tipped his hat as the ladies entered, followed by Lord Harford.

'You rescued me just in time, my lord,' Penelope said in a soft voice, as though she feared Letty might yet hear her.

Harford leaned back against the squabs with a smile crossing his handsome face. 'Rescued? I know I am to assist you with

. . . clothing? advice? But to rescue you?'

'Cousin Letty has done the most bird-witted thing.'

'Miss Winthrop has embraced the philosophy of Mr Shelley, the poet,' Miss Nilsson inserted helpfully. 'She has become an advocate of a natural diet, one which excludes all meat, fowl, and fish.'

'By Jove, you don't say!' The perfect angle of Lord Harford's beaver hat tilted as he started in amazement.

'We are,' Penelope intoned solemnly, 'to have potato-and-leek soup with bread and cheese for dinner this evening. Would you care to join us?'

'Horrors!' Harford shook his head. He shuddered at the mere thought of such Spartan diet.

'Enough of this silliness.' Penelope grinned at the shaken Lord Harford. 'As long as I am able to sneak into the kitchen, I shall see to it that Nilsson and I are properly fed. I fear that if I don't make certain the servants get food on the sly, we shall have a mutiny on our hands. One of the maids threatened to give notice just before I left.'

'Oh, dear,' Nilsson murmured, looking to Lord Harford as one does to a savior.

Not accustomed to that sort of look in the least, discounting his sisters who begged him to get them out of a pickle, Harford ran a finger around inside his collar, then began his questioning in a different line, hoping to change the topic. 'I have made a review of mantua-makers deemed suitable for a young lady. My sisters and my mother are fond of a woman named Madame Clotilde. I think she will be most proper for you.'

'I heard the name Madame Grisette mentioned. Is she acceptable? The gown she designed for a lady at the Collison ball was magnificent,' Penelope said.

'No.'

'What do you mean, just 'no'?' Penelope demanded.

'She is not suitable in the least,' Harford continued warily. His hope that he might not have to explain went sliding down the drain as his third cousin, once removed, tilted that pretty blond head and narrowed her eyes at him.

'She caters to the demi-reps and high-flyers, not at all the sort of thing for a young lady, if you catch my meaning.'

'Well, the gown was perfectly lovely, if you ask me. Nothing out of line that *I* could see.'

'Perhaps a trifle low-necked, my love, and maybe a bit daring in color. Although I am certain you would look well in vivid crimson with cascades of blond lace and ribbons,'

Miss Nilsson inserted in a soothing voice.

His respect for the companion grew as he saw her skillful handling of what could have been a touchy thing. Harford concealed a smile behind a hastily raised hand, coughing slightly as he did.

Lady Penelope crossed her arms before her, staring out across the expanse of green park. 'I expect Madame Clotilde should be well enough if your family uses her. But I do not believe I should like an insipid gown.'

'Nothing would ever look insipid on you, dear cousin.'

'You failed to see me at the Collison ball, in that event,' Penelope replied with a smile lurking in her eyes as she returned her gaze to meet him.

Seeing that her humor was restored, Harford went on enumerating the invitations she might accept, those she should not. 'My mother has promised to sponsor you at the next court presentation. You cannot truly be considered 'out' until you have made your curtsy there. Then,' he added, 'I induced her to include you — for she recalls your parents well — in the ball that she gives for my sister.'

He was quite well aware that this offering was anything but what Lady Penelope deserved. As a considerable heiress, and a beauty as well, she merited a magnificent ball of her own. However, he knew of no woman he might ask to take on the task of presenting Penelope to Society. As it was, his mother raised her brows and sighed at the mere thought.

Harford had promised her extra funds, which had done the trick quite nicely.

Penelope studied her gloved hands, smoothing the fine French kid over each finger with care. 'That is asking a great deal of your mother, sir. I beg you not to trouble her.'

'Dash it all, Penelope — or may I call you Penny? — you *must* be presented at court. I shall take care of the trifling matter of cards and all that, and Madame Clotilde can see that you have a proper presentation gown. But as to a ball, well, I know you deserve better, but unless you want me to summon Aunt Winthrop from the country, my mother will have to be it.'

'I should like to be called Penny, I believe,' she replied primly. 'I can see you know what must be done, and truly I shall try not to give you any more bother than necessary.' Penelope had never had anyone even offer to give her a pet name. Since that was a privilege reserved for families and dearest friends, of which she had precious little, she'd never had such.

'I doubt if Mrs Winthrop would care to

oversee her niece's coming-out, as it were,' Miss Nilsson said carefully.

Jonathan wasn't so sure about that. If rumors were to be believed, their cousin Ernest had frittered away a considerable amount of his inheritance. Jonathan imagined the fellow expected to forge a link with Penny, since she was devilish warm in the pocket. She didn't seem the least inclined to marry the chap, however.

'Never!' Penelope declared. 'I shall not have that woman fluttering about me with her nasty little barbs. And I feel certain that that toad Ernest would come with her.'

'Dear, it has been an age since you last saw her.'

'Yes, she came down for the memorial service for my parents and made it plain then that she would expect to control my life when the time came for me to wed. I intend to see that does not occur.'

Jonathan didn't bother to conceal his grin. Lady Penelope might be a naive little thing fresh from the country, but she had determination and she certainly possessed spunk.

They bowled along in the park, ignoring the occasional carriage, while they made their plans. Dates were fixed, arrangements were made. The weeks would be busy ones.

'You must see the mantua-maker as soon as possible. In fact, I believe I shall take you to see her this instant. The court gown takes time, unless she has an ordered one that was never claimed. That does happen, you know.'

Penelope wrinkled her brow. 'I cannot imagine someone going to that trouble, then changing her mind.'

Jonathan exchanged a cautious glance with Miss Nilsson, but made no reply. There were actually a number of reasons one might have a change of heart: losing a fortune, illness, deciding to marry before the court date, to list a few.

'I suppose I must wear something vastly insipid for my come-out ball? White muslin has ever made me look ill.' Penelope sighed and sought Jonathan's eyes with a beseeching plea that he found hard to resist.

'We shall see,' he temporized.

'Will it not look compromising if you come in with us, Cousin?' Penelope gave him a curious look, wondering how he proposed to wiggle out of this situation. Surely he had no love for sitting about while a lady picked out a design, and all that it entailed.

'For a young woman who has been buried in the country, you have some remarkable notions,' he answered in a repressive tone with a haughty stare.

'I was merely curious.' She glanced about the street down which the carriage now progressed. The shops looked terribly exclusive, just the sort she expected she must patronize to look her most fashionable. 'And we do receive the papers, you know. We are not quite the heathen you might think.' As he made no reply to this statement, she went on. 'I still do not see why I must go through all this nonsense just to acquire a suitable husband. Surely you might be able to draw up a list of possibilities — men who enjoy London, perhaps a hunting box, and travel abroad? My guardian, Lord Lanscomb, has been in the Austrian Alps for years, I believe. I cannot apply to him. Even his wife undoubtedly has not seen him in ages.'

'Clearly a blessing for both parties.' Jonathan recalled that Lord Lanscomb was a quiet man with a harpy of a wife, one who would drive any sane man to head for the Alps.

'Perhaps I must take a page from her book?'

This outrageous suggestion was not remarked upon as the carriage drew to a halt before a shop painted a pretty dove gray, with windows picked out neatly in gold. Penelope decided it was as elegant a shop as she had seen yet.

Any idea that Lord Harford intended to sit

silently in the shadows while Penelope waded through the fashion plates, Miss Nilsson at her shoulder, went by the wayside immediately. First of all, Madame Clotilde turned to him to ask what was required. Apparently he had overseen his sisters' wardrobes, being a gentleman of notably excellent taste.

Penelope sniffed faintly and bestowed a dark look on the pair. Her good sense told her that he undoubtedly was more cognizant of fashion, but *she* was to wear the items.

In short order she found her cousin had proclaimed their relationship, making it sound as though they were closer to being brother and sister. Then it transpired that not only did he know style, but he was well up on the difference in the cut of sleeves and necklines and on various colors and what they might achieve. Indeed, that languid gentleman — who had disappeared when there was work to do before his dinner — now bestirred himself on her behalf with a vengeance. Or so it seemed to her.

'A muted white, assuredly a delicate violet, and a tasteful blue — the twilight tones, I think,' Lord Harford declared in an undertone that carried perfectly well to Penelope's straining ears.

Twilight tones, indeed.

'Very feminine, not too low a neckline

— perhaps a number with a discreet ruff? I think her look ought to be one of remote gentility, a woman who is feminine and unattainable.'

Twilight tones was quite bad enough, but this? And a high neckline when every gown she had seen dipped to here? 'Unattainable?' she repeated in softly freezing accents.

'A woman of mystery, my dear. You will set your own style.' He held up his quizzing glass to study her. He spoke softly and gently, and, she noticed, rather privately, as though he didn't wish the mantua-maker to hear what he said.

She searched his face, studying the well-proportioned planes, his eyes that appeared so black, that firm mouth. Here she turned her gaze away from him. That hastily snatched kiss following his dinner still lingered in her mind.

'You do understand that my prime reason for placing myself in your hands is that I must find a husband as quickly as possible? I trust you to help me. What a pity you would not serve as a husband. It would simplify matters so much, would it not?'

His voice betrayed his pique. 'You think I would be so terrible as a mate?'

'I have seen mention of you in the papers, and distinctly received the impression that you are more than a bit of a rake, my lord. And you gamble, else you'd not be in this pickle now. My need is for someone who will marry me and go away. For some peculiar reason, I sense you might not do as I wish.'

'I'd not be a complaisant sort of husband, if that's what you mean. Any children who bear my name will be my own,' he snapped.

'My lord!' she protested in a shocked voice.

He called down the fates upon his unfortunate tongue, then turned gratefully as Madame Clotilde brought forth a pretty gown of a sunset lavender in a quite acceptable style. If he could but think of Lady Penelope as another sister needing guidance upon entering the world of the *ton*, he just might cope with this situation.

It ought not be too difficult to launch Penny. She possessed good breeding, an enviable wealth; surely it should be a simple matter to instruct her in the delicacy involved regarding Society's manners? Any lady intelligent enough to learn the art of cooking ought to comprehend the necessity to guard her tongue. Recalling her presentation at his front door in the morning hours, never mind that it had been fortuitous for him, he was reminded of another thing he must reprove.

'How fortunate your cousin is to have your judgment to assist her. Your sisters surely benefited from your taste, my lord,' Madame Clotilde said in an attractive French accent.

'My mother has always turned to me for advice.' Not to mention the wherewithal to finance that taste. 'I shall leave for the nonce, and return to claim you later.'

Deciding she was vastly outnumbered, and that after all, she had chosen her cousin because he was the most elegant person at the Collison ball — not to mention in need of her help — Penelope gracefully gave way to the inevitable.

She watched his departure with envious eyes. He would spend his leisure at his club. She had an inkling her time would be less agreeable.

Hours later, after being poked and pinned, she smiled with grim determination and not a little relief as Lord Harford returned to the mantua-maker's shop to reclaim her.

Jonathan had decided to give full measure. After all, he had won a considerable sum of money with her help. It was the least he could do for the little cousin from the country. He would offer his impeccable judgment regarding parasols and slippers, bonnets and reticules — for he well knew that little things could make all the difference in one's impression on the *ton*.

When they at last returned to the house on

Upper Brook Street, Penelope insisted Lord Harford join them for a cup of tea or a glass of something restorative, whatever his preference. The enormous number of parcels was whisked up to Penelope's room while Mrs Flint supervised a nice tea, with a bit of lovely sherry for his lordship on the side.

Once settled with the badly needed refreshment in the quiet of the deserted morning room on the ground floor, Penelope surveyed Lord Harford. Muffin wandered into the room, took a sniff of him, and promptly entwined herself about his legs, then jumped up on his lap to settle down.

'Well, really, Muffin,' Penelope said, again rather piqued at her pet.

'Muffin?' Jonathan inquired, relaxing now it seemed that Penny didn't demand he produce an acceptable candidate for her hand this instant. He failed to understand her rush to marry. Why not enjoy London a bit?

'I thought 'Marmalade' too common.'

'I see,' he replied, although he wasn't at all sure he did.

Faintly annoyed that her cat had taken so quickly to a stranger, Penelope turned the limpid blue of her eyes upon her new cousin. 'How much time do you think it will take? I should like to return to Fountains before too long. There is much to do there, and I would have this task behind me.' Then, as an after-thought, she added, 'I do hope the man you finally approve will agree to disappear quickly after the wedding. I still say it's a pity you would not suit, for I sense you far prefer London living, and I will wager you would enjoy a nice long trip to the Continent.' She sighed, obviously regretting that Lord Harford was not amenable.

Jonathan felt a rush of displeasure, although why he wasn't overjoyed that this mere chit of a girl wasn't trying to snare him into being parsoned, he didn't know. Albeit she was a taking thing, a right luscious armful. He felt pique at being so readily dismissed. 'I need time to consider the prospects. One doesn't pull a proper husband from a hat such as a conjurer at a country fair might do.' He finished his sherry, then excused himself, depositing the cat on the chair.

While he sauntered off to his club, he wondered whom he would place on the short list as a candidate for Penny's hand. For the oddest reason, not one man who came to mind seemed to be right for the position of the absent husband. With all her charms, she deserved someone better than she seemed willing to accept.

5

The presentation to Lady Harford ranked as difficult as attending court in Penelope's mind. Nervous as a small cat under the eye of a fierce terrier, Penelope put on one of her new demure 'twilight-hued' dresses — one that had a neckline up to her chin — a Gypsy hat of exceptionally proper design, along with violet Limerick gloves, then went down to wait for her third cousin, once removed.

Letty ventured forth from her hideaway to inspect Penelope. 'Hm, I detect the hand of a master of subtlety here,' she said. 'While you look very lovely, dear cousin, you are not in the way of outshining Harford's sister with a conspicuous gown. Very astute. I compliment you on your intuition.'

Far too honest to accept this encomium when she felt it unearned, Penelope smiled and shook her head. 'You must save your praise for Lord Harford. He is the one who influenced my choice, I fear.'

'Well, that is what you wished. I must say, he did well. Now, were I inclined to make a splash, I might avail myself of his taste, for I can see he has a master touch.'

'Why do I doubt he acquired it all in aiding his sisters?'

'My dear country cousin! You forget, he is a man of the town. A lady learns to ignore barques of frailty. Besides, I believe your intention is to marry a man who has other interests. I suggest that it takes such a one to know who the others are.'

Aware of a stab of disappointment, but unable to think of why, Penelope paced about the morning room, toying with the cords of her unpretentious reticule. 'I can understand I ought to be demure when meeting his mother, but do you know that nearly all of my gowns are the sort an overprotective brother would choose for his little sister? I fail to see how these will aid in attracting a gentleman to my side. Recollect that I wish someone dashing, a man who will accept my offer, then hie himself off to distant parts. 'Tis most peculiar, I tell you.'

Letty frowned in equal puzzlement, then turned as Mrs Flint entered the room with Lord Harford trailing right behind her.

The housekeeper disappeared, but Letty lingered on, more out of curiosity than for propriety's sake.

Jonathan examined Penelope with his quizzing glass in hand, missing not a fold of fabric, nor the careful tie of her hat ribbons.

When he had walked completely around her, turning her into a seething mass of conflicting emotions, he nodded. 'You'll do.'

'I'll do?' With deceptive calm Penelope continued, 'After I've spent simply ages to prepare for this *tête-à-tête* you have arranged, you can merely say that I will do?' She stamped a neatly slippered foot. 'I shall never understand men! How fortunate that I have decided to relegate my husband to a distant spot, if this is what one must contend with. Come, we might as well leave and get this call over with at once.'

Clearing his throat, his countenance carefully controlled, Harford strolled from the house with Penelope on his arm, while a confused Letty watched from a window.

During the ride over to Harford House on Mount Street, Harford ventured to say to his obviously miffed cousin, 'I cannot fathom why you insist upon a marriage of convenience. It is not the thing to turn your back on love, you know.'

She gave him a frosty look. 'I am under the impression that a great number of *ton* marriages are thus arranged. Why ought mine be any different, pray tell?'

'That simply is not so. While it might have been true in the past, most young couples today marry because they have formed an attachment. I suspect your sheltered existence has given you a narrow view of life.'

'Rubbish.'

'But you do not rule love out?' He glanced down at her face, well-concealing his interest.

'For you, it may be plausible. For me, no. By the bye, have you selected a young lady to serve as your wife?' Penelope slanted a decidedly impish glance at him.

'What a peculiar way of phrasing it.' He raised one handsome brow, while directing a reproving look at her. 'And no, I have not chosen the light of my life, the joy of my heart. Yet. And you have changed the subject when I was not tired of it.'

'Well, I am.' She gave him an exasperated glare. 'If only you were not so . . . ' She dropped the subject as his reproving look turned into an awesome frown. Apparently, for some quite absurd reason, he did not like to hear how ineligible he was as husband material. She would have thought he'd have been glad, seeing that he intended to take his time finding a mate. He'd likely search the entire country, like the Prince Charming of her girlhood fairy tales. A fine Prince Charming he'd make. Hmpf.

Harford House was a rather nice place, she decided as the butler ushered them up the stairs into the drawing room. There was a number of attractive paintings of Lord Harford's ancestors gracing the walls, the carpets looked in excellent repair, and the style of the curtains was positively enchanting. Jonathan was not the only Harford to exhibit excellent preferences, it seemed.

In the drawing room they found a slender woman, brown hair barely tinged with silver, with only a few wrinkles to mar her attractive face.

Glancing about her, Penelope smiled at the lady who had risen to greet them, and impulsively said, 'What an utterly charming room, ma'am. I am persuaded that I know whereof your son acquired his excellent taste.' Wine-colored draperies framed the windows in attractive loops, while pale cream silk decorated the walls, reflecting the upholstery of the chairs. Touches of wine and deep green accented the various pieces about the room, and the effect was of richness and elegance.

Lady Harford's eyes widened at this artless remark; then her reserve melted at the sight of the orphaned girl who was, after all, a sort of niece, a very lovely one. 'Welcome, my dear. I am pleased you appreciate what I have attempted to do in this room. It was once such a gloomy place — when I first was married, you see.'

'Your husband was most fortunate, in that

case, to find such a felicitous wife.'

'*Au contraire*, my dear. I adored Arthur and would have done everything I could to please him.'

Penelope could not prevent her gaze from jumping to meet that knowing pair of eyes across the room from her. Lord Harford leaned against the exquisite marble mantelpiece with the hint of an insouciant grin hovering about his mouth. What an utterly odious man. What a pity he had such perfect taste in all things, from what she had observed to this point, for she would have dearly liked to dispense with his tutorage.

Lady Harford ignored her beloved son, motioning to Penelope to join her on a cream-and-wine-striped sofa. They chatted for some time about the kind of things one does when first meeting, especially with relatives. Once they had sorted out the precise degree of relationship, taken note of the various peculiar aunts, not to mention the sad reduction in esteem of the present holder of the Everton title — evidently Ernest was universally deemed to be a toad — Lady Harford prepared to get to the true intent of the call.

'Now, my dear, my son tells me that you arrived at Miss Winthrop's home to make your come-out. It will never do for an unmarried young woman to sponsor you, never mind that she is an eccentric. So much more the reason she ought not attempt such a thing.'

'I believe that thought never entered her mind,' Penelope replied honestly. 'I fear I plumped myself on her doorstep before she knew what I was about. She forgot to read her mail, you see.'

Apparently Lady Harford was sufficiently acquainted with her other niece to totally understand the problem. She nodded eagerly, then continued. 'I insist you must join my daughter Charis for her ball, which is to be in two weeks. That will give you enough time to have Jonathan enter your name for the next court presentation. I shall sponsor you, but he will be such a lamb as to get the required cards for you. Charis is due to attend, and so you shall have ample company.' She turned to study her son, who still leaned against the mantelpiece. 'Be so good as to acquire those cards for Lady Penelope, dear.'

'It is already seen to, dear mother. I knew a woman of your tender sensibilities would immediately take Lady Penelope under her wing, so I stopped off at the Lord Chamberlain's office to obtain the cards for Charis and Penny. Both girls shall attend and do you credit, ma'am. I shall have the ordering of Penny's gown myself.'

'I had no idea you obtained cards for Lady Penelope as well. What an efficient son you are.' If she noticed the pet name for his cousin, she gave no sign. As to the indication Lord Harford intended to supervise the dressing of his cousin, she apparently was so accustomed to his overseeing her daughters that she made no demur on that score either.

Penelope reluctantly admired the competency of the gentleman she had selected to guide her. Clearly he had decided to expend every effort to see her quickly wedded, for the court presentation and subsequent ball were musts before settling on the man she would marry. She intended to wed someone acceptable to Society, and to do that, she must prove she merited the same regard.

'What shall she wear?' Lady Harford inquired of her son, tapping her fan against her cheek.

Penelope felt most peculiar as they both studied her. What strange people, so taken up with clothes and customs. Of course, she well knew it was part and parcel of London life. But it was the first time she had experienced such in her narrow sphere, and it was quite disconcerting.

'White and silver, I believe,' Lord Harford drawled. 'With her pretty blond hair, which must be cut — do take off your hat, Penny — and blue eyes, she will be stunning. Blond lace for the lappets, and three white feathers, with silver beads, accenting her gown, I fancy. Her ensemble ought to catch the eye of the *ton* who are present. She insists she wants to marry quickly.' This last comment was delivered with a distinctly wry note in his voice that neither lady could fail to note.

Penelope had obediently removed her hat, giving Lady Harford a look of appeal as she did.

'Naughty boy, you upset your protégée.' Lady Harford turned her reproving gaze from her son to again study her niece. 'She is a lovely girl, and seems most proper. You ought to have little trouble finding her a husband, particularly since she is blessed with a fortune. She will be a pleasing foil for Charis.'

Annoyed at being studied and discussed as though she were a statue, and in general treated like a horse one was intending to put up for sale, Penelope plopped her hat back on her head and rose. 'I shall look forward to the presentation, my lady, the ball as well. Your kindness is much appreciated. I trust your son will deliver the necessary instructions for me in due time. However, I really ought to attend to a few matters.'

Lady Harford was all graciousness in

extending the warmth for which she was famous among the *ton*. She bade Penelope a fond farewell, while insisting she use the carriage, since Lord Harford's presence was required most urgently by his loving mama.

Once they were alone, a very shrewd Lady Harford turned to her obedient son and demanded, 'Will you kindly tell me precisely what is going on?'

For once in his life, Lord Harford found it very difficult to explain a situation to his mother. At least, to her satisfaction.

⋆ ⋆ ⋆

Penny hurried down the stairs, intent upon leaving Harford House as quickly as she might, when she nearly bumped into a pretty young woman equally intent upon exiting the house, her maid trailing after her with a distressed look on her face.

'Oh, dear,' Penelope explained, 'excuse me.' Taking note of the similarity between the girl and Lord Harford, Penelope ventured to say, 'Would you be Lady Charis Trent?'

'I expect you are my new cousin. I had hoped to meet you. Come' — Lady Charis glanced apprehensively up the stairs, then back at Penelope — 'let's hurry.' She clutched Penelope's arm and urged her from the house and into the carriage. The maid scurried to follow, taking an unobtrusive seat across from the elegant young ladies.

'I am excessively grateful to you, for you have contrived to make sure my ball will be the talk of the Season.' Lady Charis beamed a delighted smile at her new cousin, settling back in the carriage with a contented sigh.

Taken aback at this bit of direct speech, Penelope blinked, then carefully replied, 'I fear I have had nothing to do with your ball, Lady Charis.'

'Oh, but you have, which is why I had to thank you right away. Mama had such gothic notions, and now that Jonathan has taken an interest — because of your joining me — he will see to it that everything is most *recherché*. You will see. Mama was in alt when he told her that he would foot the bill for the changes he wanted. He has excessively good taste, as you may know. I am most fortunate to have him for a brother.'

'Indeed,' Penelope replied, her thoughts most happily not coloring her voice. Inwardly she was quite distressed. Lord Harford had lost, or so she understood, a considerable sum of money, and now, because she had placed him in the position of helping her make her bow to Society and find a husband, he was expending a large sum on her behalf.

This would never do!

'I gather a ball is horrendously expensive, or is that another topic I must not mention?' Penelope supposed it must be costly, for she'd heard of someone who was hiring a hall rather than redoing her house for the occasion.

'Jonathan would say you must not, for he is a high stickler for propriety. But I can tell you that Mama would have dipped badly into her allowance to finance the ball. Now do you see why we are both pleased to welcome you? I believe you and I shall do quite well together.' She glanced ahead, to note Oxford Street in view. 'If you are going to Botibols for the feathers we shall need, do you know what to buy?'

'Three white ones,' Penelope replied grimly.

The girls were entranced at the enormous selection presented for their choice. Beginning to understand her benefactor a little better, Penelope picked out three small but perfect white plumes. She insisted upon paying for the three cream plumes, also small and perfect, for Lady Charis. 'A getting-to-know-you present,' Penelope said when a delighted Charis protested.

'You sound like Jonathan when he wants to do something, so you won't argue with him. I wonder how his wife will accept his dictates?'

Something froze within Penelope. Controlling her countenance, she inquired, 'I was unaware that he had fixed his interest on anyone.'

'I met her last evening at a party. She told me in the strictest confidence that they shall marry as soon as he obtains permission from her parents. I must say, I was vastly surprised, for she seems the veriest widgeon, not at all what *I* would have expected.' Lady Charis clung to Penelope's arm as they left the feather warehouse to enter the carriage once again.

'A widgeon? Well, considering his views, perhaps he fell in love with her. Is she pretty?' Penelope told herself she was glad Lord Harford had found someone to love, since he seemed to feel it so necessary in marriage.

'Rather a quiet sort of girl,' Charis said tactfully. 'I found it all quite mysterious, you know, but most romantic.' Lady Charis directed the coachman to take them to Madame Clotilde's shop.

While Lady Charis tried on her ball gown of delicate cream jaconet trimmed with knots of peach ribbon, Penelope studied the fashion plates piled on a table next to the dainty chair upon which she perched.

'Ah, Lady Penelope,' Madame Clotilde

gushed as she entered the fitting room, 'I have your ball gown to a point where you can be fitted. Is that not wonderful?'

Penelope's burst of enthusiasm quickly died when she viewed the confection of white and silver lace. It was demure and terribly proper. No *décolletage* for her, not with silver lace ruffles around the top of the gown in vast profusion. Not an inch of her arms would show, what with her gloves touching the hem of the puffed and slashed sleeves. Although she liked the silver taffeta peeping forth from the slashes, she wondered if all girls had to conceal every charm from view. Her bosom was more than adequate, her waist quite small, and Henri had told her that her skin was like the finest cream. She fully expected that her court dress would be equally depressing.

A glance at Lady Charis arrayed in her gown brought Penelope's temper to a simmer. The naughty neckline dipped to here, and glimpses of her soft arms were seen. The style was simple, but definitely enticing. The only man who might be tempted by Penelope's gown was a cleric.

Lady Charis' pretty mouth dropped open as she looked at Penelope. 'My brother chose that style?'

'He did.' Penelope sounded grim again.

Odd, how often she felt this way lately.

Sensing she was needed, Madame Clotilde beamed a smile, then said, 'You shall be a lady of mystery, of tantalizing paradox. You are so lovely and charming, yet you will not expose those charms, enticing the eye and piquing the gentlemen's interest.'

Lady Charis studied the gown on her new cousin, then looked at her own. 'I gather I am no mystery, then, for this gown is quite different.'

'But you look so beautiful, you shall capture every heart at your ball. I will be fortunate to snare even one dance,' Penelope protested.

Not totally convinced, but feeling that Lady Penelope might have the right of it, Charis nodded graciously and the matter was ended as far as she was concerned.

Penelope had other matters on her mind by now. She accepted a ride back to Upper Brook Street, then sought out Cousin Letty. She found her in the morning room with Mr Oglethorpe at her side, reading poetry aloud in a very pleasant manner.

Doubting that Letty would have the least notion as to what was proper, Penelope appealed to Andrew Oglethorpe. 'I need some information, if you please.'

Preening just a bit, happy to be consulted

when he knew that Harford was assisting her, Oglethorpe nodded. 'By all means.'

'Is it proper for a gentleman to pay for the coming-out expenses incurred by a very distant relative?' She smiled sweetly at him, looking utterly guileless.

'Never,' he declared. 'Why, if word got out among the *ton*, she would be ruined. Everyone would assume the worst.'

'The worst being that she was in his keeping?'

'Penelope!' Letty cried in shocked accents.

'Sisters, acceptable,' he said with assurance. 'Close relatives, of course. Just what did you have in mind?' He had risen from the sofa when Penelope entered the room, and now he strolled to stand by the window, glancing out at the passing carriages.

'He has told his mother that he will foot a large portion of the coming-out ball for Lady Charis and me, since there will be additional expenses. I gather it was an inducement so she would take me on.' There was no mistaking the chagrin in her voice.

'Well,' inserted Mr Oglethorpe in defense of the Way Things Were Done, 'that was only right and fair, for his mama likes to spend the blunt and he is well to grass. With a bit of ready money, she can do the ball up first-rate, and Lady Charis as well. Stands to reason that a lady of her standing would be running near low tide. Not that her son would ever let her get all to pieces, mind you.'

Glancing first at Letty, then back to Mr Oglethorpe, Penelope quietly asked, 'He is comfortably well-off? Not the least penny-pinched?'

'Well enough, although I expect no gentleman ever has enough.' Mr Oglethorpe watched the slim, demure figure that paced back and forth across the floor of the morning room. It was impossible to tell what was going on under that modest hat she wore.

'I see.' Penelope wondered if Mr Oglethorpe knew about the serious loss Lord Harford had incurred. She had expected Mr Willowby would prattle the story about. Perhaps they were more considerate, seeing that Lord Stephen Collison gained. She was thankful that she had been able to stop Lord Harford from losing an even larger sum of money. It was unthinkable that Harford go into debt on her behalf. She would pay her own way.

'What will you do, Penelope?' Letty queried in a quavering voice. She clutched the book of poetry in her hands as though to ward off an attack of the vapors.

'Do not worry your pretty head about a thing,' Penelope replied absently, in her own absorption failing to observe the attractive flush that spread across Letty's cheeks. Glancing at the long-case clock, she added, 'I had best hurry before the bank closes. I shall see you both later.'

With those enigmatic words she whirled about and left the room. In moments Mr Oglethorpe watched her enter a hackney and head off in the general direction of the city.

'I say, you don't suppose she is actually going to go to the bank!' he said, quite alarmed.

Letty rose and crossed to pat his arm. 'My cousin seems to have unexpected depths to her. I have learned in the short time she has been in the house that she is remarkably able to get her way. She is sensible and most organized, you see.'

'But what will she do?'

'Well, she cannot permit Lord Harford to pay for her come-out. You recollect she is exceedingly wealthy and can well afford to foot her own expenses. I have no idea what she will do about Lord Harford, but I expect she will think of something. She is bound to.'

The two stood at the window, side by side, contemplating a sweet young woman who looked as biddable as a lamb. Then Letty recalled that lambs could be remarkably stubborn at times, and she sighed.

* * *

Although she garnered some astounded looks when she went to the bank, it took only a brief time for arrangements to be made to Penelope's satisfaction.

The man who made all these dispositions was only too happy to see that this wealthy young woman desired to pay her bills and not incur debt. If more Society women would follow her example, he knew a great number of gentlemen who would not be driven to seek a moneylender.

* * *

The following afternoon Penelope surveyed the misty rain with a sense of unease. She had heard nothing from Lord Harford, although why she ought to, she didn't know. If he was truly affianced, he would be obliged to dance attendance on his betrothed.

She wondered more than a little about this sudden and secret betrothal. He struck her as the sort of man who would be decisive, unwilling to wait when he wanted something. If he had found his true love, would he not have sought out her parents first, to ascertain that his addresses would be welcome — and who would deny a handsome, titled man such as he — before seeking her hand? She found this all greatly puzzling.

And it angered her as well. His protestations had seemed so real, so honest. She had felt betrayed when Lady Charis revealed the secret betrothal. Although that young miss had better learn to mind her tongue. Nothing irritated Penelope more than a gossipmonger. The *ton* might thrive on tittle-tattle, but Penelope felt it did an enormous amount of harm.

A tap on her door brought the maid with a message that Lord Harford awaited her pleasure in the drawing room.

Astonished that this seldom-seen room had been pressed into use, Penelope checked her appearance in the looking glass before leaving the sanctuary of her bedroom. More than ever she felt the need for armor of a sort.

She paused in the doorway, noting that he was pacing back and forth before the empty fireplace. The room was chilly, even on a spring day, for it faced the rear of the house and not a speck of sun had entered to warm it. She shivered, but whether from the chill or the indignation she sensed emanated from Lord Harford, she wasn't certain.

'Good day, sir.' She spoke softly, almost hesitantly. Would he comment on her orders? She discovered immediately, as he whirled about to confront her.

'Aha! You! I could not believe my eyes this

morning at the missive from my man of business. That a *woman* should pay me . . . for what? Offering a bit of advice? I cannot tell you how angry I am.' He slowly walked toward her, an air of menace about him.

'I always pay my way, sir.' She clenched her hands behind her, advancing into the room with an intrepid step, her chin tilted up in a show of defiance. 'But I did not pay for your advice. I merely paid a few bills at Madame Clotilde's. True, I anticipated expenses involved with the ball. You would not deny me the pleasure of contributing to what is to be, after all, my ball as well as your sister's? How heartless, sir.'

She came to a halt before him, nose to nose, as it were. His eyes, black as Whitby jet, seemed to shoot sparks of fire at her. Refusing to turn tail, she stood her ground and continued.

'I do not cavil at your taste in selecting appropriate gowns for my come-out, for you know Society better than Mr Brummell. I do oppose any payment of expenses when I am quite able to care for my own debts.'

He took a step closer. 'You were not supposed to know about that.'

She held firm. Tilting her chin up even further, her voice shaking in anger, she snapped back at him, 'Just like I was not to know about your betrothal?'

6

'My what?' he roared at her, clearly astounded. Those black eyes still snapped with sparks, but of amazement.

'I was informed by a very reliable source that a young lady claims the distinction of being your future wife,' Penelope said in a relatively quiet tone, considering how hurt and angry she was. 'I realize I have no right whatsoever to be privy to your decision to wed, but after your recent remarks, I thought you might have given me a clue.'

'Preposterous!' He clasped her arms, staring down into her eyes with a frustrated, bewildered expression that Penelope would have sworn was real. 'I do not know what you are talking about, dear cousin.'

Penelope did not care for the sarcastic inflection in his last two words, and she tried to ignore the pressure on her arms, certain that she would end up with nasty bruises.

'I insist upon knowing the perpetrator of this taradiddle. Who told you this utter nonsense?' He gave her a shake that sent her newly short blond curls to dip over her forehead in a most beguiling fashion.

A peculiar feeling of light-headedness overcame Penelope and she attributed it to being clutched in such an abominable manner. 'Your sister — after being sworn to silence by the young lady in question, I might add.'

'Oh, bloody hell,' he murmured, clearly disgusted with the news.

'I beg your pardon!' Penelope cried with deep affront.

He shook his head, then gave her a rueful look. 'Please accept my assurances that I have no intention of being wedded to any young woman now or in the near future. I have not the faintest idea who this young woman might be.'

Had she been told by someone else of this situation, Penelope might have questioned the legitimacy of his defense. Face-to-face, as they most assuredly were, it was quite another matter. 'Oddly enough, I believe you.'

His hands slid down her arms in what Penelope considered a rather caressing motion, one that brought the most peculiar sensations to her entire being.

'Thank you for that, at least,' he murmured. 'I wonder how many others have been the recipient of these girlish confidences.'

Remarkably perceptive, Penelope, in her usual sensible custom, inquired, 'Is she trying to entrap you into marriage by claiming a betrothal that does not exist, in hopes you will be forced to marry her? What an odious thing to do. Particularly if you have not the least desire to wed her.'

'I had best find my sister and extract what I can from her about this poppycock.' He stepped away from Penelope, then stopped. 'That does not alter the reason I came here to see you.'

At this point Muffin strolled into the room to twine about Penelope's legs. A plaintive cry caused her to scoop her pet up in her arms, scratching that spot beneath the chin that always brought a satisfied purr. Penelope clutched the cat in her arms in a near-defensive move.

'As I explained before, there is no need for you to take care of my debts. I am quite able to pay whatever expenses are incurred in my behalf.' Her clear blue eyes gazed back at him without the least trace of coquettishness. Even that blasted cat stared at him with unblinking amber eyes.

Jonathan studied that stubborn, very lovely face, tilted so defiantly at him. He'd never had a woman challenge him like this. Usually they were only too happy to fall into his arms, indeed, attempted to do so at the first possible chance. Yet there she stood, that silly cat in her arms, with enchanting silver-gold curls tumbled about her head, a glint in her eyes simply daring him. To do what?

'I insist upon sharing the expenses of the ball,' she continued. 'And that is quite final. When I asked for your advice, I had no intention of becoming a leech upon your generosity, my lord. Fortunately, I am a lady of independent means. I intend to remain that way.'

Whatever rejoinder Lord Harford might have issued was lost when Mrs Flint paused in the doorway, her voice sounding distinctly upset. 'Lord Everton and Lady Winthrop are here.'

'Ernest and Aunt Winthrop?' Penelope dropped the cat, her hands flying to her face as she considered the horror of this news. She struggled to calm her temper while coping with the vexatious information.

'Good grief!' Instinctively Lord Harford drew closer to Penelope, as though to shield her from her unwelcome relatives. His, too, for that matter.

'Dear child, what is this I hear about your coming to London?' gushed the thin woman who bustled into the room, poking her nose in every direction to discover who else might be present. 'I am utterly crushed that you did not turn to your dear Aunt Winthrop to assist you. Ernest and I shall take over now, dear girl. We know what is best for you. Don't we, Ernest?' She jabbed her son in the ribs with a bony elbow.

'Yes, Mother,' replied her dutiful son, wincing at the thrust.

He had been a pudgy, not overly bright child, and the years had not been kind to him, for he was now a regular puff-guts, Penelope reflected. An unhealthy pallor clung to his rounded cheeks — from long hours spent gaming, no doubt — and he looked quite miserable. The thought of being married to this pathetic creature was beyond thinking. Take over, indeed.

Aunt Winthrop inspected with distaste the near proximity of her distant nephew to her niece. They did not frequent quite the same circles — so she had not seen him up close for some time, but nevertheless she recognized him. Repressing the desire to order him from the house, for she knew some girls might be foolish enough to prefer him to her beloved Ernest, she bestowed a frosty glare on his poor head. 'You were just about to depart, Lord Harford?'

'Actually, dear aunt, Penny and I were about to join my sister. There are so many preparations for her ball, as you may well imagine.' He gave his aunt that sort of lofty look he normally reserved for encroaching mushrooms.

'Ball? What ball? Never say you have been so precipitate as to allow someone else the pleasure of doing your come-out ball? I am desolate.' Her thin, sharp nose fairly quivered with indignation. The shock of a pet name was forgotten in the horror of learning she was too late to take charge of the ball. She had quite looked forward to spending all that money, not to mention arranging the marriage between her precious son and the heiress.

Strongly suspecting the entire display of sensibilities all a hum, Penelope took a firm grip on her nerves, tossing a grateful glance at Lord Harford before she countered, 'It is a pity, I expect, but true. Lady Charis and I have become bosom bows and look forward to sharing our ball. Lady Harford has been all that is amiable in extending her assistance to this motherless girl. Such kindness is truly appreciated.'

Deciding she might as well put on her own performance, Penelope demurely hung her head, stealing a hand to her face to wipe away a nonexistent tear. While it was true she appreciated all that the Harfords, collectively, were doing for her, she normally did not gush her thanks quite so effusively nor behave so dramatically.

Lord Harford rose to the occasion by placing a protective arm about Penelope's shoulders. 'Now, Cousin, we look upon you as one of our family. No tears, please, dear girl. Come, Mother will be waiting for us, and I know you do not wish to keep her waiting.'

Penelope favored Harford with a melting smile that she hoped might be deemed sisterly. 'How thoughtful you are, dear cousin. I shall fetch my bonnet and pelisse directly.' She glanced around to find Miss Nilsson standing in the doorway. 'Oh, dear Eva, you are ready to leave, and I tarry.' Turning back to the intruders, Penelope added in dulcet tones, 'We must see you sometime whilst you are in London, Aunt. What a pity Cousin Letty has no rooms for you. I daresay you will enjoy opening Everton House. It will happily occupy your energies, I am sure. Although I feel sure my parents left it in good repair, it has been some years, and no doubt you wish to make a few changes. Please excuse me now.'

Ernest had ignored the ancestral London residence while in Town. He had acquired quarters considered adequate for a bachelor, then spent his time in wild dissipation. Penelope would wager he wanted no part of a wife or all that was entailed in establishing his residence. After all, he couldn't gamble that money away.

Making a remarkable curtsy, Penelope swept from the room with all the aplomb of a duchess.

Aunt Winthrop stood clasping her hands as though she longed to wring a neck. Any neck. Ernest, Lord Everton, looked even more miserable, if such a thing were possible.

'I feel certain you understand how it is, Aunt Winthrop,' inserted Lord Harford with the smoothness of a diplomat. 'With the Season upon us, there is so much to be done and my mother simply insists upon obtaining my advice.' Lord Harford made a barely civil bow; then, twirling his quizzing glass in one hand, he strolled from the room, well aware he had acquired two enemies. At the doorway he smiled down at Miss Nilsson, offering his arm. 'Shall we?'

'By all means,' she replied after bestowing a distant nod in the direction of the dreaded relatives.

Alone in the silence of the room, Lady Winthrop frowned at her son, then glared at the empty door. 'Frippery fellow. I will never understand why he is doted upon so by Society. One would think his opinion was the only one worth having.' She studied the haphazardly decorated room, then debated what to do next. With her initial plans thwarted, she needed a new approach. Ernest simply *must* marry the heiress, the dear boy had such expensive tastes. And that odious nephew of hers was not going to stand in her way.

At long last she sniffed and prepared to leave, but she hadn't given up her goal. It was unthinkable that all that money should be controlled by anyone other than her son, with her assistance, naturally.

Ernest dutifully trailed after her, pointing out as they marched down the stairs — she in high dudgeon, he in resignation — 'Even the Prince Regent seeks his advice, Mama. I daresay there is not a soul in all of London whose taste is as esteemed as Harford's.'

'What is he doing with your Cousin Penelope, is what I'd like to know.' Lady Winthrop glanced about, noting the absence of the three who should have been departing as well. 'Mark my words, there is something havey-cavey here. And I intend to find out what it is.' Her angular body clothed in black bombazine — she was forever mourning someone — straightened, her nose tilted up, and she charged out the doorway, looking like an old crow about to attack its prey.

Once the unwanted visitors had returned to their waiting carriage, Penelope lightly ran down the stairs to join Lord Harford and Miss Nilsson, who had slipped into the breakfast parlor to avoid a second meeting.

'What an odious pair. How dreadful to think we are related to them,' Penelope exclaimed. 'Now that they are gone, it is no longer necessary to pretend we are to call on your mother, sir. I do thank you for your timely assistance.' She bobbed a pretty curtsy and prepared to persuade Miss Nilsson to go to Hatchard's with her.

'On the contrary, I believe I require your presence when I interview my sister, else she may claim she knows nothing of the matter.' His knowing look gave her no doubt as to what he meant.

Penelope took in his grim countenance, recalled how fierce he had appeared when he heard of the lie of his supposed betrothal, and decided he was correct. 'I believe you are right. Your sister may not be able to stand up to you as well as I can.'

Lord Harford blinked at these matter-of-factly spoken words. This outrageous girl thought she could handle him? Why, every matron and miss in Society had tried a hand at that and failed miserably. The three left the house in silence, each with most interesting thoughts not to be shared.

At Harford House all was at sixes and sevens. The presentation gowns had been delivered and Lady Charis was moaning she would never be able to cope with that hoop. 'It is simply too outdated, a hoop like this.' She gave an experimental curtsy, wobbling as she did.

'Nonsense, it can be extremely graceful,' contradicted her mother. 'Be thankful you do not have to wear a hoop as large as the one I wore at my first presentation. I was so glad we did not have to sit down, for it was truly enormous.'

'Mother,' Lord Harford said as the trio entered the sitting room, where Lady Charis had been practicing with the new hoop, 'I must speak with Charis immediately.'

At the harsh note in his voice, Charis looked at Penelope, then gasped, her hand flying to cover her mouth. 'You did never . . . ?'

'Could you think I'd not discover the matter eventually?' His tone was stiff, figure rigid.

'Well, I fancied you would know all about it, although you might have told us first, you know,' his irate sister snapped back.

'*If* I were to be married, I believe I should make my family aware of the fact well in advance of the general public, and certainly not leave it up for a whispered revelation at a ball, for pity's sake.' He gave her a disgusted look, then added, 'The least you might have done was come directly to me. I am indebted to Penny, or I should still be in the dark.'

'You mean you are not to wed Miss Dunston? But she said you are,' Charis cried, looking adorably confused.

'Miss Dunston? Carola Dunston of the pale-blue eyes and the mouse-brown hair that is forever falling about her face? The one who tripped on her gown and would have fallen on her face had I not caught her? Good God, girl, you thought I would seek *her* hand? Surely you know me better than that!'

'You mean she lied?'

'Will someone kindly tell me what is going on here?' Lady Harford inserted in an effort to bring some order to the conversation.

Penelope took pity on her ladyship and swiftly walked to her side. Taking her hand, she gently led her to the sofa, where she joined her, softly explaining, 'Lady Charis told me that your son was to wed shortly, as soon as he obtained permission from Miss Dunston's parents. He was most surprised when I mentioned this betrothal to him. Naturally he wishes to learn more of the matter. It must be set right, for that girl cannot be permitted to force him into a marriage that must be exceedingly distasteful to him, and ultimately to her as well.'

Lady Harford stared at her niece. 'You have

a rare ability, child, to speak most plainly with no roundaboutation. How fortunate for some good man.' Turning to Lord Harford, she implored, 'My dear, whatever can you do to quell the pretensions of that dreadful girl?'

'I wish I knew how many people she has told of this bogus engagement. There has been no notice in the *Times*. Yet,' he added gloomily.

Penelope began to see how she might repay Lord Harford for his assistance. 'Since you have not sought her hand from her parents, there could scarcely be any notice posted in the paper. I believe they require corroboration for this sort of notice, do they not? Unless she is extremely devious, of course. We must have a plan to counter her attempt.' Penelope gazed up at Lord Harford, her resolution clear on her face. 'We shall fix her plot, so she'll not try this again.'

Lady Harford stared at her niece, then clapped her hands. 'If I did not say this before, my dear, welcome to the family.'

Penelope felt a rare blush creeping into her cheeks at this bit of warmth. 'Thank you, my lady.'

Lady Charis plumped herself on a stool, careful to place the hoop about her so that she looked quite like an exotic mushroom.

'Where do we go this evening?'

'The Bradford come-out. Will that Dunston girl be there, do you think?' Lady Harford looked at her daughter, then to her son.

'I suspect she will attend, if for no other reason than to try to entrap Jonathan.' Lady Charis turned to her brother, adding, 'You had best stay clear of her this evening.'

'On the contrary,' Penelope countered. 'I believe he ought to ask her to dance, then manage to walk her away from that area so that we can perpetrate our own little hoax upon her.'

'And that is?' an intrigued Lord Harford inquired.

She considered the matter a moment, then said, 'Perhaps you could pretend to be enamored of someone else?'

'Who?'

'I see,' she replied, understanding quite well that he would not want to seek involvement with anyone else that would demand the same solution the Dunston girl sought.

'Perhaps,' Lady Harford said in a slow drawl, 'we might impose upon Penelope to pretend an interest in Jonathan. I feel certain you could think of some manner in which to make this sudden attachment convincing to that conniving little schemer, dear boy.'

She smiled at her beloved son, trusting he would catch her intent very well.

'I should be pleased to help with The Plan,' Penelope said, then gasped. 'Oh, Aunt, I nearly forgot to tell you, Aunt Winthrop and Cousin Ernest have come to Town. I told her Letty did not have room for them and they shall have to open Everton House. That will require some doing on her part, so we have a brief reprieve. But I do need a husband, and speedily now. And no, *I* should not think of coercing your son to marry me. Poor lamb, he has no taste for marriage without love, and anyone could see at a glance we are more likely to squabble. I argue with him, you see. 'Tis a pity, for he is handsome and probably would live the sort of life I require in a husband.'

Utterly fascinated, Lady Harford said, 'Indeed?'

'He believes me too prosaic, I suspect, for if you must know, I do not believe in love. An arranged marriage will suit me quite well, as long as your son approves the gentleman as proper and Cousin Ernest is far removed from the scene. Once I am wedded, I hope to see my husband depart immediately. Somehow, I doubt your son would be so cooperative there.' She slanted a glance at her cousin to see how he accepted this bit of wisdom.

Lady Harford could not contain her

amusement, and burst into a peal of silvery laughter, followed by giggles from Lady Charis. Lord Harford merely leaned against the mantelpiece and looked amused, or chagrined. Penelope couldn't decide which.

The tea tray was brought in and they drew chairs together so that plotting might be that much easier.

Penelope took a nibble of a dainty ratafia biscuit, then reflected aloud, mostly to Miss Nilsson, 'This is lovely. I had no idea that family life could be like this, a sort of friendly unity.'

Lady Harford caught an arrested expression on her son's face and took a long sip of tea.

* * *

Some hours later, when the party set out for the Bradford girl's come-out ball, all were primed and ready for nearly anything.

Penelope had rebelled, taking a scissors to snip at the neckline of her chosen gown, altering it into something more like those she had observed at other parties. What Lord Harford would say once he saw it, she didn't know, but she felt that it would be more in aid of catching a husband than that demure high neck he had selected for her. Really.

When she handed her velvet cloak to the maid, she turned to face Lord Harford, a fluttering in her stomach refusing to be quelled, no matter how she told herself he would never say a word.

She literally *felt* his gaze touching her, exploring every inch of creamy white skin revealed by the rather conventional dip in the front of her bodice. His eyes stopped when he reached that low point, and he took a deep breath, as though to say something.

'Remember what I said about needing to find myself a husband?' She placed a pleading hand on his ann. 'I believe this might aid a bit.'

The black look he gave her made her shiver, but she stood firm, her spine rigid, shoulders back, as she had been trained from childhood.

He muttered something she could not catch, and she decided she would rather not know what it was, judging by the expression on his face. But inwardly she trembled at that stern countenance. She accepted his arm, noting that Lady Harford had paused to chat with several friends.

'There she is,' Lady Charis whispered. 'Over there by the door.' They all looked across the room to see the mousy-haired girl dressed in a sallow shade of yellow.

‘In about an hour you must contrive to do your part. We depend on you to help with The Plan,’ Penelope declared softly.

Her words brought a proud smile to the younger girl. She nodded. ‘Do not fear, I shall be at the library at ten of the clock.’

‘So organized,’ Lord Harford murmured into Penelope’s dainty ear, disturbing a careful curl in the process.

‘I do my best,’ she replied, while searching the room for possibly eligible husband material. ‘Is there anyone here you think might be amenable to my offer?’

Lord Harford drew a vexed breath. Really, this chit was beyond all belief. He was not accustomed to being ignored while the woman at his side hunted for a better, or more agreeable, catch. Truly exasperating.

The first young cub approached, and Penelope swept off in his arms to a delightful cotillion. Lord Harford watched as she danced her way through a minuet, a quadrille, followed by a country dance that ought to have reduced her to a limp rag. She looked radiant, alive, and . . . perhaps a trifle bored, if he was not mistaken.

At the conclusion of the latest dance, he claimed her hand, ignoring the young pup who had walked forward, his eyes on Penelope’s little card that probably had his name inscribed on it. He stopped at the glare from Harford.

'We shall walk now. I do not want you to be overly tired for our confrontation.'

She sobered, then smoothed her glove so that it properly met her sleeve. 'Of course.' She strolled at his side, wondering what she could say to him.

Ahead, Charis urged Miss Dunston to walk with her, as the room was quite warm, and Miss Dunston had managed to secure a rather fast country dance.

'It is time. Shall we proceed?'

'You have not told me precisely what I must do,' Penelope reminded him. 'Only that we shall be together when she enters the room. That is sufficient?'

'Surprise is the essence of conviction, my dear cousin.'

She frowned, mulled over his confusing words, then decided she might as well go along with whatever he had planned, for she did want to pay her debt to him.

He led her into a library, where a small fire burned in the grate, casting a pleasant glow about the room. The smell of leather-bound books combined with a potpourri of meadow roses and heather to entice a reader to linger. Penelope paused before the fireplace, turning to face him. 'Well?'

'The setting should be sufficient if Charis brings her in here, agreed?' He joined her, adopting her reserved demeanor. He lit a branch of candles, then placed it on the desk so as to silhouette them to anyone who opened the door.

'I expect so. Is that what happens at assignations? It seems rather dull to me. I scarce see why I am warned against them if that is the case,' Penelope replied in a considering way.

'Impossible girl. I believe it runs more to impassioned kisses. But you wouldn't know anything about that, would you? Not believing in love, that is?' He stood close to her, his dark eyes seeming to tease her. She found them fascinating, and lost herself to everything else.

'I somehow doubt if love is necessary for kisses. Of course, I am not an expert, but it is my estimation of the matter.'

'Little fool. Your very naiveté inflames one. I am tempted to see what lies beneath that skin you dare to flaunt to the world tonight.'

'Oh, come now,' she scoffed.

'You believe yourself impervious to my charm?' He stepped closer, slid his arms about her waist, then gazed down into her nervous eyes.

'Naturally. Remember, we should not suit, my lord.' Her voice wobbled a little on those last words as she saw his head drawing nearer.

She found herself melting into his arms, for a kiss turned out to be vastly different than she expected. To think a mere touching of lips could produce such sensations, like hot and cold, trembly and afire, all at once. She dimly perceived the sound of an opening door, a gasp of horror, or something like that, but she was far too lost to do anything but concentrate on the man in whose arms she nestled. Then he withdrew and she felt adrift on an open sea of emotions.

'Well?' His voice was deep and husky.

She cleared her throat, wondering if she could speak after such a profound experience. 'Really,' she managed, 'I believe I quite underestimated the pleasure of a kiss.'

He threw his head back in a bark of laughter, delighted with her open and frank enjoyment of their kiss. No protestations, no demands, no clever ploys. Just pleasure, for he could tell she had enjoyed it as much as he had.

'Are you quite finished!' Lady Charis demanded in a soft voice, entering the room on tiptoe.

'Sorry, little sister. I believe we are satisfied

for the moment, at least.' He slanted a sly look at the bemused girl at his side. He dropped his arms away, thrusting his hands behind him, for he was tempted, so tempted, to take her in his arms again. Just to prove a thing or two, naturally.

'Hm,' Charis said, looking first at her brother, then at Penelope. 'Well, I fancy it may have done the trick. She was angry and vowed to be done with you. She called you a philanderer, dear brother. Are you one?' she inquired with a pert look.

'Scamp.'

'If Lord Harford is indeed so naughty, it is a good thing I have not lost my heart to him. It would never do to fall in love with the man I chose for a husband if he is to leave me,' Penelope avowed.

'But what if he doesn't go away, dear cousin?' Harford asked smoothly. He was definitely piqued at this little minx, who so easily accepted his kiss, then calmly declared she could never be in love with him. Surely that kiss must have affected her as much as it had him.

'Oh, dear, I hadn't planned for that. I see I shall have to learn ways to be off-putting. Perhaps you can advise me there, Lord Harford?'

Chuckling, yet vaguely annoyed, he led the

young women from the room. His appearance with the two girls, one his sister, the other his cousin, raised no eyebrows. But across the room Miss Carola Dunston narrowed her gaze.

7

Once the party arrived back at Letty's, it was to discover Mrs Flint all atwitter. Henri had arrived! He awaited them in the morning room.

Penelope turned to Miss Nilsson in worried dismay.

It was difficult for Jonathan to comprehend why the news of the chef's arrival in London could put both ladies in such a taking.

Penelope tried to explain. 'He is more than a mere chef, my lord. He is a wise friend . . . to both of us. He has always been there for me, over the years. He did more than teach me to cook, he revealed to me a philosophy of living. If he has come to town, it may be there is some trouble he seeks to tell me about. He knows how I feel about letters.'

'And how *do* you feel about letters?' Jonathan inquired, intrigued with this ever-puzzling young woman. He closed the door behind their party, for the Countess and Lady Charis had come in as well.

'Oh, I do not trust them. Recall how Cousin Letty put my letter aside and did not get my message. It is all of a piece, you know.' She nodded sagely at this comment.

There was little he might say to this argument, for she was undoubtedly correct in her estimation of what might happen. The group drifted toward the morning room.

Mrs Flint fluttered about in the entry hall, fussing and fidgeting around in great agitation. Penelope listened to her disjointed murmurings, then sent her off to the kitchen to prepare tea, thinking that would occupy her mind sufficiently.

Turning to Lady Harford, Penelope said, 'I cannot imagine what Henri will say to Cousin Letty's latest start. He does a wonderful roast duckling.' Penelope drew a reminiscent breath, then stepped into the morning room. As expected, her chef awaited her there, a breakdown of proper convention totally unprecedented in Mrs Flint's experience.

'Good morning, Henri. Is something amiss?' Penelope demanded at once, going straight to the heart of the matter, much to Lady Harford's admiration.

'Mademoiselle, I have received news of my family. I feel I must pursue this line of intelligence. There is a possibility the family estate may yet come into my hands. Stranger things have happened. So I come to London to investigate, with your permission.'

The oddly elegant chef, dressed neatly in austere gray pantaloons and a precisely cut blue coat once owned by the previous Lord Everton and given him by Penelope, stood resolutely before the fireplace, hands behind his back, mouth firmly set. He was a fine figure of a man, his forty-odd years sitting kindly on his frame. His brown hair was simply styled. Shrewd gray eyes searched those of his employer with guarded probing, a hint of worry lurking in them.

Miss Nilsson sank down upon the chair nearest the door with a gasp. '*Jag forstar inte*.'

Penelope stepped closer to her dear companion, whose great confusion was readily apparent, for she had just spoken in Swedish — a thing she rarely did unless totally upset — revealing that she understood the situation no better than Penelope.

Jonathan inserted a thought into the pause. 'Be careful, I have heard tales of men being lured to France with promises of these so-called restored estates, only to discover that all was not as warranted.' His warning appeared to be well-received.

'True, I have been cautioned by my friends as well. If I may remain as your chef — perhaps here? — I shall explore this to greater length before I take myself off to France.' His eyes beseeched Penelope with the familiarity of a servant of lifelong standing.

Penelope turned to Jonathan, explaining, 'Henri was brought home by my father from one of his trips. Henri had escaped the revolution — he was about one-and-twenty when he fled — and set himself up as chef in Austria. Papa enjoyed his cooking and Henri thought it might be better to find asylum in England, what with the way things were going. After my parents died, he came along with me to Fountains. He and Miss Nilsson are the enduring things in my life.'

Jonathan noted her warm glance at the chef, surmising the chef had indeed stood in place of a father for the growing girl, left alone all those years by her traveling parents. His look toward the newcomer grew a shade warmer.

'I believe caution and prudence are wise at this time,' Jonathan urged.

At this point Letty and the cat entered the room, both full of curiosity.

'I vow I have not had such interesting goings-on in all my time in London.' She gazed at the newcomer, pushing her spectacles up on her nose so as to better view him, before turning to Penelope.

'Letty, may my chef remain here for a time? He will be in my employ, so no drain on your household.' Penelope took her cousin's hand, hoping her coaxing might be effective. 'He is an excellent chef, I might add.'

'I eat nothing but vegetables, grains, and the like. Absolutely no fish, fowl, or meat,' Letty declared, giving the man a hostile glance. 'And this is a feminine household. I cannot see how he can be accommodated here.' She had the grace to give Penelope an apologetic look.

'I am certain I can cope with a special diet, mademoiselle,' Henri replied suavely, making a most proper bow.

'I have an alternative solution,' Jonathan inserted, sensing that Miss Winthrop was unlikely to weaken. 'As I am yet without a chef, why does he not join my household?' In his experience, poets were never the logical sort, and at this hour of the night it was best to solve matters quickly.

Penelope looked to Miss Nilsson, a silent exchange between them bringing a reluctant nod of both heads.

'That may be the best thing for all,' Penelope agreed, taking a step from Letty's side toward Lord Harford. 'Thank you, Cousin, for once again coming to my aid.'

'We do seem to have a way of assisting each other, do we not?' He meant to tease her, to remind her of those few moments they had shared so intimately, and it amused him to see how her cheeks pinkened.

Penelope hoped her cheeks did not flame with the memory of that kiss in the library. She slid a hand up to lightly touch her face, as though to test. 'I hope I should always be ready to lend a hand to a cousin in need of help. One way or the other,' she added, thinking again of the kiss. How complicated things had become. She had learned of his debt and sought his help in exchange for her rescue the day of his dinner. So much had happened since.

Jonathan motioned to his mother and sister, then Henri. 'Perhaps we had better be on our way. The hour grows late.'

Letty remained in the morning room while Penelope followed the others into the hall. Miss Nilsson still sat where she had plumped down when first appraised of Henri's intentions.

Drawing Lord Harford aside as the others headed out the door, Penelope said in a low voice, 'I shall see that you do not lose financially by this, Cousin. I have not forgotten that I offered to compensate you for your help.' She suspected that Oglethorpe did not know the half of Lord Harford's difficulties.

Jonathan drew an angry breath. Really, the

chit was impossible. 'I am well able to manage, thank you,' he replied in frosty accents. Then he recalled that she believed he had lost a large sum of money and wondered what he ought to do. He had thought it amusing at first to see how a young woman treated him when she believed him to be in dire straits. Now it was proving to be a problem.

Penelope patted his arm in a reassuring gesture, believing that he felt embarrassed about his financial reverses. She could respect his not wanting to reveal to his mother the extent of his losses. Although it was certainly silly, for how could his mother curb her spending if she thought he still possessed deep pockets?

Muffin came forward to inspect the open door, and Penelope swiftly scooped the cat into her arms, not wanting it to dash out the door to certain peril. 'I shall discuss this with you some other time, if you prefer,' she said to Harford. 'Your family awaits.'

Disgusted with his inability to set her straight in a few well-chosen words, Jonathan marched out the door and into the coach. Henri had joined the coachman up front, to Jonathan's dismay. Now he would have to endure his mother's less-than-gentle probing about The Plan all the way to Harford House.

The only good thing was that their destination was close by.

When Penelope returned to the morning room, she found Miss Nilsson sipping a cup of tea while Letty examined the dainty biscuits on the plate offered by Mrs Flint.

Ignoring Letty, Penelope sank onto the chair close to Eva Nilsson. 'Do you believe he will actually leave us?'

Miss Nilsson mutely shook her head, looking as though she was about to attend the funeral of a beloved relative.

Feeling as though her world had just received a bad shaking, Penelope reached out for Nilsson's free hand, drawing comfort from the contact.

* * *

The following afternoon brought Andrew Oglethorpe to the house once again. Penelope would have left the drawing room had she not fancied her cousin in need of a chaperon. Miss Nilsson had sent word that she was prostrated with a megrim, so someone had to do the proper.

Letty sat facing the window, while Mr Oglethorpe paced back and forth before the fireplace.

'I fail to see how you believe that your

latest work is ready to be presented to the world, Lettice,' Mr Oglethorpe declared, looking greatly torn.

Penelope took this opening to satisfy her own curiosity about her cousin's poetry. 'I should like to have you read me some of your work, Letty. Please?' Penelope ignored the dark look from Mr Oglethorpe.

'Very well.' Letty nodded graciously. She picked up a sheet of paper from the folder on her lap, cleared her throat, then commenced reading.

> 'Ode to an Inchworm:
> Small, my little creature.
> Climb, climb without ceasing
> To the top of the hickory tree.'

Penelope waited for a moment, then gave Letty a blank look. 'That is all? I mean, it seems rather short.' In Penelope's experience, poets nattered on and on about any topic that had caught their interest. Poems usually dragged on for pages of sprawling script.

Letty sniffed. 'You have no more vision than Mr Oglethorpe. This is a mode of poetry from the Far East. It requires appreciative ears.' She rose and marched toward the door. 'I can see my creative efforts are to be met with scorn. So be it. My genius will most likely not be valued until after I have gone aloft.' With that final remark snapped at her guests, she swished from the room.

'I warned you,' began Mr Oglethorpe. 'At least, I think I did.'

'I did not say I believe it to be bad, it is merely confusing. It of a certainty is quite different. When you consider her words, they do make sense of a sort . . . I mean about the little inchworm climbing to the top of the hickory tree. Although it seems a peculiar topic for a poem.' Penelope rubbed her chin with her hand, wondering how she would manage to smooth out this difficulty.

'It is one of her better efforts,' he replied, his face glum.

Penelope rose, suddenly recalling it was no more proper for her to be alone with Mr Oglethorpe than for her bewildering cousin. 'I had best go to her and see if I can improve matters.'

'By all means.' He gave a gloomy shake of his head as to what he thought of her chances. 'One of these days I shall give up on her.' With that sad reflection, Mr Oglethorpe left the house.

Penelope watched him from the window, then went off to find her cousin. When she located her back in the crowded little room that Letty used for her study, Penelope entered, then leaned against the door in the hope that she could ferret out the problem bothering Letty without her cousin stalking off in a huff. Seated at her untidy desk, Letty raised her head to give Penelope a defiant glare.

'You were a bit abrupt, Cousin,' Penelope chided.

'No one understands my work,' Letty complained with a pout.

'I have yet to hear anything written by Mr Oglethorpe, but I do not pretend to be an authority on poetry. Perhaps he is envious of your efforts.'

Letty gave Penelope an arrested look, then shook her head. 'I doubt it.'

'Odd, but I have the feeling that poetry actually has little to do with your regard for the gentleman. Would it help if you confided in me? I promise that you may trust me to keep as mute as a fish.'

Letty toyed with the pen on her desk, then slowly pushed her chair back, rising to wander about the room as she mulled over the offer. That her thoughts were in turmoil was all too evident. Her hair was a bird's nest, her gown wrinkled, as though she had spent some time crumpled on the backless sofa to one side of the room.

'He is quite smitten with you, and I

strongly suspect he longs to marry with you. Is he so poor that you cannot consider him an eligible *parti*?' Penelope gently queried. She was at a loss as to why her cousin should deliberately hurt the only gentleman who was likely to offer for her hand. She did not accept the hints that Letty had dropped that she didn't care if she remained single. Life for an unmarried woman was fraught with perils; she could attest to the truth of that.

Startled at her cousin's perception, Letty snapped, utterly dismayed at her feelings being brought into the open. 'No,' she denied abruptly. 'He is of acceptable fortune, indeed most well-to-grass.'

'He is considerate, gentle, and rather agreeable in nature. What can be the problem confronting you?'

'Mother would never consent. He is not of the aristocracy and she is a fearful snob about that sort of thing,' Letty confessed in a rush. 'His father made his fortune in manufacturing, you know.'

'I see.' Indeed, Penelope saw a great deal at this revelation. 'But he is vastly loyal to you, and seems a fine gentleman, regardless of his background.'

'His mother is of the gentry, 'tis true. I know I do not have to seek my parents' approval, being of an age when I may marry to please myself, but I would not sever the connection with my family.' She avoided meeting Penelope's probing gaze, staring at her clasped hands before strolling over to the window that over-looked a small garden.

'It would seem that you must compare your attitude toward him with the reality of his fine, noble character even though he is of the lower gentry. For he is extremely clever and certainly has improved his mind.'

'Are you so certain it would be right to wed him in spite of his background?' Letty's voice betrayed her inner yearnings as clearly as if she had spoken them. 'Oh, I do not see how he can wish to marry me,' she suddenly blurted out. 'I am a frump, with my peculiar dress and my spectacles.' She now turned back to glare fiercely at Penelope. 'However, I refuse to go without them.' She pushed the offending articles up on her nose. 'I cannot see a blessed thing without them, and I am not so vain as to believe my appearance would be greatly improved if I left them off.'

'Your dress need not be unfashionable. Lady Harford does very well with Charis. Why not seek her advice?'

'Did you?'

'Well . . . ' Penelope hesitated, not wanting to lie, yet not wishing to reveal the extent of Lord Harford's help. 'In a way.'

It was clear that Letty still had her doubts of the matter. 'I still say it would not make any difference to my looks.'

A gentle rapping at the door forced Penelope to stand away. She opened it to find Mrs Flint peering at her.

'Lord Harford wishes to speak with you, Lady Penelope.'

Thankful she could have a chance to speak with her cousin, Penelope excused herself, adding before she left the room, 'Do not think for a moment that this subject is closed. You must give poor Mr Oglethorpe more consideration. What would your life be like if he disappeared from it, never to be seen again?'

With that parting shot, Penelope sailed down the hall and up the stairs into the drawing room, where Lord Harford waited. She paused at the entrance, taking note of his attire.

As usual, he looked impeccable, his biscuit pantaloons fitting him with superb care, and that corbeau coat hugging his shoulders in a way only Weston could manage. His waistcoat had an elegant pattern, with one discreet fob displayed. She reluctantly admired his total effect of elegance. Perhaps he was a frippery fellow, as she had overheard Aunt Winthrop say. Whatever did he do with his time? Or did he spend it in endless pursuit of pleasure?

His elegance made Penelope feel rather dull in her proper round gown with its demure lace frill at the neck and sleeves she once thought pretty, with blue ribands gathering the fullness in at several places.

What a pity he was so tempting. The trouble with resisting temptation, she decided, was that it might never come again, hence her warm greeting and melting smile.

Jonathan studied Penelope, not trusting that beguiling smile in the least. He had learned she frequently had surprising tricks up her sleeve.

'I would have a word with you, Penny.'

She frowned at his repressive tone of voice, then decided she had best see to it that he was repaid for his efforts on her behalf. 'Yes?'

Rather than meet that entrancing gaze, far too direct for a lady, he looked elsewhere and began to slowly pace back and forth before the fireplace.

Penelope wondered what it was about fireplaces that made men want to walk back and forth before them. First, Mr Oglethorpe; now, Lord Harford.

'About your dress of last evening. What made you lower the neckline?'

Surprised at this topic, she bristled. 'I

explained to you that I need to find a husband, my lord. Why you thought I might attract a gentleman to my side while looking like a strayed Quaker is more than I can see. All I did was take a tuck here and there.'

'By the time you finished, there was scarce a scrap left to the bodice. You displayed an excessive amount of your charms.' He glanced at her, taking note that while her gown had a neck trimmed with a pretty frill, the fabric clung to her superb figure with wicked faithfulness. She disturbed him greatly, and he suspected he would be beating off her suitors with a stick before long. He found the thought positively depressing.

'I fail to see why it bothers you;' she pointed out in what she felt to be justifiable righteousness.

That was the problem. There *was* no real reason for him to feel like an outraged father over the low cut of her gown. She stood correct in her asssessment. Still, he could not like the attention she had drawn last night, nor could he banish from his mind the sight of that exquisite *décolletage*. Already one chap had sought permission to court her, and he had denied it with great pleasure.

'Ah . . . I shall be required — as your closest male relative — to handle the requests for your hand. It would keep the wrong sort of man away if you gave a more proper impression.'

'You aren't, you know.' At his startled glance, she continued, 'My closest male relative. That is Ernest, Lord Everton. However, I fancy you will deal with the matter better than he would, once the gentlemen know that the maternal side of the family has charge.' She took a step closer, studying him with an expression he found most disconcerting when his eyes tangled with that straightforward gaze of hers.

Penelope took the initiative away from him by turning to the subject on her mind. 'You have yet to tell me what sum you lost. I would know, so as to help as I promised.'

Angered by her disquieting effect on him, and frustrated by this peculiar craving he had to pull her into his arms, to know again the touch of that delectable mouth, he rushed into speech. 'It is none of your affair, dear cousin.'

Penelope took another step closer, flirting with the desires that teased her, desires she didn't understand in the least. 'Oh, but it is. And I intend to do what I can to see that you are solvent. As my cousin, and benefactor of sorts, it is the very least I can do.' Then, observing he looked rather red in the face, she again changed the subject. 'You will go with us to the ball this evening? And the presentation?'

'Yes, to both,' he replied. He took a step toward her, nearly touching her as she stared at him, her head tilted in a fetching way, those clear blue eyes seeming to see straight through him. A feeling that he had dropped into a well from which he couldn't get out overcame him. 'I will see you later, then.'

He suddenly backed away and hurried toward the door, as though fleeing for his life. The delighted laughter that followed after him was not pleasing in the least to one who had considered himself impervious to an assault on his emotions.

* * *

That evening Penelope joined Lady Harford and Lady Charis with a lighter heart. She couldn't have said why, precisely, unless it was the hunch she had that she had bested her elegant cousin. First he had sought to rebuke her for conforming to the fashion of the day, then had insisted she need not repay him. Why, she had always paid her way.

'There he is,' Lady Harford exclaimed as her son wended his way through the crush of people to reach their side.

Penelope turned about to see that Lord

Harford indeed approached. Her hand flew up to touch her chest at the alarming flutter within. Why must she always react so to his presence? But then, her hand concealed another modified neckline and she supposed she dreaded his scold.

The four stood conversing a short while before Jonathan reached out to take Penelope by the arm. Excusing them from her mother, he guided her to an alcove not far away.

She gave him her most obstinate look.

'You might very well look like that,' he declared, acting as though he would drop a sack over her head at the first opportunity.

'Wait until you see my presentation gown.'

'I have, and it is most unexceptionable.'

'I know.' She sighed. 'Dreary is what it is. I fancied you would approve of it. I shall not touch that neckline, however.' She gave him a saucy look; then her expression altered as she noted that Miss Dunston stared at them from a nearby chair.

'What is it?'

'Miss Dunston,' Penelope whispered. 'She stares with curious eyes. What do we do?'

'Nothing for the moment. Be prepared with that inventive mind of yours should I need you.'

With that rejoinder, he left her side, the depth of her neckline apparently forgotten.

Penelope watched as he sought out the most dashing widow present and flirted outrageously with her. It didn't mollify her that she was besieged by a flattering number of gentlemen. Glancing at her dance card, she observed that every line was filled in, with one *contra danse* claimed by Lord Harford. She wondered if they would actually get to dance, or if he would use that time to give her another scold, then took herself off to enjoy the next dance.

She left the floor, escorted to Lady Harford's side by a fairly nice man, if one didn't mind conversation about nothing but the hunting field. Still, she reminded herself, hadn't she insisted she would accept someone devoted to the hunt? She would have to find out if he ever did anything else.

Searching the room for Lord Harford, intent on having her question answered promptly, she found him absent. Murmuring something to her next partner about being utterly parched, she sent him off for a drink of lemonade while she edged her way through the crowd. With his mother and sister present, she doubted if Harford would get deeply involved with the gay widow, but something prompted her to investigate. Miss Dunston seemed missing as well.

At the closed door of a small anteroom she

paused, then peeked inside. There she found Miss Dunston confronting her cousin in a most belligerent manner.

Penelope ducked inside and quickly shut the door behind her, then advanced upon the pair. 'What has happened?'

'He has abused me in a most shameful way. I shall never be able to face Society again,' came the dramatic reply from the clever damsel.

Penelope then caught sight of a white bandage on one dainty arm. 'How gallant of him to tie his handkerchief over it. And promptly, too.'

'Penny, I swear I know nothing of this,' he muttered to her as she drew closer.

'I know that,' she whispered in reply. 'You might natter a girl to death, but you would never harm her.' She drifted closer to Miss Dunston, shaking her head in mock sympathy. 'Poor dear, to be so put upon. Allow me.' With that, Penelope swiftly reached out to tug the scrap of white from Miss Dunston's arm. As she had suspected, there was no mark to be seen.

'Heavens, this is serious,' Penelope exclaimed. 'Far worse than I expected. I suggest we apply leeches, Miss Dunston. There must be deep injury, for you have no external sign of a bruise. I insist you allow me to send you some of my special herbal potion tomorrow. There is danger in using it, but this is an extreme case. Poor dear.'

'No!' The alarm on Miss Dunston's face was almost comical. 'I shall be fine.' She jerked her arm from Penelope's light clasp, then ran from the room, murmuring incoherent words as she fled.

'When I said you were resourceful, I didn't know just how creative you could be, given a chance.' Lord Harford strolled over to the door, opening it wider so they might both leave the small room.

'How did she lure you in here?'

'Oddly enough, she said you had need of me.'

'Odd, indeed.' Penelope cleared a peculiar obstruction from her throat, then went in search of her partner, who must be most annoyed at her disappearance.

Jonathan watched her leave his side with mixed emotions. Once again she had come to his assistance. Never in his life had he been so beset by an opportuning female as with Miss Dunston. The little mouse certainly had determination. Perhaps now she would look elsewhere.

Across the room Lord Stephen Collison escorted Penelope in a sprightly quadrille. Jonathan bestowed a sour look on the pair and took himself off to locate the charming widow he had danced with earlier. Tomorrow he must escort his ladies to the presentation, then endure the coming come-out ball with all the fortitude he could muster. He might as well enjoy himself this evening. Yet he could not shake off the sensation that something was missing from his life.

8

'I feared it would be more trying,' Penelope said as she eased her hooped skirt through the door, then followed Lady Harford and Charis up the curving stairs to the first floor and into the drawing room.

Charis spun about, carefully managing her hoop, and cried, 'That really was not so frightful. It was very kind of the Queen to say such lovely things to you, Penelope. I daresay all of London shall hear of her gracious condescension. Even the Prince eyed you with more than interested notice.'

'Charis,' Penelope cried, 'what folly you speak. I feel certain it was all owing to my distinguished company.' Her eyes sparkled with mirth at the remembrance of the Prince Regent's appraising gaze. 'You attracted a great deal of attention.'

Charis giggled, then turned to her mother with soft words.

Penelope smoothed the white silk of her skirt, which seemed to go straight out from her waist, so full was her hoop, then caught sight of herself in a looking glass on the far wall. What a fantastic image. The modest bodice of her gown was a delicate silver above a white petticoat edged and trimmed in silver lace and beads. Blond lace lappets draped gracefully over her shoulders, and the three white plumes in her hair nodded ever so gently as she moved. She looked for all the world like a princess from her childhood book of fairy tales.

'What has happened to Jonathan?' Charis waltzed to the door, peering down the hall. 'Ah, my dear brother comes now.'

Penelope felt her heart constrict as the handsome figure of her mentor entered the room. He was dressed in the finest of court clothes, his elegance almost too much to endure. His court suit was of a blue and black weave, with an oldfashioned — but proper for court — edging on his coat of tasteful embroidery in cream silk. His cream satin waistcoat was also edged with cream embroidery in the same design, a touch of admirable refinement. He was indeed fortunate to have such well-formed legs, for the tight-fitting breeches and clinging white hose certainly left nothing to the imagination and assuredly would have revealed any defects. She could see none.

Suddenly aware that she had been staring, Penelope bent her head, clearing her throat before saying, 'I believe Charis completely captured the affair. She was by far the prettiest girl to make her curtsy.'

Lady Harford watched the pair who had been regarding each other as gingerly as two strange cats. 'I believe our family honor has been quite nicely upheld by you girls. All we must needs do now is prepare for your ball.'

Considering all she had seen in the entry and up the stairs, Penelope wondered aloud, 'What is left to do, ma'am?'

'Actually, very little. By tomorrow evening I believe we shall be in readiness. You shan't fail me, dear boy?'

Jonathan had been surreptitiously examining the dainty curve of Penny's tiny waist, the thrust of her full bosom above the broad sweep of her hooped skirt, and just barely caught his mother's words. 'Of course, dear mother,' he said with the polished suavity of a courtier. He took another glance at Penny, wondering how a gown whose design had seemed so unassuming could look so downright . . . seductive on her. 'I shall make it a point to arrive a shade early if you like.' He darted a look at Penny again, then left.

Penelope had discovered that when most gentlemen accepted invitations, they fully intended arriving quite late. It was considered acceptable by Society. Penelope thought it abominable manners. She bestowed a wry smile on his lordship, wondering to which group he belonged.

* * *

The following morning, Penelope was awakened rather late by Miss Nilsson. The maid followed her in with a tray of hot chocolate and toasted buns with shaved ham on them. Both ladies had discovered that if they ate in their rooms, they might sneak what they wished up on the trays.

A gorgeous bouquet of flowers nestled in Nilsson's arms. She held out a card, saying in an amused voice, 'I believe that if you remove the center of this nosegay, it becomes a posy for you to carry this evening.'

The bold handwriting suited Lord Harford, Penelope decided as she perused his card. 'How lovely. He really ought not have been so extravant if he is hard pressed for funds. Nilsson, I must see to it that he gets that money. He refuses to reveal his needs to me. Discover if you can the name of his man of business. I would deal with him rather than through my banker. One must guard the tender susceptibilities of gentlemen,' she concluded, making a face at her companion.

'Are you quite certain he will not be offended, my dear?' Miss Nilsson placed the bouquet in a vase, tossing a cautious look at her employer.

'Nonsense,' the practical Penelope declared. 'Now' — she attacked the pile of toasted buns with a healthy hunger — 'we must organize our day. I do hope that Henri has settled in at Lord Harford's place.'

'Indeed,' Miss Nilsson murmured, her voice and manner now greatly subdued.

Taking note of her companion's wan face and sad droop, Penelope resolved to make her a nice tonic, something to drive away all thoughts of melancholy. However, it would have to wait until tomorrow, for Penelope very much doubted if she would have a spare moment today. She had promised to take her things to the Harford house as soon as she was dressed this morning, then assist with last-minute details.

Lady Charis took note of the magnificent floral offering from her brother when Penelope brought it along, but only commented that he was doing his usual best. It deflated Penelope's pride a touch, but she decided she was being a peagoose to place undue importance on mere flowers.

When the girls were dressed for the ball in their pretty white muslins — Charis with rose accents, Penelope with blue and silver — they joined Lady Harford in the drawing room.

Charis was delighted to find Lord Harford had managed to arrive before them, and exclaimed her pleasure.

Jonathan noted that the demure neckline he had approved for Penelope's coming-out gown now dipped somewhat lower, displaying a vast expanse of skin once again. He decided his best course was to pretend not to notice her naughty conduct. He never seemed to make any headway with a rebuke anyway.

Over to one side of the room, Eva Nilsson sat in the shadows, her soft gray sarcenet gown seeming to make her disappear in the gentle candlelight.

Dinner proved to be a challenge. Lady Harford had invited a number of young gentlemen, Lord Stephen Collison included, as well as girls making their bows to society. Penelope found herself seated between Lord Stephen and Lord Harford, something she thought to be a dilemma, and had said so to Lady Harford when viewing the place cards.

'Dear girl,' her ladyship replied, 'I do never trust those other boys. Lord Stephen is a darling, and of course my son will do all that is proper. You are a great heiress, and as such must be guarded from fortune hunters.'

Penelope wondered a little at the secretive smile her ladyship possessed, but had not complained any more. She had no wish to be saddled with a man who was all to pieces and on the prowl for an heiress. While she did not demand a husband of equal fortune, she expected to marry a man of rank who had a respectable background, as was her due.

Lord Harford partnered his sister while Lord Stephen took Penelope's hand to walk her out for the first dance of the ball, once all the guests had been welcomed.

If her heart did not flutter, nor that peculiar heat creep over her when coming close to Lord Stephen, Penelope accounted it to the ire she so frequently felt when near her cousin. She enjoyed dancing with Lord Stephen, taking pleasure in his skill.

'I suppose you have been fending off proposals for your hand,' he said as they paused in the country dance, watching the others. 'I heard your cousin is a dragon, guarding you and your fortune well. Word has seeped out that Harford, not Everton, is the one to approach.'

She was silent at this tidbit. Harford ought to have told her about every one of the gentlemen who requested to court her. When the dance concluded, she accepted Lord Harford's hand, while Lord Stephen smilingly claimed Charis.

'What a chore this must be for you, my

lord,' Penelope said in a seemingly demure manner.

'I have not missed that neckline, Penny. You are fortunate I have not insisted you fill it in with a fichu or round of lace.' He led her through the first movement of the country dance, the warmth of his hand as he held hers distinctly felt even through their gloves.

'Indeed? And you think I would obey your demand? You forget yourself, my lord.' Her eyes flashed with the blue fire that so frequently flamed when near this top-lofty man.

'Take care, my little termagant, or I shall have Miss Nilsson remove all those altered gowns to be repaired.'

Penelope gasped, utterly outraged. 'You would never!'

He failed to reply, but the sly expression on his face gave her the clear impression there was nothing he would not do if he so chose.

Penelope fumed in silence, completing the dance with automatic grace. Abominable, detestable man. She had merely requested he assist her in finding a husband, not asked that he stand custodian over her.

As they circled the room following the dance, she touched the matter which had been simmering in the back of her mind. 'I would have you tell me precisely how many offers for my hand you have received to date, sir. I have the most peculiar notion that you have not told me of them.'

He had the goodness to look uncomfortable. Clearing his throat, he said, 'Perhaps we ought to seek a glass of lemonade, I find I am uncommonly thirsty.'

'What do you conceal, my lord?' she demanded in a silken voice.

Resigned to a fierce wigging, he looked down into that disapproving face. 'Watkins, for one. The fellow is a scapegrace, a thoroughly wild fellow, so naturally I rejected him.'

'Naturally,' she replied smoothly.

'Willowby, as well. I knew you could not wish such a frippery fellow as that. He hasn't a feather to fly with, and while he might be complaisant, you could never depend upon him to remain so.'

'I can scarcely pull cape with you over that, can I?' she said with deceptive calm. 'Anyone else?'

He continued, naming several others, listing his objection to each with irrefutable logic for each denial and a sound reason as to why he had not consulted with her. When he finished, he waited for her to speak. He hadn't long.

'Although you have indeed pointed these

men out to me at various times, I think it positively wicked that you would conceal the offers from me,' she said in a tight voice. 'I am persuaded that I do not suffer from an excess of vanity. You might have told me. I doubt I would succumb to sham proposals, my lord.' She gave him an angry look, then continued, 'However, I have no intention of combing your hair in public.'

'I am indeed thankful for small mercies, Cousin. But you must understand, my dear, that it is not the easiest of matters to discover a potential husband who would meekly do as you insist. You are rather lovely to be left alone in the country.'

While secretly mollified at his explanation, she gave no inkling of her reaction in his words. 'And to think I trusted you to guide me to find the sort of husband I want.' She gave an indignant sniff.

'Do you still feel the same way about being left alone? You have not altered your opinion since coming to Town?'

Memory of those odd sensations that had gripped her when close to Lord Harford returned, but she was saved from a reply when her next partner presented himself. 'I believe I shall reserve my answer to that, sir.' She whirled off on the arm of young Patterson.

Concealing his thoughts beneath a bland façade, Harford crossed to solicit the hand of the young lady he had asked for this dance. He then found a place in the set that Penelope and her partner had joined and proceeded to put her utterly out of countenance by giving her knowing looks whenever their eyes met.

Penelope was provoked at how frequently her gaze strayed in Harford's direction. Quite deliberately, especially after that uncomfortable dance, she set about keeping as great a distance between them as possible until she chanced to see him with that brown mouse of a girl, Miss Dunston.

Words exchanged earlier with Lady Harford returned in her mind. Penelope had queried her hostess at the inclusion of the drab girl. Lady Harford had replied that while she felt the girl to be more than a little peculiar, Mrs Dunston was an old friend, and she could not slight her daughter.

Penelope felt the girl to be unbalanced, what with her odd habit of staring at Lord Harford with such a fixed gaze. Penelope felt a stirring of unease when Miss Dunston offered a glass of wine to Lord Harford. What a strange thing for the little mouse to do, a bold action for one usually so timid. It brought to mind the other incongruity, when the girl had importuned Harford with false accusations.

Penelope drifted across the room, skirting several groups who sought to include her in their numbers, until she reached Harford's side. She paused only once, and that was to make a request of one of the footmen.

'Miss Dunston, how charming you look. I trust the herbal potion I sent you did the trick? You seem quite in plump current this evening.' Penelope shifted closer to Lord Harford, eyeing the contents of the glass Carola Dunston had handed him.

Seeming confused by the kind words from one she obviously considered an adversary, Miss Dunston blushed and shook her head before nodding. 'I am well, thank you.'

'Good.' Penelope turned to Lord Harford, smiling in an artless way. 'Cousin, do let me have a sip of your drink. I asked the footman to bring me something, but I shall faint from thirst before he ever finds me.' She took note of the amount that had been consumed, then took a sip from the glass, grimacing at the state. She glanced at her cousin, then cried in dismay as she tilted the glass to allow the contents to fall on the floor. 'How clumsy of me! How fortunate your footman comes now.'

Harford gave her a quizzical look, even as

he began to notice a most peculiar sensation creeping over him.

Penelope swiftly took the glass of milk from the tray proffered by the puzzled footman, thrusting it into Lord Harford's hand with a terse command to drink it. Then she requested the servant mop up the spill as soon as possible.

By now Harford felt obliged to place a hand on Penelope's shoulder for lack of a column to lean against. 'I feel dashed queer,' he muttered in her ear. Thinking she had taken leave of her senses, yet unable to resist her direction, he obediently drank most of the honeyed milk.

Penelope took the glass from him, polishing off the remainder, then requested the footman bring more.

At Penelope's precipitate action, Miss Dunston had turned deathly pale and begun to back away from them. She glanced about her, then said, 'I see my mother beckoning. I had best go.'

Penelope gave her a frustrated look before admonishing, 'If you think to escape lightly, you are foolish beyond permission, my girl.' She watched Miss Dunston flee to her mother's side before turning to Lord Harford.

'What is happening? I feel bloody peculiar.'

'I have a notion, my lord. Something your mother said earlier gave me a suspicion of the girl. I fear she is dangerously unbalanced; more than a little peculiar, as your mother put it. Unless I miss my guess, she put a bit of henbane in your wine, hoping God only knows what. Had you consumed that entire glass, you would have undoubtedly failed to be with us on the morrow.'

Harford allowed Penelope to nudge him down onto a chair while he sorted out his thoughts. 'Poison? Egads!'

When the footman appeared with the two more glasses of sweetened milk, Penelope silently offered one to Lord Harford, who obediently consumed the contents. She drank the second glass. The footman backed away, his confusion at the odd behavior of her ladyship's son and guest obvious.

'I am glad my intuition led me to act. She behaved quite out of character. Do you wish to rest? I believe we might quietly leave the room so you could recover in peace.'

He nodded his agreement. Once they had found the sanctuary of a small anteroom that was unoccupied, he studied his surprising cousin. 'How did you know what it was, and how to combat its effect?'

'Miss Nilsson taught me to distinguish the beneficial herbs from the dangerous ones.

Henbane is often used in small quantities for a purgative. It is also a narcotic, like opium, and will induce sleep. Miss Nilsson explained that in Sweden they have found it can be very dangerous if not used with care. A little too much, and death can result.' A wry smile crept over her face. 'In some countries it is used in love potions, for it produces a strange effect on the senses. Doubtless Miss Dunston knew of this, but was careless in her dose.'

'A love potion? Good grief. My mouth feels dry and my heart has been beating in the most peculiar way.' He rubbed his forehead as though dizzy.

Penelope refrained from commenting that her heart usually beat in an odd manner when she was near him, and she hadn't taken any herbal love potions, either. 'Rest, and it should pass before long. I shall close this door when I leave, so you'll not be disturbed.'

'What about you?' He gave her an alarmed look.

'I spat out that sip I tasted, and took the precaution of drinking some milk.' With those words Penelope slipped away from the room, thankful her cousin was to be fine and that she had been able to use the knowledge Miss Nilsson had so diligently poured into her head over the years spent wandering about the estate and developing her herbal garden.

Seeing a footman in the hall, she requested he stay with his lordship until he felt more the thing.

When she returned to the ballroom, she searched the room to discover that Miss Dunston was no longer present. Upon asking Lady Harford about the missing guest, she was not terribly surprised at her answer.

'Miss Dunston? La, that puzzling child left merely minutes ago. I pity her poor mother, to manage a husband for that girl. She really is the strangest creature.'

Deciding not to upset her ladyship in the middle of her daughter's come-out ball, Penelope murmured agreement, then strolled along the edge of the room until claimed by Lord Stephen for a cotillion.

It was not until the next day, when summoned to appear at Harford House on Mount Street, that an explanation of all that had happened was demanded of her. Penelope explained everything, and Lady Harford exploded.

'It is infamous that chit be allowed to go free. Why, she might have killed Jonathan!'

'And who knows what she will do next?' gently inserted Penelope, quite in harmony with Lady Harford.

It was decided to approach Mrs Dunston instantly with the charge. When told of her daughter's action, that good lady nearly fainted, promising to remove her daughter from London at once and seek help for her.

The drive back to Harford House was depressingly silent. Thinking of herbal potions had brought the matter of Miss Nilsson to mind once again, and Penelope decided she had best mix up something that would remove the melancholy mien from her dear companion's face.

It was not to be as easy as she thought. After leaving a grateful Lady Harford and Charis, Penelope could not find an apothecary who carried precisely what she desired. She might have known that fresh germander speedwell could not be found in the heart of the city.

The third one she consulted said, 'I have seen a plant of that in the Physic Garden over in Chelsea. Pity it is open only to an apothecary, or you might get a snippet of it there.'

'Could you give me a permit to visit, since you are a member?' Penelope was vexed to find that the place was generally not open to the public. It ought to be, she fumed. It was not as though she wished to decimate the garden.

The man took note of the elegance of the young lady, then the gold coin offered for his assistance, and succumbed. 'Of course.'

With the piece of paper tucked in her reticule, Penelope headed in the direction of Chelsea in her carriage after giving her new coachman the direction. Wanting to keep her work a surprise from Miss Nilsson, she had slipped from Cousin Letty's house with no one being the wiser. Now she complacently sat back as they neared the river.

When the carriage stopped, she left the vehicle and hesitantly approached Swan Walk, taking note that it ran like a country lane, green, peaceful, and quite rural. The warmth of the sun brought forth the scents of hundreds of flowers and herbs in a near-heady aroma. Penelope closed her eyes for a moment and thought herself back at Fountains. How her heart ached for her dear home.

As she neared a magnificent iron gate, she glanced back at her new coachman, suspecting he thought her a bit mad to be out in the country just to visit a garden.

All she had to do was to get inside, then locate the germander speedwell. Miss Nilsson's countryman, Carl von Lime, or Linnaeus, had named it *Veronica chamaedrys*. Eva Nilsson said she had once viewed his famous botanical garden, and proclaimed it superb. Over the years she had worked with Penelope to develop a splendid botanical garden at Fountains. Penelope was anxious to get this business of finding a husband over with so she might return to her estate and see how her new greenhouse progressed.

The gate swung open silently, and Penelope eased inside, holding her pretty new violet pelisse away from the catch. The breeze tugged at her bonnet, but the violet ribbons held it secure. She debated which way to go first.

Two picturesque cedars stood not far from the banks of the Thames. She recalled reading that the tops had been shattered in a storm back in 1809. It was a pity, she mused, while hunting about for the speedwell. An aged gardener shuffled over to her, admonishing her with a rake held high in one hand.

'You can't come in here. Very private, this place is.'

She waved the paper under his nose, rightly guessing he probably couldn't read and it didn't make the least difference what was written upon it. She ignored him, although she was most polite in her attitude.

The old man seemed nonplussed, not knowing what to make of this well-bred member of the gentry entering the garden to prowl about in a skulking manner. He retired to a shed to watch her with wary eyes.

There was a pond set in the center of the garden. She tripped on a piece of rough flagstone while skirting the edge of it, and fumed at the damage to her slipper. Beyond an ancient cork tree, once called Jesuit bark, she espied the offices of the society. She thought that might be where the lectures were given, and hoped no one was about today.

After a bit of study, she determined where the low-growing herbals were located, and made her way over the unevenly flagged walk to the spot. Quick scrutiny found the plant she sought. It was a pity that speedwell was the thing that worked best for Nilsson. Another herb might have been a good deal simpler to find. But, caring for her companion as she did, nothing would prevent Penelope from taking an ample cutting of this plant, sufficient to make a supply of the remedy.

'Here, you can't do that!'

This time, the gardener was accompanied by another man, a younger one. Both were extremely irate and Penelope began to wonder how she would manage to get out of here with the cutting still in her possession.

She rose from where she had knelt, assuming her most haughty pose. 'I beg your pardon?'

Both men stopped, taken aback at her

composure. The younger man took a step forward. 'See here, miss, you can't come in here and dig up the garden. It ain't allowed.'

'But I have not dug it up, merely clipped a bit of herb for a special remedy.'

'There are no women apothecaries. What do you want with the herb?' the man demanded, motioning the gardener to go away on some errand.

'I need it for a potion. My companion is not well.'

'There are sufficient mixtures to be had at any apothecary shop.' He narrowed his eyes, suspicion seeming to emanate from every muscle. 'I must request you to leave.'

'Would a donation to the society be welcome?' Penelope asked, assuming that, as usual, she could buy her way out of trouble. She eased the bit of speedwell into her reticule, praying he would not notice her deceptive action.

'Are you trying to bribe me?' he demanded, looking incensed.

Penelope hastily shook her head, aware she had blundered badly. 'Never. However, it has been my experience that most public gardens are usually in need of funds. I had read that the Physic Garden had been having a spot of difficulty. Perhaps I was wrong?'

The man was torn between accepting

needed money and teaching this young chit a lesson, but his desire to get the better of the young woman who dared to so blatantly ignore the rules won.

'I have called the constable, young woman. We shall not tolerate this sort of desecration of our garden.' He assumed a pose somewhere between lecturing and threatening.

Whirling about, Penelope was dismayed to discover a constable bearing down upon them, fire in his eyes at the wild description he must have been given, judging from the look on his face. The old gardener limped along behind him, rake in hand, looking for all the world like an avenging devil.

'But you cannot do this,' she pleaded, wondering how it would look in the papers when it was revealed that Lady Penelope Winthrop, heiress to a vast fortune, had been placed in jail for pilfering a bit of herb. Or worse yet, would they dare hang her for the deed? She was well aware that penalties were harsh for seemingly slight infractions of the law. Not long ago she had read of some poor soul hanged for cutting down some hop vines. Was taking a bit of herb any less serious? Why hadn't she remembered this before?

Bolder still, now that he had reinforcements from the local constabulary, the garden's keeper stormed and raged at Penelope until her head ached with the noise of it all.

Helpless to stop the disaster that had befallen her, she stood silently as the constable moved to take her into custody. 'I would that you send for my solicitor. Do you know who I am? You are doing injury to Lady Penelope Winthrop, I shall have you know, my good man.'

'Ha! And I'm old farmer George himself. A likely story, that one is.' The constable, his blue suit stained with splotches of ale and food, grinned, revealing a missing front tooth. 'No real lady would come here without no maid to attend her, now, would she?'

'My carriage awaits me,' Penelope cried, growing desperately afraid as she stumbled along Swan Walk toward the main road. Here she was proved wrong. Her cowardly coachman had taken himself off to London, leaving his mistress behind. He apparently had wanted no part of an unsavory scene and felt no loyalty to her.

What had seemed a mission of mercy now assumed dire consequences. For the first time in her life, Penelope was utterly terrified. What if her solicitor failed to appear in time, provided they actually sent for him? Would she be able to get word to Cousin Letty or

Lord Harford? She had a pitiful few shillings in her reticule, and she feared that little sum would be taken from her. Stupidly, she had tucked the cutting deep inside her little bag, hoping to buy her way from her dilemma and have the herb as well. Now it would serve to convict her of a crime, it seemed. She had a vision of herself on the gallows at Tyburn Hill, her neck firmly in the rope, hanging for all to view. She shuddered at the very image.

'Is there some problem here?' The masculine drawl carried the boredom of the elite class, revealed a touch of the dandy's disdain for contretemps.

Tearing free of her captor, Penelope spun about, then cast herself into her savior's arms. 'Lord Harford! You have come!' With those dramatic words that impressed the hearers to a considerable degree, she swooned completely away.

9

Everything appeared extremely hazy, blurred, as though looking through a dense fog. Then she heard retreating footsteps and felt a cool waft of air on her face, and the fog drifted away.

Blinking her eyes, she slowly sat up, wondering where she was and what had happened. Then she glanced up and saw him. Lord Harford. And everything returned. In the distance she saw the stiff figure of the constable, his blue suit clearly visible, marching hurriedly off toward the center of Chelsea. Of the gardener and the disagreeable young man, she saw nothing.

Swan Walk was peaceful and tranquil in the soothing afternoon stillness. Sunlight sparkled and danced on the Thames and songbirds warbled away within the Physic Garden. A breeze swayed the tops of the old cedar trees seen over the garden fence, bringing with it the scents of gillyflowers and rich herbs. There was nothing around to indicate that a young woman had been so threatened only moments before.

Suddenly realizing that she clutched her

reticule to her with a death grip, she relaxed her left hand, then rose uncertainly from where she had been placed. Lord Harford stepped closer to offer his hand.

Shaking her head to clear all remnants of fog from her mind, she sensibly inquired, 'What happened?' When a reply was not immediately forthcoming, she continued, embarrassed at the silence and that he should see what had happened to her, 'I assure you I have never fainted before in my life, not even when the news of the accident of my parents came. How vexing, to be sure,' she murmured. 'I thought I was to be hanged, or at the very least transported to Botany Bay. However did you persuade them to go away? And without placing charges?' Then, observing the altered expression on his face, she continued, 'Or did they, and I have merely staved off the day of reckoning?'

'You bacon-brained pea-goose!' His exasperation rang in every syllable. 'To go haring off beyond the city with an unreliable coachman, no maid, and not obtaining permission for a cutting is outside of enough. You deserve a punishing.' Hands on hips, he shook his head in disgust while he stared at the young woman who looked frightened and badly shaken. Her bonnet was askew, and blond curls tumbled about her head in charming disarray. Her eyes were enormous, their blue of a startling intensity. He stepped toward her to place his arm in support, certain she was about to collapse again. He had never suffered such a fright in his life and was totally unprepared to deal with it. What he wanted to do was to clasp her in his arms, to shield her from the harsh world. Since he couldn't, he chose to censure. Judging by her face, he was making a royal hash of the matter.

The fear left her face, to be replaced by blazing temper. 'Well, and how kind of you to ask how I fare!' Those wide eyes now flashed with indignation.

'You are safe enough for the moment. Unless you tumble into another disaster.' His voice was rough with what she could only assume was anger or annoyance.

'Remind me to mind my own business next time I suspect a woman is out to give you a love potion,' she muttered as she bent to brush off her pelisse. There were twigs, and bits of soil from where she had knelt in the garden. Avoiding the critical eyes of her cousin, she checked her front and back to be sure she would not disgrace them both. She didn't think to adjust her bonnet.

He bowed his head for a moment, then finally spoke while placing one of her hands on his arm. 'Do you have any idea of what a turn I had when I saw your carriage come back empty with your fool coachman babbling something about the constable? By the bye, where *did* you hire that man? At any rate, I managed to wring from him just where he had left you. I arrived none too soon, my girl. You were well and truly about to discover what the interior of the nearest jail looked like.'

Stunned, as the memory of her recent danger returned, Penelope retreated to lean on the trunk of the beech tree against which she had been placed earlier, leaving the support of his arm for something a bit more solid. 'Oh, dear. I hope the potion proves to be worth it.'

'Potion?' he demanded in the most silky of voices.

'Yes,' she replied absently, looking about until she espied Lord Harford's lovely curricle waiting not far away. His tiger stood by the horses, ready to walk them if need be. The scent of oiled leather and horses was comforting in an odd way, for it was so very normal.

At the prolonged silence, she looked back at Lord Harford, adding, 'Miss Nilsson has been sadly out of curl of late. I wished to buy some germander speedwell, for that makes the best potion for such a melancholy. The fresh is the most desirable for this sort of thing, and I ought to have realized it could not be found in the city. But the third apothecary I went to was so obliging as to give me a ticket to the garden.' Recalling her possession of that slip of paper, she dug into her reticule and pulled it out in mild triumph.

'Did you show it to the gardener?'

'Yes, but you must know the man could not read. And I quite forgot to show it to that horrid young man who came rushing out of the building. Indeed, he scarce gave me a chance to defend myself.' She took several unsteady steps in the direction of the carriage, then added, 'I perceive our system of justice has a number of flaws in it. For a person to be near death due to a mere snipping of an herb is beyond belief.'

'You would go off by yourself,' he reminded her. 'Did you not tell them who you were?' He went to assist her into the curricle, then, seeing what a difficult time she was having, picked her up in his arms and gently placed her on the cushioned seat.

At this unexpected display of gallantry, she gave him a bemused look before answering, 'Most definitely, I did. And the fools made fun of me. They refused to believe a word I said. And then you arrived. You may be the most annoying man on earth, but I confess I was excessively glad to see you,' she allowed, the admission reluctantly dragged from her by her compulsive honesty.

At this bit of frankness Lord Harford gave an abrupt bark of laughter. Then he climbed up beside her, nodded to his tiger, who released his hold and ran around to jump up behind them as the curricle set off for London.

'This bit of idiocy could have put paid to your chances of ever contracting a respectable marriage, my girl.' His voice held strong shades of disapproval, such as she frequently heard from Miss Nilsson.

She drew slightly away from him, turning to bestow a studied look on her rescuer. 'I believe you are refining too much upon it. In my experience money can overcome any number of obstacles, especially when combined with impeccable background.'

'Breeding still accounts for a good deal, but having windmills in the head is not a desirable trait in a wife or prospective daughter-in-law,' came his swift response with a wicked chuckle, followed by a hurried glance at her flushed face. She was fast forgetting her narrow escape in the heat of argument. He, in turn, was learning more about this impossible cousin he had promised to help find a husband.

Without due regard for her choice of words, she snapped, 'Lady Harford thinks I am quite acceptable.'

'But then *I* am not marrying you, am I?' he said in the most bland and lofty manner.

'More's the pity,' she flared back at him. 'If you were inclined to wed, then ignore me, this nonsense might all be avoided.' She sighed a great gusty sigh, as one monstrously put upon.

'My dear girl, if we were to marry, I seriously doubt I could ignore you. I might wish to throttle you from time to time, but never could I ignore you.' There was the barest hint of sensuality in his voice, one she caught and that made her tremble slightly.

Instead of his words bringing the retaliatory remarks that would normally have leapt to her tongue, Penelope found herself musing on what he had said. How would it feel not to be ignored by his lordship? His kind regard for his mother and sister bespoke a man of strong sensibilities. Indeed, his quick and timely chase to Penelope's rescue revealed a man who held his obligations in high esteem. She well knew that being the head of such a family carried vast responsibilities with it, and he did not shirk his duties. An eldest brother might seem arbitrary and even cruel to his younger brothers and sisters, but he was virtually a slave to his family's interests. After all, he was but a tenant for life of the estates, and the authority they gave him to live like a lord was quite circumscribed. He couldn't sell what was entailed, nor could he deprive his family of any fair settlements. All of a sudden she saw herself as a rather onerous charge, one dropped in his lap without due consideration for his wishes in the matter.

He negotiated the corner to Upper Brook Street, then looked down on her bent head with puzzled concern. 'Do you feel that everything has a price? Beware, my dear. There are some things which cannot be bought for any amount.'

Penelope suspected that his regard was one such thing, and of a sudden she desperately wished she might have his admiration.

The carriage was brought to a halt precisely in front of Letty's house. He came around the carriage to assist Penelope, holding out his hands to her.

She stared at those hands a moment, then said in a very subdued voice, not daring to look into his dark eyes. 'I am the veriest sort of fool, my lord. It is a lowering reflection to realize that you have given of your valuable time to come to my aid. How silly it makes me feel.'

'What's this? A contrite spirit? Never say you admit you have been foolish beyond permission. Poor Penny. I vow you shall be meek enough to satisfy Mrs Drummond-Burrell.'

'You may keep your spurious sympathy, my lord,' she said, utterly vexed with the man, her usually composed self distinctly frayed.

He lifted her down, his hands staying at her waist a few seconds longer than absolutely necessary. 'Well, it is good to see your color restored and your temper back to normal.'

Penelope backed away from him as it dawned upon her that much of this raillery had likely been deliberate. Indeed, she wondered if the scoundrel had meant a word of what he'd said.

'Oh!' she said, piqued beyond belief. Sensibly refusing to dwell on what had happened, Penelope walked into the house, followed by Lord Harford. Once inside, she calmly turned to face him. 'I thank you for your timely assistance, Cousin. I trust that I shall not require help again while in London.'

'Nor I,' he murmured, bowing properly over her hand before leaving the house. He had sounded quite dubious.

Penelope was about to march up the stairs when Letty bustled down the hall from her little study, her features fixed in a frown.

‘I was about to mix up a potion for Miss Nilsson. Is something amiss?’ After the events of the past few hours, Penelope did not welcome the thought of additional dilemmas. She intended to mix up that restorative for Miss Nilsson, then curl up in bed for a time of reflection.

‘It is the most vexing thing. Your cat seems to have disappeared. One moment she was here, the next she was gone.’

Since Muffin was accustomed to free rein of the meadows at Fountains, Penelope could well understand her longing to be rid of the house.

‘Don’t fidget yourself, Letty. After a quick check here, I shall take myself off for the nearest spot of green, and there she will be. Which way would that be?’ Although she had been in London for a short while, Penelope’s sense of direction had not asserted itself. She thought that Hyde Park and Green Park were not very distant, but which way, she couldn’t have said.

Letty walked to the door with Penelope, pointing out where Green Park and Hyde Park were to be found, then apologizing again for the cat’s disappearance.

‘For you may know that Mr Oglethorpe was here and I quite forgot that the cat had come into the drawing room as well. When that man left, I fear the cat walked out with him.'

'Be careful, Letty,' Penelope said with boldness, moved to speak what was in her heart. 'I have heard it said that every man has a limit to his patience. I fancy that Mr Oglethorpe will demand an answer from you before long. Be certain the one you give is the one you mean with all your heart.' Penelope hoped that her words of caution would not upset Letty. She had come to like both Mr Oglethorpe and her peculiar cousin, and thought they suited each other very well. It would be a pity if false pride stood in the way of their happiness.

'You are nothing if not direct.'

Another look at Letty's annoyed face, and Penelope marched up the stairs to check under her bed where the cat liked to hide. Not finding her pet, she came down again and was soon off to the park, reluctant feet marching along the walk in search of her wayward cat.

What was the matter with her? What she considered a sensible outlook seemed taken by others as unusual and unfeeling. She had no desire to wound Letty. Poor dear, torn as she was by her loyalties and feelings, it was a wonder she even noticed the absence of one marmalade cat.

'Muffin,' Penelope called in a soft voice. 'Come, kitty, kitty.'

No ball of orange striped fluff came running to greet her. 'She is undoubtedly chasing after a mouse, or possibly up a tree after a bird,' she muttered to a stray dog who had run up to investigate. 'Shoo,' she admonished the dog. Muffin would scarcely return if a dog were in view.

She strolled along deeper into Hyde Park, after finding it the closest, peering beneath bushes, behind trees, and around any clump of wildflowers she happened upon. Fortunately, it was not yet the fashionable hour for carriages to converge upon the park. She shuddered at what the ladies of Society would think if they found her at her worst, without her maid, and scampering across the grass. Minutes passed, her concern growing. The delicious scents of spring, occasional bursts of wildflowers, and the abandoned singing of the resident birds failed to register. Penelope was worried.

Several riders approached, but Penelope paid them no attention, figuring that if she ignored them, they would ignore her. It didn't work quite as she hoped. She skirted a large oak, hoping to get on the far side, and thus out of sight.

'I say, isn't that Lady Penelope over there?'

came a familiar voice.

Startled, Penelope looked up to discover Lord Stephen cantering across the grass in her direction. Behind him were Mr Willowby and Sir Aubrey Preston, as well as a fourth gentleman. She was dismayed to find that when he lifted his head it was none other than Lord Harford. Double drat! He must have dashed home to ride out with his friends.

Lord Stephen reined in his bay, then slid down, walking up to meet Penelope with a quizzical look in his eyes. 'Alone in the park? I say, Lady Penelope, that will not do.'

'Oh' — she waved her hand vaguely about in the air — 'my maid is somewhere nearby. We are looking for my cat, who escaped from the house earlier.'

'Her cat is gone missing,' Lord Stephen in turn relayed to the others, who had lagged somewhat behind. 'What color is it?' demanded Sir Aubrey.

Penelope explained the size and coloring of her pet, helpless to prevent their joining in the search.

'Another contretemps, Lady Penny?' came a dulcet voice too close for comfort, a voice she had come to know all too well. He joined her, looking about for the cat.

'I did not request your aid this time, my

lord,' she retorted in lofty tones, albeit very quiet ones. She had no desire to argue with him so others could overhear their words.

'You are without a doubt the most shatter-brained female I have yet to meet,' he replied in repressive, although equally soft, accents. 'Not even Charis would be such a goosecap. If your maid is anywhere this side of Upper Brook Street, I shall be amazed.'

'I no doubt suffer from a disgraceful want of conduct, my lord,' she said with a deal of composure, considering all that had befallen her this day. 'However, my concern for Muffin brought me here in haste.'

'Without due regard, and you completely forgot you are in the heart of the most gossip-loving city in the world.' The touch of irony in his words was not lost on her, but she refused to yield an inch.

'Oh, I seriously doubt that. Why, I have it on good word that the Italians are no better than we. Nor the French, for that matter,' she added thoughtfully, gazing across the park while searching for a wisp of orange. 'Besides, I expected to be nearly alone, but for the nannies and their charges. 'Tis not the fashionable hour as yet.'

He shrugged, finding it impossible to counter her excuses. 'Your bonnet is still askew. Allow me.' He glanced about; then, seeing that the others had gone afield, he took the liberty of straightening her chip straw bonnet, retying the violet ribbon that precisely matched her pelisse. He stepped back to study the effect of his work, then caught sight of her face.

'Now, do not be in a pelter. I doubt if the others will have noticed your problem.' His tone was fatherly, kind, and his voice as smooth as fine satin.

'Please, do not say another word,' she said through gritted teeth, although why she should feel such ire was rather silly, for he had just performed a kindly gesture.

'I know,' he said sadly, 'you had rather be left alone.'

'Actually, I would rather find my cat, so that I might return to Letty's house and rest,' she retorted, though without her earlier spirit.

Concerned at her sudden lack of animation, Lord Harford remounted his horse, a splendid chestnut, and trotted off in the direction opposite to where the others had gone.

Penelope watched him leave, then turned to resume her own search. She was pleased he had left her alone. That depressed sensation within was merely concern for her missing pet.

Lord Stephen cantered up to where

Harford rode, a smile lighting his face. 'Hullo, words with the heiress? But then, you have no need for her fortune.'

Harford gave him a curious look, but said nothing, although he seemed to invite further confidences.

'I fancy that you,' Lord Stephen continued, 'like everyone else, believe my competence quite adequate, as does my father.' It was evident that Lord Stephen did not agree with this view.

'You are not precisely a pauper,' Harford reminded his friend.

'Does one ever truly have sufficient? Tell me, what are the conditions for marriage to the lovely Lady Penelope?' The offhand curiosity didn't fool Harford in the least.

A wry grin crept across his lean, handsome face. Harford glanced at his friend, then resumed searching the brush for a glimpse of orange. 'I fancy you'd not find it too difficult to handle.' Then the thought that Stephen might not honor Penny's stipulations occurred to him, and the image of Stephen taking her to bed flashed across his mind. Frowning, he glared at Lord Stephen. 'Are you serious?'

'Why not?' the other replied flippantly. 'I'll wager I can find that blasted cat and she will be so grateful that I will have her hand in a trice.' He did not sound in the least as though he contemplated something as solemn as matrimony, more like a lark.

An irrational anger gripped Jonathan. This was precisely what Penelope had claimed she wanted: a gentleman of acceptable birth and patrimony who would wed her, then take himself off to a merry round of dissolution in London and points abroad. He found it immensely distasteful.

'Tell me, how do you feel about traveling on the Continent?' His voice was austere, reflecting his inner turmoil.

'If she wishes it, travel would certainly be no hardship,' Lord Stephen said with an insouciant grin.

Jonathan wondered how he would feel when he discovered his travels were to be sans his bride. With Stephen, one never knew. He might find it quite pleasurable.

'How much has she told you? What does she seek in a husband?'

'I fear you will have to inquire of the lady as to that. My only task is to see that no fortune hunters ask for her hand.' Harford's face had fallen into grim lines, and his tone was so repressive that it brought a speculative look from his old friend.

Lord Stephen studied him for a few moments, then replied, 'I see.'

Just what he thought he saw was not

revealed. And Harford decided it best he not inquire. For some peculiar reason, he found the notion of Penny married to this dashing fellow a dismal concept.

'There it is,' Lord Stephen exclaimed under his breath. He slid from his horse, softly ordering it to stand, then stalked the tigerish cat with the stealth of a hunter. He pounced, clutching the squirming bundle of fur with a smug expression on his face. 'I told you I would find it.'

Harford nodded, then watched as his old friend marched toward Penelope while holding the cat at arm's length, lest he get cat hair on his splendid blue coat.

'Oh, Muffin, what a naughty cat you are, to be sure!' Penelope held, her arms out to receive her pet, smiling at Lord Stephen with considerable warmth.

Off to one side, Lord Harford watched the little scene enacted before him with a wry face. Stephen had always been a clever one, even back in their schooldays. Yet there was an inconsistency in character, a wanting you might ignore in a friend, but that you would never countenance in a husband for a relative. Harford assured himself that he was merely looking out for Penelope's interests. But if she thought she was going to marry Lord Stephen Collison, she would find unexpected opposition.

Mr Willowby and Sir Aubrey watched Lord Stephen and Penny walk off toward the far end of the park with amused, rather ironic expressions. They turned to join Harford, shaking their heads.

Sir Aubrey spoke first.

'I say, old chap, that's your cousin he is dangling after.'

'A very sensible cousin, I might add. I doubt he'll get far in his pursuit.' Harford brought his horse in line with theirs, and they continued walking for a bit.

'His debts have been mounting,' Willowby offered, annoyed with his friend for chasing off after an heiress. Willowby was in geater need; his pockets were near empty.

Harford spurred his horse to a respectable canter, his mind churning with this new piece of information.

* * *

'Fie, sir, you must return to your friends,' Penelope urged. 'I would not deprive you of a lovely ride this afternoon. As you can see, my cat does not like being out and not free.' She glanced down at the squirming orange bundle in her arms.

'It's a feisty little thing.' He didn't offer to

take the cat from her, knowing that orange fur would not be at all the thing with his blue coat. Besides, he held the reins in one hand and his horse required attention.

Penelope wondered if he would have come haring off to Chelsea to rescue her from the clutches of a constable. Or would he have cared? Then, fearing she did him a great injustice, she smiled with greater warmth as they came to the house and he hurried ahead to rap on the door for her.

'You were very kind to escort me home, sir. I daresay my maid gave up the hunt some time ago and is even now waiting for me with trepidation.'

His eyes danced with a hint of mischief; then he bowed over her hand, holding it with unseemly boldness, she thought.

'I was hoping you would consent to a drive with me later on?' Seeing she was about to shake her head, he continued, 'Perhaps tomorrow? Chasing this scamp must have tired you, and I am an utter beast to think of urging you to endure another outing. Tomorrow? I beg of you?'

Trying not to frown at his sudden flare of interest in her, Penelope slowly nodded her head. 'Tomorrow would be lovely, say about five of the clock?'

'Until then, fair lady.' He jauntily performed

an elegant bow, then vaulted up on his bay, cantering in the direction of the park with nary a look around to see if anyone might be in his way.

Mrs Flint closed the door behind Penelope, then murmured something about Miss Letty being upstairs again in the drawing room with that nice Mr Oglethorpe.

Not wishing to intrude, Penelope tiptoed up the stairs, then around the landing, hoping to get past the door to the drawing room without detection.

'Ho, there,' Mr Oglethorpe's voice rang out. 'You found the animal.' He came striding out of the drawing room, his long legs making short work of the distance. Letty followed behind him, peering around his lean form to see if the cat really was present.

'Actually, Lord Stephen Collison found him for me. That naughty cat had managed to get clean to the far side of Hyde Park. I vow I don't know when I have walked so much.' She hoped to get away from the romantic pair of poets. They could best reach an agreement if left alone.

'When Letty informed me that the cat had gone missing, I was truly distressed. I came over to offer my services in the hunt.'

'You were too late,' Letty said, walking around to study the cat. 'However, it seems to have enjoyed the run in the park.'

'But I appreciate his caring, Letty. It was a very thoughtful gesture. Lord Stephen would not hold the cat, you know. I suspect he feared acquiring a dusting of orange hair on that elegant blue riding coat he wore.'

With a self-conscious look at his own bottle-green coat, fitted by Weston himself, Oglethorpe stepped forward. 'I should be pleased to help you with the animal.'

Penelope laughed — in a kindly way — and shook her head. 'I think you had best compare odes with Letty while I retreat to my room and make repairs. It was brought to my attention that I am in sad need of such.' Memory of those dark eyes that had bored holes into her when he revealed his scorn for her behavior came back, and her cheeks flamed.

Clutching the cat more tightly to her chest, she quickly ran up the stairs to the second floor, where her bedroom was located. The room was empty. Where Miss Nilsson might be didn't cross her mind.

Dropping Muffin on the bed, Penelope turned to her looking glass, utterly horrified at what she found there. The once neat line of her violet pelisse was not at all as it ought to be, snagged, dusty, and somewhat stained as well. While her bonnet had been straightened, it was not at the proper, fashionable angle. Oh, she appeared to be worse than a frump. She had the appearance of a hey-go-mad miss, a young woman with more hair than wit, to be sure.

She tore off the offending bonnet, removed her pelisse — wondering if it was totally beyond salvage — then sank upon her bed to caress her reprehensible cat.

'Muffin, I fear I am not cut out to be a member of the *haut ton*. I have the birth and wealth, but a sad want of conduct.' Never would she forget his cutting tone as Lord Harford denounced her foolishness. It seemed she had quite sunk herself beneath redemption as far as he was concerned. Why that bothered her so greatly, she didn't pause to examine. She buried her face in the orange fur, and ignored the trickle of tears that crept from her eyes.

Muffin, as undemanding a pet as might be found, snuggled closer, offering comfort and understanding that no human seemed about to give.

Penelope sniffed, thinking to herself that life couldn't become more grim than it was at this moment.

10

Penelope was allowed little time to dwell on her misdeeds. Between paying social calls with Lady Harford and the adorable Charis, and trying to persuade Letty that she would be utterly miserable without Mr Oglethorpe in her life, lamenting her shortcomings had to be tabled for private moments, of which there were few.

Henri had come to call on them, putting Mrs Flint in a stew, not being accustomed to a mere servant presenting himself at the front door. His suave continental manner placed her in a greater quandary, for although she knew he was a chef, now at Lord Harford's elegant establishment, he possessed an address many men of the *ton* might envy. Truth be known, he set poor Mrs Flint's heart all aflutter.

Penelope concealed her amusement when the dear lady informed her in tremulous tones that that Frenchie was here to see her, and in the morning room, no less!

'Henri, what have you to report?' Penelope asked with a glum countenance. She knew she ought to be happy that he might find his family, or at least his estate. She made an effort to smile, hoping she did a better job of it than Miss Nilsson, who, in spite of the concoction Penelope brewed up for her, still looked the melancholy Swede.

'Very little, I am sad to say,' he replied after bowing low over Miss Nilsson's hand and offering her a small nosegay. His attentions brought a blaze of pink to her cheeks and a flustered glitter to her eyes.

Her simple dove-gray gown was subtly becoming, outlining pleasing curves and flattering her delicate coloring. She studied the bouquet of pale primroses with demure eyes. Her hand strayed up to tuck a soft blond curl beneath her dainty cambric-and-lace cap, her one great vanity. All of Miss Nilsson's caps were exquisitely embroidered in white with elegant flowers in attractive patterns and of the very latest style.

Since Miss Nilsson and Henri had frequently been at vociferous odds while at Fountains, Penelope found this new behavior distinctly curious. Was she to be surrounded by lovelorn souls? It seems to be the case, for Henri had eyes only for Miss Nilsson.

'You may as well tell us what has happened up to now.' It hadn't been all that long, Penelope realized, a matter of five weeks since coming to London, but so much had happened to her that she felt it near a lifetime.

'I have decided to take my chances, now that peace has uneasily settled over France. I confess that I do not trust Napoleon, but I feel impelled to investigate. It would mean a great deal for me to regain the family property.' He ostensibly spoke to both women, yet Penelope had the feeling that it was to Miss Nilsson that the words were sent. 'It would free me . . . ' His words faded off, leaving Penelope to wonder precisely what it would free him to do.

'When do you leave?' Miss Nilsson braved the answer she obviously feared.

'This week, once I can make arrangements with Lord Harford. I have a dinner this coming Friday I would not wish to miss.'

Penelope studied his face, thinking how much dearer he was to her than her own father. He had been present all her growing-up years, carefully friendly, offering fatherly advice on neutral subjects, but answering her questions on more controversial topics as well. Often she had persuaded him to discuss the concept of love. They argued amiably, for they far from agreed on the subject. He had called her his little *cynique*, casting concerned looks in her direction when he thought she wasn't watching him.

'Henri . . . if you find it necessary to leave early, I shall take your place in the kitchen.' She raised a hand to silence the objections she could see forming in his mind. 'I shan't have the least difficulty, and you know it. Plan the menu, do the shopping, and let me know if I am required. I shall keep Friday open, just in case.'

Miss Nilsson muttered something in Swedish that Penelope was just as glad she didn't catch.

Penelope bade her dear friend and former chef good-bye, then found something she simply had to obtain in a rush, leaving Miss Nilsson alone with him. Later, she alluded to the matter, but not a hint could be drawn from her companion. Whatever their feelings for each other, it was a very private matter. The stoic countenance presented by Eva Nilsson gave not a clue.

That Wednesday evening found Penelope with Lady Harford and the delectable Lady Charis Trent entering the formidable doors of Almack's. They passed the array of flowers and potted plants, handed their tickets to the man on duty, then walked up the stairs to the ballroom.

Penelope watched Lord Harford's sister curtsy to the first patroness with all the aplomb of a duchess, and decided that the girl was naturally born to the role. That she was being courted by a pleasant young man who was also heir to the Duke of Farncombe might partly account for her polish. Lady Harford was a great one for practicing.

When Penelope approached the intimidating figure of her distant relative, Mrs Drummond-Burrell, she found Lady Harford at her side. 'My dear, allow me to present your relative, Lady Penelope Winthrop, a connection on your mother's side, I believe.'

Her relation was a notably proper person; for being relatively young, she possessed a dignity that was unassailable. To think of her having such power in Society was almost shocking to Penelope.

Princess Esterhazy smiled, then tapped Mrs Drummond-Burrell on the arm with her fan. 'You must introduce us all to your relative, Clementina, for as such she comes with the highest commendation, does she not?'

When the ordeal, for that is how Penelope considered it, was over and they had passed along to the far side of the room, Lady Harford beamed smiles on all she met, while murmuring to Penelope, 'Your future is settled, for with the approval of the patronesses you will everywhere be sought.'

Penelope shook her head, amused at the

whims of these fashionable people. 'I fancy a husband would be pleased to know his wife had been approved by the doyennes of Society, but I think it all a deal of nonsense.' At the shocked expression on Lady Harford's face, Penelope continued, 'However, I shall confine my remarks to the acceptable, in hopes that some good may come from the evening.'

It was her second evening here. Mrs Drummond-Burrell had not attended the previous occasion, thus the lack of introduction. For some reason, Lady Harford had decided not to pay a call on her either.

Lady Jersey had been the one to extend the promise of a voucher, for Penelope could manage to be very prettily behaved when she chose. Doubtless Lord Harford played a part as well, for Penelope had observed he had teased and lightly flirted with Lady Jersey while present at a ball that Penelope had also attended. There were many ways of attaining what one wanted, she knew.

Lord Stephen sought her hand for the first minuet. 'Lady Penelope, you are indeed a graceful dancer, a credit to your teacher.'

Penelope smiled, but didn't reveal that her French chef, Henri, had performed the task. Upon reflection, she decided that her chef must have had a background far above his present station to even know the steps of the dance, let alone have mastered them. She whirled about and dipped, while wondering if she would again be found in Lord Harford's kitchen come Friday.

'You look positively enchanting, my dear,' he whispered as they met in the pattern of the dance.

'How kind you are,' she murmured back, wondering if Lord Stephen would come up to scratch, and did she truly want him if he did? One thing for certain, she would — unless she might persuade Lord Harford to perform the task — be required to inform him of her stipulations for the marriage. Somehow, after observing Lord Stephen at various balls and parties, she suspected he would find her demands easy to follow. He seemed far too dashing a man to think of settling into humdrum domesticity.

The hour was advanced when a faint stir at the door caught Penelope's eyes. Her Aunt Winthrop and Cousin Ernest entered the room. Eugenia Winthrop was gowned in black, with jet jewelry dripping from her ears and cascading across her bony chest. Neither the dress nor the jewelry she wore improved her appearance.

Ernest, the present Earl of Everton, looked even fatter than when last viewed; his yellow waistcoat striped in bright purple strained the brass buttons that attempted to hold it together. His lavender velvet coat pulled at the shoulders. As for those breeches that were required wear at Almack's, it was truly a pity he couldn't have been allowed something else. He simply didn't do them justice.

Penelope couldn't refrain from glancing at Lord Harford, who, as he had at his appearance at court, looked splendid in his garb. His black jacket matched his eyes, and the black breeches, hose, and shoes contrasted sharply with the snowy white of his stylish waistcoat and cravat. Restrained refinement. She felt quite drawn to him, although she did not understand this emotion in the least.

Penelope sought to avoid a confrontation with Aunt Winthrop and Cousin Ernest for as long as possible. At long last, Aunt Winthrop managed to corner her when the gentleman who had partnered Penelope was so neglectful as to deposit her near her aunt rather than Lady Harford.

'My dear girl, why did you not permit me to bring you here? I flatter myself that I have connections in the highest places. I feel certain I could have obtained the voucher you sought, without your going to strangers.'

'Lady Harford has been all that is kind, and

she is also my relation,' Penelope reminded, trying to edge her way toward Lady Harford without being obvious.

'Hmph,' Lady Winthrop snorted in an inelegant manner.

Penelope thought her aunt looked nothing more than an anxious crow waiting to pounce on a bit of grain. She gave a pointed look at the scrawny hand that darted out to clutch Penelope's arm in a viselike grip. 'I beg your pardon,' she said with the proper air of a lady.

'My dear,' the older lady's calculating voice whispered in a most confidential manner, 'I was thinking you really ought not to wait with announcing your betrothal to dear Ernest. He is utterly beside himself with anxiety over the delay.'

Penelope glanced to where Ernest reclined at the side of the room, looking like a bizarre pumpkin. If anything had upset him recently, it was more likely to be the tardiness of his dinner.

'Dear aunt, I was unaware that there was to be a betrothal, at least between the two of us. Listen carefully to my words, ma'am. I have no desire to marry your son.'

It was likely that Ernest could easily be persuaded to frequent the environs of London, or even the Continent, now that the tables of France were once again available to him. She doubted he was interested in her, or in sharing her life or bed, for that matter. But she could not contemplate being his wife. Not even in name. She hadn't thought she would have such scruples, but there it was. She wanted something more. The image of Lord Harford as he had queried her about her attitude toward marriage came to mind. She refrained from a sigh.

'Nonsense, my girl. Such missishness is not to be tolerated. Why, marriage to the Earl of Everton is a plum to be desired.' She shook her finger beneath Penelope's nose.

Penelope longed to inquire why Aunt Winthrop hadn't sought the hand of a willing young girl for her son. However, she strongly suspected why the union was so desired; Ernest had gone through too much money and his dear mama worried there would not be sufficient to keep him in the style she wished him to adopt. Aunt clearly wanted the entire estate under one control again. Penelope had heard a rumor or two that the family, the Winthrop branch, that is, was furious that the previous Earl of Everton had divided his estate the way he had, bequeathing all the unentailed money and Fountains to Penelope. Apparently they expected her to be endowed with a decent portion, and nothing more, if that.

What a pity Aunt Winthrop had not sought out Penelope's solicitor. So much of this bother could be done away with. Or could it? Was there a way that Aunt could compel a marriage? Penelope tried to think, furrowing her brow as she continued to ease along the side of the room in Lady Harford's direction.

'Ah, Penny, I believe this is my dance.'

'How true, Cousin,' Penelope gushed in relief, even though she knew very well that Lord Harford had not sought her earlier to request a dance with her.

Aunt Winthrop sputtered indignantly at the sound of the pet name conferred on her niece by Lord Harford. 'Unseemly! In my day . . . '

No more could be heard as Lord Harford led Penelope out on the floor, then partnered her in a gay cotillion. Nothing could be discussed during the dance, for it was an energetic one. When it concluded, she gratefully walked with him to where the refreshments were to be found.

'Lemonade, please,' she replied in answer to his questioning nod at the tables.

'You exchanged words with your aunt before I rescued you from her grasp?' He handed her a glass of surprisingly cool lemonade, then strolled along the room with her on his arm, trying to appear they discussed nothing more than the weather.

'She is most insistent that I wed the toad.' Because of the proximity of other people, Penelope declined to avoid using his name.

'Money problems? I can see no other reason why she would consider allowing another to get close to her darling.'

'I suspect she wants to control the estate as it once was.'

'Ah.' They walked a bit; then he said, 'You cannot bear the thought?'

'Odd, is it not? I thought I might be able to marry just anyone, but I find I must draw the line somewhere before him.'

'You might find someone else before she can force the issue.'

'But who? Since you will not be so obliging . . . '

'Dear girl, when and if I wed, *I* shall do my own proposing.'

Penelope thought he sounded exceedingly huffy and said so. 'You make me sound the veriest hoyden, and I have not precisely asked you to wed. I merely said it was an excellent solution.'

'You ought to marry for love, not convenience.'

'There are reasons for eluding the bonds of passion, my lord. 'Tis greater than mere virtuousness. Passion bursts into flames and burns brightly for the moment, then dims to become the ashes of love. While I admit to desires, I have no wish to be left with naught but ashes. They are but cold comfort indeed. Better not to love at all.'

'You admit to desires?' he said with the faintest of voices, one Penelope strained to hear.

'I suppose I ought not. I fancy it is not proper in the least.' She recalled those most improper kisses. 'You see, I've not discussed that subject with either Miss Nilsson or Henri.'

At this, Jonathan stopped to stare down at the young woman at his side, clearing his throat.

'Well, and I would never mention it to anyone else, my lord.'

'I wish you could call me Jonathan, Penny.'

'That has nothing to do with the matter at hand.' She gave him a teasing look, dropping her lashes once, then raising them, so her large blue eyes met his gaze. 'I wondered if Lord Stephen might do.'

'Stephen?' Jonathan recalled their discussion in the park, when Stephen wagered he could marry Penelope if he so wished. With a flippant attitude such as that, Stephen could easily promise to keep her stipulations, then break them for a lark. He was capable of taking her to bed, only to dash off to London or the Continent, uncaring of the consequences that might be left behind.

'What is it? In the past you have not hesitated when I mentioned his name.' She wondered what emotion gripped Lord Harford, for she dared not call him Jonathan, particularly at Almack's.

Jonathan wondered how he might caution her against Stephen without sounding like a jealous, spiteful person. He was mulling the matter over when the man in question appeared before Penelope, his jaunty good looks and rakish air giving him a definite appeal. Jonathan noted with satisfaction that Penny didn't seem all that eager to take off with Stephen. She clung to Jonathan's arm with a decided reluctance to leave him, he thought.

'Our dance, my fair one.' Lord Stephen extended his arm with the supreme confidence that she would gladly accept his partnering.

She nodded. 'As you say, sir.' After a proper curtsy to Jonathan, she walked off with Stephen, with no coy backward glances or indication she was sorry to go.

Jonathan decided that he had done more worrying this past month than in his entire lifetime. He turned from the sight of his cousin in the arms of a good friend to seek his mother.

'Ah, there you are, my dear. The last time I saw you, you were strolling in the direction of the refreshment room with Penelope. Tell me, does not Charis look charming on the arm of David Howell? He's heir to the Duke of Farncombe, in case you forget. As Marquess of Lisle he has a sizable estate, and stands to inherit quite nicely.' The smugness in her voice might be forgiven, considering the splendid connection her daughter would make, not to mention the feeling of success at attaining one of the supreme catches of the year for her remaining daughter. It was an achievement any mother might envy and probably would.

'How does she feel about him?'

His mother shot him a conscious look, then said, 'She declared to me that it mattered not if he was penniless, for she utterly adores him.'

With a wry expression, Jonathan shook his head. 'I daresay she thinks that, but as long as she truly has a regard for the young man, he has my blessing. I suppose I am to be favored with a visit from him in the near future?'

'Would tomorrow be too soon?' She laughed softly at his expression of mock dismay.

'Definitely April and May,' he murmured, chuckling until his mother spoke again.

'I worry about Penelope. Do you really believe she will find the man to suit her purposes? She said something yesterday about being anxious to return to Fountains to see how her greenhouse was coming along. Jonathan, she cannot go haring off in the middle of the Season and still expect to find a husband, especially the sort she wants.'

'Cousin Ernest is willing to marry her.'

'Heavens, he is such a toad. I do not care if she merely desires a *mariage de convenance*, she is too lovely to be shackled with him. What if he . . . ?' She gave a delicate shudder at the thought of Ernest taking advantage of his vows to actually consummate the marriage. Provided one of his girth was actually capable of such a thing, that is. Her own husband had been as slender as her son was now, right until the day he was killed in the accident. They had had a most satisfactory married life, and she failed to understand why Penelope felt as she did about the subject.

'Unthinkable, I agree. Of course she must not marry him. Tell me, do you think Lady Winthrop would take matters into her own hands to place a notice in the *Times*?' He watched the progress of Penny on Stephen's arm as they moved down the center of a country dance. That smile she flashed him was far too trusting. Jonathan could see only hurt in store for her if she settled on Stephen.

'I had not considered the possibility, but that woman is horrid. I would put nothing past her capabilities.'

'That is what I thought,' Jonathan replied, drawing up to his full height as he considered the problem before him. The slender minx was fluttering her lashes at Stephen, flirting with him like the veriest of coquettes. Off to one side he observed that Lady Winthrop had not missed the little scene either. Drat that girl. For someone who insisted on how proper she was, she had the ability to entangle herself in one situation after another.

When the country dance ended, Jonathan promptly presented Penelope with a very acceptable young man as a partner, one that could not possibly alarm Lady Winthrop. Thereafter, he made a point of casually bringing around one potential partner after another, all unremarkable, and quite presentable. Not one of them was the sort to drive a girl into a passion, he supposed. At least Twysden, with his excessively receding chin, certainly wasn't.

His mother playfully tapped his arm, whispering, 'Whatever are you about, dear boy? I have never before seen such a collection of *almosts, not quites*, and *perish the thoughts*.'

'I hope to calm any apprehensions Lady Winthrop may have acquired after seeing Penny gaze at Stephen with those cow eyes.'

'Cow eyes? Really, Jonathan, that is most unkind. He is entirely presentable, and you know it. However, as a possible husband, I should not like him for Charis.'

'Nor for Penelope. He made me a wager that he could win her hand, and indeed, it looked promising when he found her lost cat. She bestowed a very fond smile on him as he gingerly handed the animal to her.' He gave his mother a wry glance before turning again to watch Penelope. 'I fancy he did not wish to get cat hair on his new blue coat.'

'But he is charming,' Lady Harford admitted. 'However, he is not the most dependable boy.'

'Indeed. Perhaps someone ought to tell her that.' He touched his mother on the arm, then moved to where Penelope fanned herself after finishing a lively country dance.

'Are you willing to go home now?'

'I suppose you will lecture me?'

'I shall leave that for Miss Nilsson.' He found her shawl, gathered a reluctant Charis and his curious mother, before leaving the hallowed halls of the most fashionable assembly rooms in all of London.

Aunt Winthrop nudged Ernest into following them out the door. The groups silently awaited their carriages. Lady Winthrop tilted her head in a listening attitude.

At last Lady Harford murmured, 'Really, it is too bad of them, to allow the streets to be so congested.'

'It is not a broad street,' Penelope observed, taking care to remain safely between Charis and Lady Harford, with Lord Harford behind her.

'There are times when one must wait for hours for a carriage,' Charis added quietly, for she had been affected by the grim presence of her distant relatives. Lady Winthrop had that depressing capacity to put others into the dismals without half-trying.

When at last the Harford carriage was maneuvered up before the awninged entrance, they hurried in, then drove off with a collective sigh of relief.

'Was there ever such a woman as that?' Charis wondered aloud.

Little more was said about that other pair, for Charis desired her brother be informed of her dearest David's intention to call on the morrow. Upon learning that there was no reason to deny the marriage, indeed, who would not welcome such an alliance, Charis giggled happily and bounced with delight.

Penelope felt a deal of pleasure at her cousin's happiness. The glow enveloping the girl seemed almost tangible.

After Lady Harford and Charis went into their house on Mount Street, Jonathan continued on alone with Penny. He was glad his mother had understood his need to discuss certain things with his cousin and had not questioned this change in procedure.

'Penny, I wish you would reconsider this matter of your wanting a marriage of convenience. I cannot live with myself if I don't urge you to contemplate a union based on love rather than expediency.'

'I told you before that I do not trust love. My parents loved each other, or so they said. They also said they loved me. Since I rarely saw them, it seems they loved me better from a great distance.' She gave him a gentle, sad smile. 'The rare instances they appeared, it did not seem to me that love, if that is what they knew, seemed so desirable. They quarreled frequently.'

'Even people in love are not in harmony all the time.'

'We quarrel frequently, but we are not in love,' she snapped. 'Nor could we be.'

'What an exasperating young woman you are.' He clenched his hands in his lap, wanting badly to shake some sense into her, then continued. 'You must be careful about Stephen.' He picked up her hand as the carriage came to a halt before Letty's home. 'Just be on guard. You do not really know Stephen. He may not be what he seems. How do you know but that he doesn't seek your fortune? What is to say that Stephen might agree to your stipulation, and then, once wedded, change his mind?'

Tired of his constant caviling, Penelope turned on him, the light from the flambeau in front of the house revealing her annoyance. 'Perhaps I *shall* change my mind, sir. Maybe I shall try to find a man who can love me for myself and not my fortune. Or would that be too difficult?'

'Not at all. You do have your . . . moments.'

'Oh! What a wicked man you are.' Her eyes flashed with an emotion he couldn't identify. Anger? Pique? 'Tell me, have you ever been in love?' she demanded.

Startled by her question, Jonathan lightly replied, 'Dozens of times, I can't recall them all.'

'Then I doubt you could have been serious,' she pointed out as conclusive proof to the vagaries of so-called love.

'I was serious at the moment,' he informed her in all earnestness, his amused face in the shadows.

She pulled her hand from his, turning her face away from him, so he had no idea what she might be thinking. 'I think that is horrid,' she said in a muffled voice.

He reached out to take that charming face and bring it about so he might look at her. When she raised her lashes, he took note that her eyes seemed to sparkle with suspicious brightness.

'You're laughing at me!' he declared with irritation.

'You are so absurd. You adjure me to find a lover, then admit you have never truly known what it is to love. How silly you are. Come back and talk to me of love again when you know what it is.'

She moved restlessly, wanting to leave the carriage. All this nonsense about love was definitely unsettling. Glancing at him again, her tongue darting out nervously to moisten dry lips, she said, 'Well?'

'Well, indeed.' He drew her closer, then deposited a fierce, although brief, kiss upon a very startled but softly inviting mouth.

He escorted a silent young woman into the house, then promptly left. He feared very much that he already had met her demand. The devil of it all was that she'd probably not have him in a million years now.

11

Penelope trailed up the stairs to her room, dragging her shawl behind her, ignoring the tangled fringe as it caught in the top post of the banister.

Her cat saw the captured fringe, and thinking it a game, began to stalk it, then pounced. The tug and thump brought Penelope's gaze to the floor, where Muffin now rolled in a field of paisley. Instead of continuing the new game, she picked the cat up, then wandered up the next flight of stairs and around the corner to her room.

Muffin protested this treatment. Penelope dropped her shawl on the bed, then snuggled Muffin close to her as she went to the window to stare out at the night. Faint light from the partial moon somewhat lit the scene below, sending just enough light into the room so she might make her way about.

Almack's, Jonathan, and Lord Stephen whirled about in her brain. Images flickered; Jonathan scolding her, picking her up, cradling her close to him before gently placing her in the carriage. He had never fully explained how he came to her rescue at the

Physic Gardens. For a man who had the reputation of being a dandy, and as such rather indolent, he certainly found fault with her over every hair-splitting thing. All she had asked him to do was to aim her in the right direction. He seemed to want to be involved in her every step.

And was Lord Stephen the right direction? She pulled a small slipper chair over to the window, reluctant to light a candle. She wanted to think, and the quiet of the night was a good time to do it.

The important thing now was to escape marriage to Ernest. It was quite plain that Aunt Winthrop intended to pursue that event. As Penelope dimly recalled, it was said that Eugenia Winthrop did far better than Bow Street at getting what she wanted.

And what was Penelope going to do about her altered feelings for Lord Harford? He must see her as the most tiresome of charges. As to that teasing kiss this evening, well, he had just admitted he didn't really know what love was. It stood to reason that he simply couldn't, having fallen in love dozens of times. And he had the audacity to declare he had been serious each time!

She thought back to the come-out ball, where a premonition had prompted her to order the milk, Culpepper's remedy for too much henbane. Why she had suspected that drug, she wasn't sure, except that it was easy to procure. Yet it could be deadly, not a drug to treat lightly. And Miss Dunston seemed the sort to desire a love potion. As though a love potion would really work.

Penny frowned again. Why had she been so attuned to danger for Lord Harford? Why had she even cared about what happened to him? For he was the veriest quibbler. Yet she had felt as though he was a part of her, in some peculiar way. It had to do with this surge of emotion she felt whenever she saw him.

And then the next day he came tearing after her. What a strange experience, finding herself in his comforting arms after the terror of her arrest. That ordeal had haunted her for some time, yet she suspected that his taunting her in his typically maddening way had lessened the impact of what she had undergone.

So where did that leave her now? She shook her head. It was hard to tell what Aunt Winthrop would do next. Perhaps if Penelope announced a betrothal to Lord Stephen, it would defeat her aunt. The problem with that notion was that Lord Stephen seemed content to flirt and dance with her, nothing more. Although he had been gallant when he had found Muffin. Lord Harford had merely sat on his horse and looked annoyed. Penelope admitted she was most confused.

There was no one else who half-appealed to her as a husband. Mr Willowby was almost nice, Sir Aubrey did not quite succeed, the others presented to her were complete 'perish the thoughts.' Lady Harford had described a number of gentlemen in that manner and Penelope had found it amusing. Now she discovered the designation most apt.

Deciding that her thinking process was sadly muddled, she deposited the cat at the foot of her bed, then swiftly undressed herself, scattering pins on her dressing table in her hurry to get to sleep and blessed insensibility.

Morning brought a note from Henri. In his spidery French, he wrote that he had a chance to leave immediately. The menu was all set, the food to prepare would be waiting, and he would be eternally in her debt if she would cook for him. Nothing he had planned to serve would be beyond her capabilities.

But would Lord Harford discover that she was in the kitchen? That was the largest problem she could see. It was one thing to cook for him before she had made her appearance at Almack's. It was quite another to risk her reputation by sneaking into his house to cook a dinner for his friends again after she had been accepted by Society. If word of this got out, she would be ruined, and not even her pots of money would get her a proper *parti*.

Henri knew nothing of this aspect of the arrangement. She could only hope that among them — she, the cook, the maid, and Mr Darling — the dinner could be pulled off with no one the wiser. God forbid Lord Harford come to the kitchen on any errand. The letter explaining the chef's absence would be given his lordship the next morning. After all, he knew that Henri had planned the trip.

'I shall be gone all day tomorrow, Nilsson,' she informed her companion over their chocolate, who raised shrewd brows in acknowledgment of the information and what it entailed.

'If anyone inquires for you, I shall say you have gone on a mission of mercy. And I believe that to be the case. *Ja*?' She paused, then added softly, '*Minst sagt*.'

'To say the least,' echoed Penelope in English. Miss Nilsson knew what chances Penelope took, yet she felt sure her companion also wished Henri Godspeed on his journey, with a safe return.

That evening Penelope joined Lady Harford and Lady Charis at a small musicale at the Sefton home. The Countess Sefton was the kindest of the patronesses and she and her earl welcomed the select group with gracious charm.

When Penelope saw Lord Harford taking a seat with the musicians, she turned questioning eyes to Charis.

Charis dimpled a winsome smile, holding a fan before her face so she might explain without another overhearing her words. 'Did you know that Jonathan plays the flute? He is vastly accomplished. You play too. I overheard you trying the pianoforte at our house.'

Deep in consideration over this new aspect, Penelope merely nodded with modest grace.

Charis sat back with a speculative look on her face, then excused herself for a few moments, returning with a smug expression that made Penelope wonder a little. She might have been more curious, but her mind was still on Lord Harford and his multifaceted personality.

The music was utterly delightful. All the players were of professional caliber, although of the peerage and gentry. Penelope sighed with pleasure as the music of Haydn and Bach floated about her in rhythms that ranged from delicate to profound.

When the pause came for refreshments, she made her way to Lady Sefton's side. 'In truth,

I nearly dreaded a musicale,' she confided with a smile, 'having heard dire tales of them. This is positively delightful, ma'am. I am so pleased to join you this evening.'

'I understand you are musical, my dear.' The agreeable lady beamed at her. 'Promise me that you will play for us.'

'Oh, no, I am not as accomplished as those we have listened to this evening.' Penelope shrank from the thought of performing before such a select group, particularly Lord Harford.

Nothing would do but that Lady Sefton had her way. Any musician who ventured to her house on the evening of a musicale was persuaded to perform. The pianist yielded his place with quiet insistence, eager to hear another play.

Penelope gathered every bit of her poise, glancing first at Miss Nilsson, at Lady Harford, and at the traitorous Lady Charis, before she went to the pianoforte. She avoided meeting Lord Harford's gaze.

'I suggest we try this piece, if it suits your abilities.' Jonathan gestured to the music, shifting the candles so she might see better. She looked like a dream he had conjured up in that frosted lavender and silver gown, with the once-demure neck-line now dipping so low it would take his mind off the notes if he stood too close.

She nodded, thanking the heavens for a simple piece that she knew well. In moments the charm of Bach's *Jesu, Joy of Man's Desiring*, floated out over the room, his flute taking the choral melody. Never had she played so well; it was as though the duet was inspired. She decided it must be the atmosphere, when they brought the piece to its conclusion to the enthusiastic appreciation of the group.

Penelope began to leave, and was restrained by one of the other musicians. 'I feel sure you can join us for the Vivaldi. You play uncommonly well.' He set the music before her, nodding to the others to gather around, and before she had a chance to protest, they began the concerto, *The Four Seasons: Spring*. It was quick and sprightly in the opening, and Penelope had to concentrate, part of her wishing she was in her seat, the other part taking great delight that she could play with so fine a group. It was exhilarating, to say the very least. If she was a bit cautious in her approach to the music, the others led her on, making allowances for her.

During the second, slower, movement, she appreciated the musicality of the others. The violinist led each of the performers along with him in little duets, drawing each out. When they reached the animated conclusion, she was almost sorry the performance was at an end. She felt breathless, as though she had faced a challenge and emerged triumphant.

During the confusion following their performance, the gentleman who originally was to play the pianoforte came up to her. She blushed with embarrassment at his kind words.

'You ought to have performed, sir. I am indeed sorry to have intruded.' She gave him one of her direct looks, with a contrite smile.

His words were cut short when Jonathan made a slight gesture with his hand, and the gentleman, whose name Penelope never did catch, melted away.

'Must you captivate everyone in London? I had no idea you played so well.' He bent over her hand, bringing it to his lips with a languid grace, then glanced up, an impish look in his eyes. 'You can cook too. So unanticipated.'

'I could say the same about you.' She tried to overlook the way he held her hand. 'You are full of surprises.' She hoped no one had heard what he said. 'Why did he bring up the subject of cooking now, for pity's sake?'

What else he might have said was lost, for Charis came up, bubbling with her enthusiasm for the fine pair they made, her brown curls bouncing with her animation.

Penelope grimaced at her choice of words,

then scolded her cousin. 'And just what made you think I might play well enough to join that group? It would have served you right had I been terrible.'

Charis giggled sweetly, retorting, 'I heard you at our pianoforte one day after you came. I thought you'd do well enough.'

'And you planned this?' Suspicions rose in the back of her mind, and she spun about to challenge Lord Harford with her eyes. He looked faintly guilty about something.

'It is getting late,' reminded Miss Nilsson in her quiet way. 'You have a full day tomorrow. We had best leave.'

Jonathan walked at her side, then stood with her while waiting for the family coach. Tonight there would be no private conversation. 'What do you have tomorrow that requires extra sleep?' he inquired, amused at her blush.

'Ah, a philanthropic meeting of a sort, sir — the Benevolent Society for Refugees.' She exchanged an oblique glance with Miss Nilsson.'

'Your chef is involved in this?'

'Oh, assuredly,' she agreed, thinking that *that* certainty was the truth. The conversation turned to music all the way home, for which Penelope gave sincere thanks.

The next morning she quietly dressed once

Miss Nilsson shook her awake, then ate the shaved ham on buns and drank her hot chocolate with appreciation.

'We must do something about Letty. I dare not think of anyone dining here, not that it is my privilege to invite such, but even to encourage her is folly. Perhaps if I speak with Mr Oglethorpe, he will think of something.'

'*Ja*,' agreed Miss Nilsson. 'Turnips and carrots are very tiresome.'

'Not to mention rice and the rest.' They exchanged rueful smiles, then Penelope donned a plain medium-blue round gown of light kerseymere and the paisley shawl that Muffin liked so well. Her hat concealed her face well.

'I shall not disgrace you or Henri,' Penelope promised. 'Say what you think best if someone asks for me.'

With that, she slipped down the back stairs, far from Letty's room, then off to enter the hackney that awaited her. Miss Nilsson had thought of everything, it seemed.

This time Penelope felt more at ease in preparing for the evening's dinner. It was to be much the same group of men, from what Mr Darling said. They gathered to enjoy fine foods, sip excellent wines, and gossip, as near as she could figure out. Only now, a wager was not involved.

After being assured that his lordship had gone out, Penelope tiptoed into the upper part of the house, admired the fine table setting in the dining room, then took a look about her.

A beautiful console table inlaid with lapis lazuli, porphyry, and various colored marbles stood against the wall, having pride of place in the hall below a tall looking glass framed in gilt. The dining table was inlaid with brass, and the chairs drawn up to it were an elegant curving design.

She wandered on, peeking into the library, taking note of the marvelous collection of music that was piled up on the far side of the room. Had she seen this before, she might have been prepared for last night. She still glowed when she thought of the gentle compliments showered upon her from the one she admired.

On an impressive desk she observed a buhl inkstand, with his seals, a tray holding his pen and nibs and other impedimenta for writing, everything neatly arranged. Feeling like a spy, she backed from the room, then hurried to the kitchen before she could get caught.

The remainder of the day was a whirl of activity. She sat for a brief bite to eat at Mr Darling's insistence, then plunged into the final preparations for the meal.

Mr Darling wrote out copies of the menu for each guest. Following that, he made trips to the wine cellar, bringing back bottles of sherry, Madeira, Johannesburg, Bordeaux, sauternes, champagne, Tokay, Malaga, and Lafitte.

'Mercy!' Penelope declared. 'They shall all be under the table if they drink every bit of that.'

'A different wine for each dish, I believe, Lady Penelope,' Darling replied with a smile.

She sniffed, knowing that what he said was likely true. Just because she rarely drank didn't mean she was unaware of what others consumed. And what was not drunk at the table would be returned to the kitchen.

Before dinner he uncorked the various bottles, except the champagne, setting that to cool. Penelope decided that she ought to taste each of them to see what complemented which food, according to Henri's notes. She enjoyed the Johannesburg, for it was light and delicate. The Bordeaux was fine, if a bit dry for her taste. The others, she sipped, her head to one side, listening to Darling's evaluations with growing appreciation for the finer points of wines.

Was she a bit tipsy? Oh, not foxed, just a little elevated? Insufficient food in her stomach, the warmth of the kitchen, and the relaxed feeling that followed the finishing touches to the dinner that went up to the dining room in course after course contributed to the state.

She giggled at Cook, who surveyed the meringue decorated with Chantilly cream and angelica. 'It looks like a wedding cake.' She hiccuped, then giggled again. 'Fine thing to serve a party of bachelors. I ought to put a ring in for luck; whoever gets it is the next to wed.'

Cook smiled at the nonsense, then looked concerned as Penelope took off a simple gold band she always wore and plopped it into the sweet.

'My lady,' she protested, 'you may never see it again.'

'Oh' — Penelope tilted her head and loftily waved her hand at Darling — 'he'll get it back to me. Won't you, old man?' She hiccuped again and forgot to apologize.

Darling and Cook exchanged concerned glances.

When a bottle of Johannesburg returned to the kitchen not quite empty, Penelope poured out the remaining trifle and slowly sipped it down, thinking that Jonathan lived very well. He must have ordered a lot of wine when the peace came, for he didn't seem the sort to be financing the enemy by buying smuggled stuff. Of course, this particular wine was imported from the vineyards along the Rhine.

She rose on legs that seemed to be oddly unsteady and wondered if Darling would be so good as to call her a hackney, or perhaps a sedan chair. If she could have the men come into the house so she could merely step right in, and not have to negotiate the steps, it might be just the thing, she decided with another hiccup.

She heard the door open behind her and turned, opening her mouth to make her request. Her mouth gaped open, but not a word came out, for rather than Darling, Jonathan stood there, looking like a winter storm.

'Oh, dear,' she finally managed to say.

'I rather hoped you had not gone as yet.' In contrast to his severe expression, his words sounded smooth, yet somehow rather dangerous.

'You knew I was here?' She gave him a wary smile. 'Odd, I thought you'd never guess that I took Henri's place. I'm a very good cook. You said so yourself,' she enunciated with extreme care, for the words seemed peculiarly difficult to say.

'I brought the remainder of the champagne down so we might have a toast to a very good dinner.' He strolled over to the table, placing the bottle down while waiting for glasses, then watched her.

'That's nice.' She beamed at him with all the goodwill of a slightly tipsy lady.

'And to return your ring, which I recognized immediately,' he snapped out as he poured the sparkling wine into the two flutes Darling had hastened to place on the table. 'Thank God I was the one who got your piece of nonsense. Whatever possessed you to put it in the sweet? I can only hope that no one else observed the dratted thing. Here.' He held out the ring and her glass.

She took the ring, unable to cope with both at one time, then accepted the champagne, ignoring Darling's frantic motions from behind Jonathan's back. 'I must say,' she said while trying to focus on him after taking a healthy sip, 'this seems to be the nicest of all. Very nice,' she pronounced, drinking every bit of champagne with delight.

Her legs were getting distinctly capricious in their willingness to hold her upright, so she abruptly sat on the stool that Darling had rushed to place behind her.

Lord Harford took a closer look at her, then turned to his butler. 'Just how much has she had this evening?'

'I tried to warn you, sir. I doubt the young lady is accustomed to wine. She has tasted each of them, at her insistence, I might add, sir.'

'Oh, dear, er, heaven,' Jonathan said, exasperated.

'Darling, would you please get me a sedan chair,' she said slowly, with extreme care. 'I do believe it is the better choice.' She smiled like a proud child who has completed a difficult recitation.

'I shall take you home in my carriage. Where is Henri? Not at the meeting of the Benevolent Society for Refugees, I fancy?'

'He's gone to France. I didn't tell you because I wanted to help him and he didn't want to ruin your dinner party. I'm a good cook,' she repeated. 'You said so yourself.'

Jonathan issued some terse orders to Darling, then scooped up Penny in his arms, wishing he could do as he pleased and not as he must. Darling hastily took the glass that was slipping from Penelope's grasp before it fell, then he disappeared.

'Oh, this is lovely,' Penelope said, quite agreeable to anything. She snuggled into Jonathan's arms, placing her head against his strong shoulder with a sigh of contentment. She reached up to stroke that utterly irresistible face before slipping her arm about his neck.

Jonathan took a fortifying breath, then

marched up the stairs, through the baize door, and into the entry. While awaiting his carriage, he sought a chair in the dim recesses of his library.

The aroma of leather and sherry, fine old books, and the scent of her rose perfume mingled together. He looked down at a very drowsy face. Bemused, he said, 'You shan't feel in plump current tomorrow, I suspect.'

'Aunt Winthrop is coming to call. She does not like my cat,' murmured Penelope in reply. 'I shall sleep in, and the old girl can go away.'

Amused, Jonathan shifted her a little, then said, 'If she gives you any trouble, please call on me. Can you remember that, I wonder.'

'Oh, yes,' Penelope whispered, sighing with delight at her place of repose. She would cheerfully remain here all night rather than face her aunt in the morning. 'In fact,' she mused aloud, peeping up at him, 'I should like to sleep right here.' With that, she snuggled more comfortably into Jonathan's arms, one hand curved trustingly about his neck, and closed her eyes. Fatigue, worry, and more than a little wine had caught up with her. She snuffed out like a candle.

Jonathan nestled her close to him, leaning his cheek against her tousled blond-curls. What was he to do? He bent his head while tilting hers, bestowed a loving kiss that he ruefully conceded she wouldn't remember. He would.

'Your carriage, sir. Oh, I say, sir,' Darling said, utterly dismayed at the sight that met his eyes.

'You have never seen this lady, nor do you know her name. Correct, Darling?'

'Absolutely, sir.' The butler assisted his employer from the house and into his carriage with great care, keeping an eye open for others who might be out. The street was silent; not so much as a curtain twitched.

Jonathan settled on the cushion on his coach, content that Darling would give directions to his coachman.

'Darling,' murmured Penny in her drowsy state, snuggling more closely to Harford.

'Would that you meant that, little termagant,' muttered the elegant Lord Harford into a blond curl.

* * *

There were fiendish little hammers at work in her head. The soft light coming through the blinds that had been let down when Jonathan carried her up to her room, turning her over to a dismayed Eva Nilsson, seemed blinding to Penny.

She rolled over to find that a definite

mistake. Her stomach seemed a bit squeamish this morning and did not take kindly to being jostled about. 'I do believe I had a shade too much wine last evening.'

'Are you able to dress? Your aunt shall be here before long and I cannot be two places at once.'

'If I am careful, I believe I can manage. Soda water?' she queried as Miss Nilsson handed her a glass.

'It will soothe you.' She busied herself about the room, leaving the blinds nearly closed, softly fetching a simple rose gown from the wardrobe to give Penelope some needed color in her cheeks.

'Could you hurry, my dear? Time is fleeting.'

Penelope set down the empty glass, amazed that Nilsson had been right. She felt considerably better. That hideous ache in her head had eased. Obediently she stepped into the pretty rose gown with the demure ruff, then stood still while Nilsson pinned her up before nudging her onto the bench in front of the dressing table.

While she brushed the lovely blond curls, Nilsson said, 'The dinner went well?'

'They drink a shocking amount of wine, I discovered, in addition to eating well. I do believe I tasted every bottle.' Her eyes met

Nilsson's in the looking glass. 'You needn't laugh at me. I suffer terribly.'

'How much do you recollect of the evening, particularly the end of it?' Nilsson put away the shawl and hat that had come over this morning, looking at them with raised brows.

Penelope gave her a wary glance, then dropped her gaze. 'Not very much.' She saw the gold ring on her finger and recalled, 'He returned this to me, said he had found it. You know what that means, Nilsson. He'll be the next to wed. I wonder if I should warn him.'

'Whom would he marry?'

'Well, I doubt it will be me,' Penelope said sadly.

'Now, now,' said the faithful companion, rather amused in spite of it all. 'Never give up hope until the cause is totally lost.'

'Is that another of your Swedish sayings? It sounds like, 'Don't give up the ship' or something.' Penelope gathered up a rose shawl, then her cat, drawing comfort from its devotion to her, and slowly made her way to the drawing room. It would never do to receive Lady Winthrop in the morning room today.

'My dear girl, you look positively ghastly,' Aunt Winthrop boomed in a cheerful voice.

Penelope restrained a shudder with difficulty. 'Good morning, Aunt. We must talk,' she said, deciding to cut the chitchat and reach the heart of the call, thus trim the call as short as possible.

'Ah, you have reconsidered and seen the light. You shall be a lovely bride, my girl. Ernest is a lucky man and you are most fortunate indeed to wed the Earl of Everton. It will be a white satin-and-lace wedding at St George's, Hanover Square. Ernest looks well in light blue.'

'I shall not marry Ernest!' Penelope noted her aunt's anger at this bit of plain speaking and took courage.

'On the contrary. You *will* marry the dear boy. The entire family has agreed. We act as one and intend to convince your guardian that it is in your best interest, not to mention the estate's, that you marry Ernest. Since Lanscomb never comes back to England, it will be a simple matter. He won't bother over you, never has in the past. A simple matter to get him to sign a paper consigning you to my care. And I shall sign the papers for the wedding. The Court of Chancery will be on our side.'

'I shan't do it.'

'Oh, but you shall. Perhaps if I take your cat as hostage, it might help.' She reached for Muffin, who had been sniffing at her skirts. The cat, not liking to be picked up, dashed away, hiding beneath the sofa where Penelope sat.

An aggravated, yet undefeated Lady Winthrop sailed out of the house, leaving a discouraged Penelope behind.

'She will not get you, Muffin,' muttered Penelope, 'nor me either,' recalling something Jonathan had said to her last night. He had told her that if Aunt gave her any trouble to call upon him for help. Like it or not, she would do precisely that.

Rising from her chair, Penelope gathered her cat, wrapping her shawl about them both, and walked from the room, fuming as she contemplated life as Lady Everton. Jonathan *must* help her.

12

'You quite see the necessity of my consulting you, do you not?' Penelope inquired of Jonathan, while perched uneasily on the edge of a leather chair in his library. She had rather hazy memories of this room, and she stifled with difficulty the most improper yearnings that crept up inside her. Surely he would be the gentleman, and kind enough not to remind her of her unladylike behavior.

Miss Nilsson had insisted upon coming along, to Penelope's relief. She glanced at her companion for confirmation of the urgency of the matter at hand.

'Indeed, Lord Harford, I believe Lady Penelope has the right of it,' she said in her lilting accents.

'Explain to me precisely what she intends to do.' Jonathan turned from Miss Nilsson to Penny, wondering how she felt this morning. He suspected she would never say a word, no matter what. She was definitely a game 'un, as his young brother would say.

'My aunt claims she will write to Lord Lanscomb in Austria, demanding that he release me into her care, and that to marry

Ernest will be in my best interest, not to mention the estate's. She intends to send papers along for him to sign. In truth, her reasoning is not far off, for he does not take the slightest interest in me, never has. Once she has those signed papers from him, she can go to the Court of Chancery with my guardian's blessing, and doubtless they will agree with her, never mind that I protest. All they care about is my guardian's permission.'

Lord Harford twiddled the pen he had been writing with before Penny came precipitately into the room, with Darling huffing at her side. He felt uneasy in her presence, yet she had given no indication that anything unusual had transpired last evening. Looking at her now, her shawl draped provocatively around her, that soft rose gown clinging so sweetly to her figure, it was not a simple matter to abandon the images and memories of last night. He cleared his throat before attempting to speak once again.

'I am not exact on this law, but I seem to recall that if a guardian is overseas or induced by wrong motives, the parties may apply to the Lord Chancellor, or several others.' He stared off into space, trying to remember what he knew of the Marriage Act. He was well aware that it was responsible for winging any number of lovers across the border into

Scotland for a hasty, if legitimate, marriage.

Penelope clasped her hands and nodded, hope shining from her eyes. 'I certainly could claim he is being offered the wrong motives. Besides, as my relative and head of the Harford family, do you not stand of some importance in this?' She felt reassured by his nod, although she suspected her father's family had the greater authority in this case.

'It will take some time for your aunt to communicate with Lanscomb. That gives us an opportunity to approach the Lord Chancellor on your behalf before she can hear from him.' He gave her a casual glance, then added in his slow, rich drawl, 'It might help if you were to present a betrothal to one of acceptable birth and breeding, not to mention wealth, as your alternative.' His heart nearly stopped as he waited for his little love to reply.

She fixed her eyes on Jonathan, sitting so composed and calm across from her, and felt trembly when she remembered what transpired here last evening. Her gaze strayed to the high-backed chair where she had curled up so contentedly in his arms. Why, she near ached with longing to be close to him again. How could she think of another man as a husband?

'I suppose you mean Lord Stephen,' she

offered with extreme politeness but a distinct lack of enthusiasm.

Jonathan concealed a smile behind a raised hand which rubbed over his upper lip. 'Do you wish to marry him?'

'Whether I might or no, I fear Lord Stephen is no more than flirting with me. I seriously doubt he wishes to become leg-shackled.' She gave Jonathan a wry look that said volumes about her feelings regarding the dashing Lord Stephen, if she but knew it.

'Any others?' he probed.

'Mr Willowby is all you said, and I scarcely know Sir Aubrey, so I doubt he would suit.'

'I fancy that were I to present myself to the Lord Chancellor with the support of my friends, I should have little trouble being heard or acquiring the necessary permission.' Jonathan cleared his throat again, struck by sudden nervousness, pausing several moments before he continued. 'As to a suitable betrothed, may I offer my poor self?'

Penelope thought immediately of his financial situation, and her heart, rather than grow hard, went out to him with deep sympathy. It must be a tremendous strain for him to be the head of such a great family, with a mother and sister who delighted in spending his money, and all the other claims — such as hers — upon his time and energy, not to mention fortune, such as it might be at this point.

'You cannot wish to wed me, my lord,' she replied mendaciously. 'Should it rather be a betrothal until my aunt takes herself back to the country? She finds the city distressingly expensive. She complained it would cost them two thousand pounds to keep Everton House going for the Season, and that, you may be sure, vexes her exceedingly.'

'Is that an acceptance of my offer, Penny? I suppose it is no more than I deserve, being so unloverlike.' He glanced at Miss Nilsson, who rose silently to slip from the room. It was doubtful that Penelope was the least aware of her departure.

Jonathan rose from his desk, then walked around it to confront the demure figure perched on the chair. He leaned over to draw her to her feet. He held her hands a moment, then released them, gently placing his arms about her shoulders to bring her closer. She did not resist.

'Would it be so distasteful? To be betrothed to me, that is? Or for me to be your husband?' He studied her face, then slowly, so as to give her time to pull away if she wished, he claimed her lips in the very sweetest of kisses. It was light, but demanding, seductive, yet not going beyond that barrier that existed between them.

Penelope melted. All thought of holding back from his kiss fled her mind at the touch of his lips. Heaven could be no better. She slid her arms up to wrap them tightly about him, clinging for all she was worth to his solid and satisfying form. If a drop of water had chanced to fall upon them, doubtless it would have sizzled.

It was Jonathan who drew back from the embrace. He said, rather amused at their predicament, 'I fear I have well and truly compromised you, my dear Penny. Shall we consider our betrothal as a fact?'

Embarrassed at her wholehearted reception of his kiss, Penelope nodded, eyes downcast, quite unable to speak for a few moments. He must think her a sad wanton.

'Very well, I shall take the necessary steps. Do you trust me to do what is right for you?' His eyes fixed a keen gaze upon her, suspecting that her trust was not something she bestowed lightly.

Penelope held her breath for a moment. Never had she completely trusted another, particularly a man, she realized. Could she bring herself to trust Jonathan? Then she thought of all his many fine traits: his patience and loving kindness to his mother and sister, his appreciation for lovely things, his music, and last of all, his concern for her. Aggravating he might be at times, but he did care what happened to her, and for that she must extend him her trust.

She nodded. 'I do, sir.' Clear blue eyes raised to meet his reflected the complete trust she placed in him.

'I believe you can now claim the indulgence of the use of my first name, Penny.'

'And you are to persist in calling me by that silly pet name as well? No one has ever given me such.' She stepped away from him, giving him a nettled look. The strings of her reticule were being fearfully mangled by nervous hands, his only real clue to her inner feelings.

'Then it's about time, is it not?' He walked over to ring for Darling, who arrived with suspicious promptness.

'I believe there is another bottle of that champagne that Lady Penelope enjoyed so last evening. Would you be so kind?'

'Indeed, sir.' Darling beamed a smile at Penelope, then left. Moments later, he returned — amazingly soon, considering the distance of the cellar — with the carefully cooled and opened bottle of the fine wine.

Miss Nilsson followed the butler into the room, studying the flushed face of her charge with intent eyes. 'Am I to wish you happy, my dear?' she said, her lilt quite pronounced in her emotion.

'Well,' Penelope said with caution, 'we have agreed that Jonathan and I shall announce our betrothal. 'Tis a blessing that betrothals are not quite as binding as they once were, is it not?' She darted a look at Jonathan, then returned her gaze to her companion, finding it safer. 'He plans to approach the Lord Chancellor to explain what Aunt intends to do, claiming that she is abusing the truth and that her motives are far from pure in her application to my guardian. As the head of the family, Lord Harford stands in higher estimation than my guardian, I should hope.' Regarding the mention of marriage, she said nothing.

'No doubt that is true,' Miss Nilsson replied, accepting a flute of champagne from Darling with evident pleasure.

'We should be able to obtain an Order of Court, which, when approved, will stand the same as the consent of Penny's guardian,' Jonathan added with relish. He placed his glass on his desk, then unlocked and opened a drawer. A small velvet pouch rested in his hand when he turned to face Penny once again. From the pouch he withdrew an exquisite ring. It was of delicately worked gold with a fine sapphire in the center.

Penelope sighed at the sight. How could she ever bear to part with such beauty? Especially when it came from Jonathan?

'I believe this will go with those lovely eyes of yours, my dear.' He placed the ring on the appropriate finger, noting with pride that it fitted perfectly. His guess had been staggeringly accurate when he'd gone to the jeweler to have it sized.

Penelope duly admired his taste, then expressed concern when he informed her that it was a family ring, given to each countess in turn upon the promise of marriage.

'I should dislike thinking that I had deprived Lady Harford the pleasure of wearing this magnificent ring.'

'Actually,' he said, well pleased that Penny looked on the ring with such marked admiration, 'she gave it to me some time ago, in the hope that I might get around to selecting a bride one of these days.'

Penelope gave him a dismayed look, feeling a fraud, for he must wish his family and friends to believe the announcement of their betrothal, and what would they think when it came to an end? She said nothing more on that score, however, feeling it impolite to argue the point.

When the four drank a toast to the betrothal, even though one of them thought it to be a sham one, Penelope was observed to have a distinct shimmering in her eyes.

A rather annoyed meow came from the doorway. There stood Muffin, glaring at all with indignant eyes.

'Oh, bother!' Penelope exclaimed. 'Poor kitty. I forgot that I brought her along for her safety. Aunt says she thinks she might kidnap Muffin, knowing how I care for my cat. May I leave her here with you?' she pleaded, one slender hand reaching out to touch Jonathan's ann. 'Darling assured me that Cook will watch after her.'

'I would be the veriest scoundrel to deny you the security of your pet, my love. Of course it may stay here. Did you have the least doubt?'

Muffin gave Jonathan a disdainful look, then stalked over to the high-backed leather chair and jumped up. She inspected her chosen spot with haughty eyes, turned about three times, then settled down to place her chin on her paws.

'I do believe she has decided to accept your hospitality, my lord,' Penelope said, trying not to laugh.

'I shall do my best not to be overwhelmed at her condescension.' He exchanged an amused look with Penny, hoping this would be a giant step to reaching a feeling of harmony between them.

They strolled from the room, Jonathan musing aloud on the various things that needed to be done, and in what order, in a highly organized fashion.

An admiring glance from Penelope improved his self-regard, for it was plain she put much stock in his words, and that made him feel very good.

'I believe I shall see about an appointment with the Lord Chancellor, also do a bit of visiting with those gentlemen I mentioned earlier, the ones I thought might be of help. I can depend on them to remain tight-lipped about what we intend. It would never do for your aunt to find out what's afoot.'

'Good grief, no. I would not put it past her to persuade Ernest to hie off to Scotland with me. She is a very determined woman, you must know.' Penelope gave Jonathan a concerned look, then tightened her shawl about her before taking her leave.

Jonathan stood for a moment after the two women left, wondering at his boldness in proposing to Penny as he had. Did she imagine that the betrothal was only to last for a short time, then to be dropped? Little fool. He had no intention of allowing her to go free ever.

He wandered up to his room, thinking

about the lovely duets they could have, flute and pianoforte. He surmised, from the depth of her response to him, that they could create more than beautiful music together. She proved to be a never-ending source of delight to him. Provided, of course, that she didn't drive him mad first.

Once suitably attired in the first stare of fashion, Lord Harford sauntered off to his club to find the first of his quarry. It proved to be easy to obtain support, for the fellow had no liking for Everton and thought Lanscomb a dashed loose screw for taking his duties as guardian to a beautiful young heiress so lightly. He didn't deserve the honor. If the gentleman had thoughts about Harford's position in the case, he kept them to himself.

The others proved to be equally agreeable. They fully believed the tale, knowing Harford to be a truthful, honorable man, who was, in addition, a prince of a good fellow. They also thought the heiress a lucky young woman to have captured the splendid gentleman who was held in such esteem by those who knew him.

Thus it was with anticipation of success that Lord Harford approached the office to the Lord Chancellor to request an appointment. It was promptly granted, for who would dream of denying the darling of Society, the man who could get along with both Tories and Whigs by being the consummate diplomat? Not to mention his friendly association with every premier hostess in London? Or his impeccable background as head of the house of Harford?

'Splendid,' Harford said as he left the office after a highly satisfactory chat, thinking that marriage to Penny would be a pleasure. He couldn't wait.

* * *

At Letty's house, Penelope sat in the drawing room, gazing fondly at the ring when she thought no one was watching her.

Mr Oglethorpe read poetry in a pleasing voice, while Letty sat on the sofa listening, her eyes flashing from him to Penelope.

> Let not ambition mock their useful toil,
> Their homely joys, and destiny obscure;
> Nor grandeur hear with a disdainful smile
> The short and simple annals of the poor.

Letty glanced back to him, wanting to discuss this peculiar development with her cousin rather than hear noble sentiments about the workers. 'I trust Thomas Gray did not actually work on a farm himself, did he?' she inserted in one of Andrew's dramatic pauses.

'No, but he wondered what they might have accomplished had they been given the opportunity, rather than despising them as some do.' His disdainful look was totally lost on Letty, who had turned her attention in the direction of her cousin.

Penelope had seized an opportunity before Letty joined them to beseech Mr Oglethorpe to think of something that might deter Letty from her vegetable eating. Andrew saw an opportunity to assist both his cause and Penelope's.

'By the bye, dear Lettice, do you know what I heard? That poet, Shelley, the one who wrote the pamphlet on a natural diet, is an atheist!'

Letty, who never failed to attend divine services unless she was at death's door, paled. 'No!' Her plump little hand fluttered up to her throat. The revulsion in her voice might have been amusing had it not been so important to convince her of the fallacy of her thinking.

'True. Heard it from a good friend, so I went up to where Shelley lives, to find out for myself. There is no denying it. Has been for a long time, ever since he was at Eton.'

If ever a woman looked torn, it was Letty at the news that her admired advocate of a natural diet was an atheist.

'I hear his marriage to Harriet is in danger, for he espouses Godwin's notions against wedlock. Seems he prefers free love, whatever that is. Not to mention he declaims loud and clear of the tyranny of the government.'

This proved too much for Letty. She could never tolerate a radical atheist, much less someone who would plot the overthrow of her government. 'What shall I do?' she wondered. 'I had such faith, and now it is gone. I cannot consider a recommendation from a man like that.' She glanced at Penelope in alarm.

'I quite agree,' Penelope replied. 'I believe a sensible English diet, with a moderate amount of vegetables, fish, meat, and fowl included, is to be commended.'

'Quite right,' agreed Mr Oglethorpe, glancing at Penelope with a glimmer of amusement.

'I expect you are correct,' Letty said doubtfully, giving in at last.

Penelope avoided looking at Mr Oglethorpe, but she hoped he knew how grateful the entire household was to him. She rose, murmuring something about consulting with Cook, then drifted out of the room before Letty had a chance to quiz her more on the sudden appearance of the sapphire ring.

In the kitchen there was rejoicing to discover they would be able to resume a normal diet, with all the foods they had either been denied, or had to smuggle into the house, Penelope supplying the funds.

When she returned to the drawing room — for although she trusted Andrew Oglethorpe, she well knew that Letty would scold if propriety did not prevail — the first thing she saw was that Letty's little gold-framed spectacles did not perch on her nose as per usual.

'What? Have you mislaid your spectacles?' Letty, upon occasion, was known to deposit her spectacles, then forget where she put them.

'Andrew has taken them from me. He says he'll not have me reading a thing until I agree to what he proposes.'

'I should say the man is indeed desperate. Had you better not listen to what he has to say, then?' Penelope exchanged an understanding look with Andrew, one that Letty could not see.

Letty sat stubbornly silent, looking like a plump little brown hen on a nest, with her Devonshire brown gown trimmed with blond lace gathered about her. Her gray eyes seemed troubled but determined.

'Do you know what he demands as a ransom?' Letty asked of Penelope, ignoring the man who now sat beside her, those missing spectacles peeping out of his pocket.

'I might venture a guess, but I should rather you told me.'

'He has again asked me to marry him.'

Sympathy for his plight could clearly be seen in Penelope's eyes by the patient-no-longer Andrew Oglethorpe. 'Aye, I am an anxious man to have this business settled. You see, she has never said no to me.'

'I might yet,' Letty said with a pout.

'Letty, do you recall what we discussed some days ago?' Penelope inserted at this point. 'I believe it is time you took yourself in hand and faced the issues that concern you. Why not discuss them with Mr Oglethorpe?'

The plump little bird on the striped sofa turned to the man she considered 'her' Andrew, then admitted, 'Penelope told me to think about what life would be if I did not have you about. I have done so.'

Andrew and Penelope waited with suspended breath to hear her conclusion.

At that moment Aunt Winthrop bustled into the room without so much as a by-your-leave, and settled on a chair near Penelope. She ignored the two on the sofa, except to favor them with a basilisk stare.

'Good afternoon, Aunt,' Penelope said with a strained civility. 'Mr Olgethorpe has been favoring us with a selection of poetry. Since he and Letty have something they wish to discuss, perhaps you and I might retire to the morning room?'

Aunt Winthrop looked horror-stricken at the very thought of leaving Andrew and Letty alone in the drawing room, and cast her niece a dark look for even suggesting such a thing.

'I might have known something ill would come of your sharing a roof with a poet, even a bad one.'

Letty stiffened, but said nothing in her defense.

Andrew Oglethorpe compressed his lips, but politely kept his silence as well.

Letty then looked resigned and perhaps a bit amused that her awaited conclusion would have to be delayed.

'My dear, I have sent off an express to your guardian. Although rumor has it that he intends to return to England soon.' She bestowed a sly, superior look on her niece.

Penelope schooled her features so that her aunt wouldn't know whether this news dismayed her or not. 'I have never met him. I wonder what he is like.'

'Never mind that. I suggest you concern yourself with bride clothes instead. I shall take you to my mantua-maker, who has a way with flounces, if I do say so.'

It was to be hoped that the revulsion Penelope felt did not show on her face. Aunt Winthrop's gown was of execrable design with an excess of flounces which did nothing for the skinny figure they floated about.

Knowing full well that her aunt intended to spend Penelope's money on the gowns, never a cent of her own, Penelope bridled. 'I have my own mantua-maker, thank you. She has my measurements, and that avoids the tedium of standing for ages while the tape is applied.' Penelope allowed for no argument, but swept on to another matter. 'Tell me, how does Lord Everton feel about your plans? I have scarce seen him since that first day you came to Town.' If this was a gentle reminder that the supposedly love-struck swain was less than attentive, it missed the mark.

Lady Winthrop directed an arrogant look at Penelope, dismissing the other two as unimportant. 'He has been much occupied, my dear girl. When one is as important as Ernest, there is much to do. He has been consulting with various warehouses as to the refurbishing of Everton House and is even now selecting the wall hangings. I suppose he ought to wait for your approval, but he has always displayed elegant taste, so you need not fear his choice,' she simpered.

Penelope recalled the yellow waistcoat striped in purple and nodded, barely suppressing a shudder at the outcome of such 'elegant' taste. She could only be thankful that she need not marry the man. How she would relish informing her detested aunt that marriage to Ernest could never be.

'Have you accepted your fate, then, niece?' Lady Winthrop bared her yellowed teeth in a smile, reminding Penelope of an aging horse.

Letty interrupted at this point. 'You would refuse Penelope the delights of the Season, Aunt?' It suddenly occurred to Letty that if she married Andrew, she could shed the name she shared with her detested relative. 'There are concerts, balls, and routs to attend. Once she is married, I daresay she will wish to spend her time in the country.'

Penelope could see the old lady thought this fine, for it would relieve her the burden of managing the town house. Not for a moment did Penelope believe her aunt would permit Ernest's bride the satisfaction of having one thing her way.

'Well . . . ' Aunt Winthrop faltered.

The sound of footsteps on the stairs, followed by an exchange between Mrs Flint and a decidedly male voice, focused all eyes on the doorway.

'Dear cousin,' exclaimed Penelope as she rose decorously from her chair to cross the room. 'You know our aunt, of course, as well as Letty and Mr Oglethorpe. What brings you here so early in the day?'

'I am pleased to see you have not forgotten our expedition to the theater this evening. I trust Letty and Oglethorpe will join us as well, for it is by way of celebration.' At the black look from his aunt, he added, 'Have you not informed Aunt Winthrop, my dear? Naughty girl. But then, perhaps you thought she would observe your ring.'

Her aunt popped up from her chair to peer at the ring now displayed for her benefit on Penelope's slim finger, her hand held possessively in Harford's. Lady Winthrop knew the sight of the Harford sapphire without being told what it was. Anger burned in her eyes when she looked up at the pair before her.

'Think to out-fool me, do you?'

'I doubt if anyone could do that, Aunt,' Harford said respectfully, ignoring the tug from the hand he clasped firmly in his. 'You see, we found we suit admirably well. Is that not correct, Penny, my love?'

'You said nothing to me, girl,' her aunt accused.

'You gave me little opportunity. Besides, I

wished Jonathan at my side when we gave you the happy news.' Her sideways glance at Lord Harford made him clear his throat as though uneasy.

'I have been duped and misled by the girl I believed good enough for Ernest,' Lady Winthrop declared, definitely aggrieved.

'You see, dear aunt, I told you from the first I am not the one for him. You will no doubt find someone more suited.'

'I heard Miss Dunston is back in Town.' At Penelope's indrawn breath, Harford added, 'She was not feeling quite the thing, but her doctor declares there is nothing wrong with her. She would make a most biddable wife.'

Penelope could see her aunt was mulling over the aspect of a wife who would not interfere in any way with the plans Lady Winthrop had for her son. After terse farewells, they watched her depart, then turned at the outpouring of questions from Letty and Andrew Oglethorpe.

'What happened?' Penelope demanded quietly when the others subsided.

'Smooth as glass,' Harford replied, wondering if Penelope realized that there was no way she might extricate herself from the upcoming nuptials he had arranged. 'I presented our case to the Lord Chancellor, along with the range of support from my distinguished friends. It seems our beloved aunt has made a number of foes among the *ton*. Even he had heard of her from his wife. There was no problem in the least, and I have the Orders of Court in my pocket. In fact, I intend to visit Doctor's Commons tomorrow to obtain the special license.'

Andrew Oglethorpe nodded sagely, taking the hint from the look directed at him. He would follow suit, since there was no impediment to a marriage between himself and Letty, her being of age. He'd wait no longer, regardless of her family. Harford gave his blessing. That was good enough.

Clasping her hands nervously before her, Penelope began to pace back and forth before the fireplace, seeing it a very fine spot with no furniture to impede her progress. 'You think this step is necessary?'

'I do,' he intoned, then drew his little love out the door to leave the others with a moment of privacy for what he suspected was on Oglethorpe's mind.

Ignoring any propriety in leaving the others, Penelope turned her attention to the other menace that plagued them. 'And what about Miss Dunston? Is she really returned to London?'

'Yes, indeed,' Harford gravely replied. 'It seems her most worthy doctor found her quite normal, given the set of circumstances that would put any young miss in a pelter. He told her mother he considered henbane an effective medicine for colds and sleeplessness, and suggested she not fail to keep it in the house. You may imagine what tremblings this information gave me.'

'I wonder how many other love potions she has found?' Penelope was torn between amusement and exasperation.

13

Jonathan was greatly tempted to gather her worried little self into his arms, if only to reassure her there was no need for concern. He had an idea.

'But you see, Penny, my love, when she discovers that you and I are to be wedded, she will look elsewhere to fix her attentions. As well, she will recall that private and incriminating dalliance of ours in the library and believe she knew it all beforehand.' His face wore the pleased expression of one who has answered all questions.

'Oh, that,' Penelope murmured as they slowly neared the foot of the stairs.

'Someone might have believed her rantings, had she dared to make them known at the time,' he reminded.

'I should have thought of that.' How foolish he must find her.

Lord Harford gave her what she deemed a rather superior smile, then kindly replied, 'I suspect you were finding it a bit difficult to think of anything at the moment.'

Of course it was the truth, but he need not have said so. 'Wicked man,' she said with a shade more fervor.

'My mother wishes you to come over immediately, if you would. She feels we must make a few plans.'

Just as Penelope was about to reply, Letty and Mr Oglethorpe came from the drawing room to the head of the stairs, a sheepish expression on Letty's plump face — her glasses once again in place — a distinctly satisfied one on his. They drifted down to where Penelope and Jonathan stood with watchful expressions.

'An announcement, by the looks of it,' Jonathan said close to Penelope's ear.

'We have decided that I am to marry Andrew,' Letty said at length, while pushing her little gold spectacles up on her nose. Her satisfied look might have been attributed to their restoration but for Penelope's knowledge that Letty was as besotted with Andrew Oglethorpe as he was with her.

Penelope held out her arms in a happy sharing of joy. Letty, fussy and inclined to waver, accepted the felicitations, declaring they would have to have a family celebration.

'You must join us at Harford House. Mother will want to wish you happy. I hope you might be able to come now?' Jonathan gave Andrew Oglethorpe a significant nod.

Sensing that more could be found in the

invitation than met the eye, Andrew agreed they could go, for the poetry had lost its hold on them for the nonce.

Letty discovered one of her paisley shawls draped over the bust of Caesar, and Penelope accepted a light pelisse from Miss Nilsson.

'Please come with us,' a thoughtful Lord Harford urged the companion. 'You are one of the family and this is to be a gathering of the clan, minus Ernest and his mother, of course.'

Gratified beyond speech to be included, Miss Nilsson hastily picked up another shawl from the pile that seemed to accumulate in the entry, and joined the exodus.

Lady Harford welcomed the news of Letty's coming marriage to Mr Oglethorpe with delight, hugging Letty and exclaiming over the rightness of the connection.

It seemed to Penelope that with Lady Harford's approval Letty relaxed considerably. If she might tell her mother that none other than Lady Harford found the marriage quite the thing, her mother certainly ought to see reason. Besides, she would now be in a position to help her younger brother attain the schooling at Cambridge that he so ardently desired. That ought to be significant as well.

After Lady Harford ordered an elaborate

tea, she directed them all to take their places, including a puzzled Lady Charis, who had slipped in late.

'Now,' Lady Harford said with complacency, 'we shall discuss what is to be done.'

'Forgive me, my lady,' Penelope offered hesitantly, 'but what *is* there to do? Letty has accepted Andrew, Jonathan insists on going to Doctor's Commons tomorrow. What, precisely, needs to be planned?'

Lady Harford gave a wise nod. 'We must see that your odious aunt does not spoil things.' She exchanged a meaningful look with her son that Penelope failed to see because she was watching Letty shyly settle by her Andrew.

'Since we have already had the come-out ball, and all of you girls are nicely established with highly acceptable gentlemen, present company quite lauded, we can allow nothing to upset our plans.' She frowned. 'I understand Miss Dunston has returned to Society. I suggest we be on guard. Who knows what might be in another potion?'

The footman and a maid entered bearing magnificent trays loaded with everything Lady Harford deemed necessary to stave off dire hunger. Tea poured, cakes offered, and all returned to quiet again, Lady Harford turned to a happier subject.

'Charis and David shall be married here, so she tells me. Since only family will attend, our private chapel will suit admirably.' Many of the *ton* preferred private ceremonies away from public scrutiny.

'Next in precedence are Jonathan and Penelope. Where do you wish the wedding to be, my dear?' Lady Harford looked to Penny for an answer.

Penny looked askance at the smoothly spoken question. How could she say in front of everyone who was here that the betrothal was only temporary? Although why his mother had not been told, Penny couldn't understand. She seemed to know everything else that was going on around town and within the near relations. But then, Lady Charis might possibly tattle the tale to her David, and he mention it to another, and so on, but still . . .

'Would you prefer a quiet wedding here at our chapel, my dear?' Jonathan inserted blandly.

'Oh, yes, that sounds lovely,' Penny responded gratefully. Since Lord Harford was only too well aware that there would be no wedding, he was the one person Penny might trust to arrange matters so there would be no difficulty later on.

'Are you sure, my pet?' Lady Harford said

with a delicate frown. 'There is none closer to you?'

'You are my family,' Penny declared, wishing they were to be more intimately connected.

Lady Harford nodded, then turned to Letty. 'And you, my dear? I fancy your mother will come up to town?'

'I should rather marry quietly if Andrew does not mind. I have decided I'll not impose on Mother to come to town.'

Since Letty's dear mother had made a lifelong study of mastering the art of being imposed upon, nothing more was said on that score.

'I shall take care of the matter at once, my dear,' declared the gallant Andrew, pleased there would be no obstacle in the way of his marriage to Letty after all this time. It seemed as though he had courted her forever.

Penny rose from her chair, placing her cup on the tray before crossing to face Jonathan. 'What can we possibly do about Miss Dunston?'

Jonathan looked past her to his mother. 'I rather thought we might introduce the young lady to Ernest.'

There was general laughter at this, while Lady Harford nodded with enthusiasm.

'The very thing. I shall give a small ball to

announce the betrothals, I believe, nothing elaborate. Gunter shall cater it, so we will not need to hire extra help. Simple; a few flowers, nice music, good friends. I love to play match-maker!'

'I admire you, Lady Harford. You make it seem so effortless.' Penny suspected it would be anything but.

'You girls shall do the invitations right now, so I can send them off by the footman. I drew up a list this morning, just in the event we might have need of it.'

She shepherded the three girls to a table where a stack of cream cards sat with an abundance of inkwells and pens. Handing them the list she had prepared, she set them to work. Then she urged the two young men out of the room and down the stairs.

'I truly believe that the sooner you obtain those special licenses, the better, especially you, Jonathan. I have heard a rumor that Penelope's guardian has written that he expects to return to London before long. Heaven knows when that may be. If you do not want your future spoiled, best go at once.'

'I'd not have anyone think I marry Penny for her wealth.' Jonathan well knew the most absurd rumors could filter through Society with no foundation other than speculation, and, in some cases, spite.

'How could anyone get such a foolish notion? I have received no pitying looks, and Silence Jersey has not been here to pry for ages.'

'You know the reason we became entangled in the first place was that she thought me in need of funds. That was why she made the bargain, remember?'

At Andrew's blank expression, Jonathan made some vague explanation, then turned to his mother, whose wisdom he respected.

'That *is* a problem. Well, surely she is the only one who would think such a thing. You might tell her you have made a fortune on the 'Change.' She nodded a dismissive smile while trying not to look worried.

She shooed them out of the house, then strolled back to confer with her housekeeper. Lady Harford was not quite as confident as she pretended. The source for her information regarding Lord Lanscomb was the Countess Lieven; she knew what was going on in the capitals of Europe better than many of the king's men. It was fortunate that the countess had taken a liking to Penelope, and passed the critical information along regarding the Austrian officials and their traveling companion. No doubt she had gleaned the tidbit while at the Esterhazys'.

Married at fifteen to Count Christopher

Lieven, young Dorothea revealed the influence of the patronage of the Empress Maria, who supported her following the death of the Baroness von Benckendorf, Dorothea's distinguished mother. To put it mildly, she was a haughty young woman, and feared with good reason, for she had acquired a surprising amount of influence in the English capital. Society had embraced the aristocratic girl with open arms, adoring her airs and graces. Lady Harford grimly smiled to herself as she settled down with her housekeeper. The countess was not called 'the Snipe' without justification. She could be a dangerous enemy. Perhaps she might also be an ally, if she thought the cause entertaining. What delight it would be to saddle that toad Ernest with a most deserved wife.

⋆ ⋆ ⋆

Penny had her doubts that a ball was necessary, but who was she to deny Lady Harford her pleasure? However, the money aspect bothered Penny. Since she was, she felt, responsible for much of the situation, she ought to help pay for it. Poor Lord Harford ought not bear the brunt of it, and she doubted it would occur to Letty to assist. After the invitations had been written and sent off with two footmen for prompt delivery, she did something about it.

The gentleman at the bank looked askance at Penny when she requested another transfer of funds to Lord Harford's man of business. It was amazing how the hint that she was to be the next countess cleared the way for what she wished. It worked like magic.

Once her conscience felt at ease, she took delight in assisting Letty to select a gown for the ball. Under the guise of choosing something for herself, she persuaded her eccentric cousin to join her in a shopping expedition. Letty peered over her gold spectacles with suspicion, but in the end came along.

At the mantua-maker's, Letty plumped herself on a chair, reluctant to so much as look at a fashion plate. It took Madame Clotilde's skill and Penny's blandishments to convince her it was absolutely necessary.

'Do you want your mother to learn you looked like a provincial at your betrothal ball?' Penny chided at last.

Letty jumped up and turned to the mantua-maker. 'Madame Clotilde, if you can but do something with this pudgy self, you will have my eternal gratitude.'

It was accomplished with greater speed than Penny had dared hope. A simple gown of delicate peach muslin trimmed discreetly in gold ribbon was chosen in short order.

Her own gown, an affair in twilight-lavender sarcenet with silver ribbons trailing down the back, was the most elaborate she had ordered yet. It was scandalously expensive for a sham betrothal, yet she deemed it important to make everything seem real. The thought of appearing on Jonathan's arm wearing the shimmery, floating gown pleased, especially when she considered the low neckline that nicely revealed her rounded bosom.

The impossible Miss Dunston would be present. Who knew what might be going on in the girl's strange mind? Jonathan seemed to believe it important she be convinced the betrothal was genuine. Penny wondered if those love potions might actually be effective.

* * *

'Do I pass your inspection, dear brother?' Lady Charis spun around before Jonathan to display her gown of Florence satin in a pale willow green. Ash-brown curls were dressed high on her head in clusters threaded with silver ribbon.

'David will be enchanted.' Jonathan knew what would please her and, in truth, she looked lovely.

'Did Madame Lieven accept?' he inquired of his mother in an undertone, not having had private conversation with her for several days, what with all the dashing about London required of him. He felt great satisfaction that the special license now rested in his desk drawer.

'Actually, she called on me. I was able to drop a number of hints, along with a subtle request she influence the marriage of the Earl of Everton in the right direction. Lady Winthrop is such a fool that the persuasions of a lady of such distinction will doubtless convince her.' Lady Harford gave her son a bemused look. 'You really believe this will work?'

'It had better. I am tired of her importunings, not to mention the threat of a love potion in my glass.' He smoothed the worry from his face, then turned to charm the guests that entered the house. When word had filtered through the *ton* that a terribly exclusive party was being held at Harford House, with only the cream invited, not one excuse was received.

Penny surveyed the elegant throng of exquisitely gowned ladies and superbly groomed gentlemen with curious eyes. Where was the elusive Miss Dunston?

'Before I point out our quarry for the

evening, I should like a word with you, my pet,' Jonathan growled softly into Penny's wary ear.

'Whatever are you upset about, sir?' she inquired with what she hoped was an elegant lift of her brows. He had caught her off-guard. She hoped the assemblage of guests would keep whatever bothered him to a minimum of fuss. There were people everywhere, strolling up the stairs, meandering through the various rooms. They were in twos and fours, gossiping or merely chatting, but around.

'Do not tilt your nose, my sweet,' he continued as he skillfully ushered her to a small anteroom off the drawing room, where the glittering elite of society gathered. A branch of candles had been lit; Jonathan hastily lit another, then turned to face her. 'Now I can see your expression. Why? Why did you do it? Did you wish to embarrass me?'

'Do not tell me you are annoyed because I transferred a paltry few pounds over to you? What utter rubbish. I have told you before that I insist upon paying my way. I have discovered that quite often wealthy people are only too happy to have others pay their bills. I do not accept that. You shared the cost of the come-out ball. There is no reason on earth that I not help now. Tell me, were my father alive and he insisted upon paying a portion of the expenses, would you deny him?'

At the reluctant shake of Jonathan's well-bred head, she went on, becoming more amused than annoyed. 'So what is the problem? Men!' she exclaimed, turning to walk to the door. Before she could open it, she found a restraining hand on her arm. She paused, giving him an expectant look.

He first bent his head, then met her eyes with a candid gaze. 'Do not repeat it. I will take care of all bills. I am not at *point-non-plus* yet.' He glanced at the door, then back. 'And promise me that you will be careful around Miss Dunston. Who knows what lurks in her mind?'

'I had no intention of accepting a glass of wine from her hands, you may be sure. I have no need of a love potion.' Aware that they had defied propriety for too long, she sighed, then slipped from the room, closing the door on the grim man behind her.

Lady Harford motioned to Penny the moment she entered the drawing room. In the background a string quartet played a very lovely waltz. Countess Lieven stood chatting with Lady Harford. Both of them looked intent upon something of import.

'You wish to speak with me?' Penny dipped a gracious curtsy to the two ladies, curious as to what they might have to say.

'Your Aunt Winthrop has arrived with Ernest in tow. He looks more like a stuffed pumpkin tonight than anything else,' Lady Harford reported quietly.

'Ernest believes that all food exists to be eaten, or so I've been told. Aunt tries to discourage him in his other belief, that money exists to be spent.'

Countess Lieven smiled, a wry lifting on one corner of her mouth. As one who had collected such power in her short life, she managed her countenance with a poise beyond her years.

'Come,' she urged, 'I wish to meet your so-plump cousin. And the unusual Miss Dunston as well, I believe. I know many who are suspected of dire things; I have yet to meet someone who resorts to using love potions.' Her lashes fluttered over her large expressive eyes as she followed Penny to where Lady Winthrop fussed at her son. Her appearance had the happy effect of rendering Lady Winthrop speechless.

'Madame Lieven, may I present my aunt, Lady Winthrop, and my cousin, Lord Everton.' Penny edged back a bit to watch her aunt make an utter fool of herself, while Ernest merely stood looking like one.

The countess tolerated it for a few minutes,

then with a wave of her hand silenced the older woman. 'And now for the other,' she murmured to Penny, who turned to see Miss Dunston approaching with Lady Harford.

The introductions proved absurdly simple. Penny began to appreciate the extraordinary gift the countess possessed. She skillfully implied that Miss Dunston had her approval as the next Countess of Everton without actually saying so. She flattered without complimenting, cajoled without asking. It was a scene not to be missed.

It was hardly surprising that Lady Winthrop suddenly looked upon the Mouse far more kindly. As for the girl in question, the bewildered expression on her face made it difficult for Penny not to laugh.

Later, while strolling away from the trio, Penny smiled at the countess. 'I am most grateful to you, madame. My aunt is nothing if not persistent. I did not relish life as his wife.'

'Hm,' the countess replied, 'a Toad, a Mouse, and a Crow. They ought to make for an interesting household, no?' Her eyes lit up with delightful mischief. 'I adore such nonsense, for I refuse to be bored.'

Before they parted, the countess paused to place a cautioning hand on Penny's arm. 'If I hear more of the arrival of Lord Lanscomb,

I shall let you know. He is most assuredly on his way to England, but we do not know when he arrives for certain. He travels with members of the Austrian court. I hear things, you know. They may wish to stop for a bit in Brussels. Perhaps the deed were best done before he arrives.'

With that last word of advice, she floated off, her slender figure soon lost in the throng so eager to listen to her frequently acid-barbed words. If Lanscomb was with the Austrian delegation, one might be sure that the countess would be aware of it and their progress. Jonathan believed she acted as an agent, reporting to the court of Russia, for it was said she was expert in drawing out secrets. No one could deny she was an attractive woman, undoubtedly useful, and, Penny suspected, quite unscrupulous in achieving her aims.

'What happened?'

'The countess worked a touch of magic, I believe. As she so quaintly phrased it, a Toad, a Mouse, and a Crow ought to make an interesting household, no?'

Jonathan looked over the heads of the crowd to where Lady Winthrop stood chatting with Mrs Dunston. Their offspring eyed each other, Ernest with apathy, Carola with curiosity.

'Lovely. It is too early to say if we shall succeed, but I believe we will keep our distance, nonetheless. Who knows what might be lurking in that dainty reticule that hangs over her arm?'

'The countess informed me that Lord Lanscomb travels with a group from the Austrian court. I suspect she uncovered that information while keeping track of diplomatic moves.'

'And what advice did she give you, for she loves to meddle.' Jonathan bestowed a knowing look on Penny's troubled face.

'She suggested it might be well were the deed done before Lord Lanscomb arrives. Do we truly believe he will accept Aunt Winthrop's demands without seeking you out first?' She gave Jonathan a distraught look.

'It is not merely to wed you to Ernest that she plots, it is to recapture the fortune your father bestowed upon you. She feels that ought to be in the Everton coffers once again. There is strong sentiment for that sort of thing among the older generation.'

'She informed me the entire family supports her. I fancy that might have an effect on Lord Lanscomb as well.' Penny gave a worried look in the direction of her cousin and Miss Dunston, then turned away. 'Perhaps you would feel better if I purloin that dainty reticule that intrigues you so much?'

'If you can manage to accomplish such a thing with deftness and no suspicion, I think it might be interesting.'

Penny went in search of Miss Nilsson, wondering how on earth she had managed to get in such a fantastic position. Once sighted, she approached her companion quickly. 'Come, we have a little work to do. I wish you to distract Miss Dunston a moment while I spirit her reticule away.'

Instead of a horrified gasp, Miss Nilsson sensibly replied, 'In aid of the cause?'

'Most definitely. Lord Harford thinks something interesting may be concealed in it.'

'By all means, my dear girl.' The two strolled along the side of the room, nodding and smiling until reaching the place where Aunt Winthrop still chattered with Mrs Dunston. Penny would have wagered that by this time her aunt would know the amount of income the Dunstons could boast, their lineage, and anything else considered pertinent.

Miss Nilsson fired the opening salvo. 'Have you attended the opera lately?' she asked Miss Dunston.

Never having been asked the like, Carola blinked, then shook her head. On her other side, Penny jostled against her as though nudged by another. She apologized profusely while Miss Nilsson murmured on about some scrap of gossip. Torn between the apology and the naughty gossip, Carola Dunston did the natural, concentrated on the gossip.

Penny drifted away from the conversation to where Lord Harford stood to one side, giving him a significant look and a faint nod.

He immediately made his way to her side. 'Did I remember to tell you how exquisite you look this evening? Lavender and silver are definitely your colors. Although,' he added, quite destroying his compliment, 'that neckline is too low. Why bother, my pet? Just invite me to sample.'

She swiftly walked down the hall and around the corner to a small room where accounts were done. She rushed inside, then dropped the purloined reticule on a table.

Harford had followed her, and he whistled when he saw what was inside the little bag. He pushed aside the usual handkerchief, bottle of scent, pins, and fan. 'A vial, and two packets of powder, plus a tin of gray tablets. I suspect there is enough potion here to place our entire gathering in love. Or at least in a charitable mood.'

Jonathan reached out to stroke a finger along one gloved arm, wishing he could do as he pleased. Reluctantly he said, 'I suppose you had best return that reticule to Miss Dunston. She might scream to the ceiling if missing her reticule, but she can hardly complain to anyone over the loss of the love potions, can she?'

'We are not certain it is love potions,' Penny said slowly while she complied with his suggestion, dropping in the articles to be returned one by one.

'Tell me this, would you take some of it? Any of it?' He scooped up the vial, packets of powder, and the tin, slipping them into a hidden pocket in his coat.

She shook her head, then paused by the door. 'I told you before, I have no need for that sort of nonsense. I shall make my restoration at once.' While she fled from the room, she reflected she loved Jonathan to distraction but wished he might love her without such help.

She wended her way through the guests, reaching the side of her quarry without incident. It was a simple matter to exclaim, 'You have dropped your reticule, Miss Dunston.'

The haste with which the girl retrieved her possession confirmed to Penny that the reticule had most likely contained what they suspected. She murmured some vague words, then turned with relief as Lord Stephen tapped her on the shoulder.

'I have not seen you dance once this evening, and the music is delightful. Come,' he persuaded.

Penny chuckled at his pleading, and walked with him to become part of a little group who were at the moment beginning a *contra dance*. It was a sprightly dance, and there was little time for conversation. She skipped up and back, dipped and swirled, smiling and thinking how good it was to be away from Miss Dunston and Ernest.

The Mouse's plot had been foiled, and Penny had managed to snabble that reticule as though a practiced thief. Amazing what one could do when determined.

When the dance ended, she fanned herself, feeling rather warm. 'That was charming,' she told her partner in a dismissive way.

'You found that excessive. Let us find something cool to drink.'

The notion appealed, and she willingly went along with him to the next room, where refreshments awaited all.

They stood to one side after picking up glasses of what Lady Harford had said was the Prince Regent's punch. Penny gasped when the liquid touched her throat, for along with oranges, lemons, pineapple syrup, and green tea was Jamaica rum, brandy, and arrack, not to mention champagne.

She took a few sips, then declared she was not thirsty after all. Memories of her bout with being tipsy returned to tease her.

'Lady Penelope,' Lord Stephen said after he had stopped chuckling at her, 'I do not pretend to know what is afoot at Harford House, but I sense something is going on. You have looked troubled this evening. Dear lady, if I may ever be of service to you, please do not hesitate to call upon me.' He picked up her delicately gloved hand and held it to his lips. 'Do not forget.'

As if she could. One never knew when help might be required; she well perceived that.

On the far side of the room, Jonathan slipped the contents of a packet into a glass of wine and then the other one into one glass of lemonade. He stirred them both, then sauntered over to where Everton stood with Miss Dunston.

'I trust you are enjoying yourselves this evening? May I say I have never seen you in better looks, Everton,' he announced to his dumbfounded cousin. 'Accept my compliments with this wine. Here is a lemonade for you, Miss Dunston. These balls can become so warm, can they not? Such a crush of people.'

Helping himself to a glass of wine from a passing footman, he raised his glass to Everton, then sipped. The others drank as well, unable to give offense by refusing.

When all glasses were empty, Jonathan drifted away, a most devilish smile curving his lips. Would it not be interesting to see what developed now?

14

The presentation of the multiple betrothals seemed to be an anti-climax as far as Penelope was concerned. The *ton* delighted in the novelty, however.

Lady Harford climbed the two steps to the musicians' stand to raise herself above the crowd just a little. She had drawn Charis and David along with her, Letty and Andrew, and Penelope and Jonathan following closely behind.

'My dear friends,' she began after the curious crowd fell silent, 'you cannot begin to know what great pleasure it gives me to offer you the entrancing news that our family is to be favored with not one, but three happy occasions very shortly. My daughter Charis is to wed David Howell, Marquess of Lisle.' She paused a moment while this coup sank into the minds of her Society friends.

'In addition I wish to reveal the coming marriage of Lady Penelope Winthrop to my dearest son, Jonathan.'

The gasp that followed this announcement was all that she might have desired. That the dashing, elusive bachelor had succumbed to the lure of the intriguing heiress would be food for speculation for days to come.

'I also wish to announce the betrothal of my niece Miss Lettice Winthrop to Mr Andrew Oglethorpe.' She beamed a warm smile to include Letty in the near-family, thus eliciting a great deal of conjecture. It was known that Miss Winthrop had spurned all the hopeful suitors over the years, preferring her eccentric solitude to marriage. That the fantastically wealthy Mr Oglethorpe had chosen her as his bride and that she actually agreed offered another feast for the gossips.

Once a toast was drunk to the young couples, Lady Harford made her way through the throng of socialites, accepting the envious congratulations from all in her path. For although there were petty snide thoughts by a few, most genuinely liked the pretty, gay Lady Harford and were pleased for her good fortune.

Penelope chanced to find herself brushing past the Countess Lieven, who gave her a lazy look from beneath her long dark lashes. 'You have kept me most amused, *chérie*.' She glanced at Jonathan, then back to Penelope. 'I wish you well, my dear.'

Aunt Winthrop pushed her way through the crowd until she confronted Penelope, noting Jonathan's protective position with displeasure. Ernest and Miss Dunston had followed, but both looked perplexed, as though they had no idea what prompted Lady Winthrop's actions.

'Well! You cannot have sought the consent of your guardian, miss. I shall make known your foolish behavior to him, and he will make short work of this nonsense, you may be certain.' Her eyes narrowed with malicious pleasure.

Penny's gaze flickered toward the Countess Lieven, who still stood close by. There was a faint wink of one of those impressive eyes before she nodded ever so slightly.

'We are all in the clouds, Aunt. I would that you not spoil it for us this evening. Anything new that you have to say may be presented to my solicitor,' Penny said in an amazingly calm voice. Perhaps coping with love potions and arrests and subterfuge in the kitchen allowed her to rise above this detestable woman? Turning to Jonathan, Penny said, 'I believe we are to join the others in a dance.'

The delicate strains of a waltz floated over the room, and Penny drifted into Jonathan's arms, as Letty fumbled her way along with Andrew. His face looked strained, possibly from the tread on his toes of Letty's plump feet. Yet he seemed happy for all that.

Charis and David drew smiles from

everyone, with their charming performance of the dance. The six whirled around the floor in gentle rhythm, swaying and dipping in a rather nice manner. At a motion from Jonathan, others slowly began to join them, the first being the Countess Lieven and her escort. Since she was the one who had introduced waltzing to Almack's, one might expect she would be a most accomplished waltzer, which she was.

Once the dance concluded, Penny gave the slender Russian an envious glance before confiding to Jonathan, 'I do believe she is the very best of us all. I expect she had a good deal of practice while at court in Berlin before coming here. I heard she was shockingly young when they married her to the count. I believe I had rather wait a bit, politics notwithstanding.'

'I understand she was placed in the hands of the Empress Maria at a tender age. I daresay she might sympathize with you on the subject of forced marriages.' His hand slid around Penny's waist to guide her to one side of the room, and she felt the heat from it radiating out as though the sun had chanced to beam upon her.

As the evening advanced, Penny threaded her way through the gathering, accepting the felicitations with composure. What, she wondered, would they all say when the betrothal was dissolved? Chuckle with glee, undoubtedly. Her vision flew to the three witches of Endor, their caldron transformed into a Sheraton tea table with Society matrons substituting admirably in their place.

Lord Stephen presented himself before her, looking at her with chastising eyes. 'Fair one, you leave me utterly desolate. You might have warned me.'

'Anyone who looks less forsaken I cannot imagine,' she replied with amusement.

'One dance? A cotillion?'

Still amused at his preposterous display of love lost, she agreed, first catching sight of Jonathan doing the proper with Miss Dunston.

During the movement of the dance, Lord Stephen found opportunities to speak. 'You intend to become the perfect English wife?'

'But, of course,' Penny replied with a smile. 'What do you believe the requisites to be?'

'Oh, a woman easy to live with, one who can make her own little world and be content in it.' The dance separated them for a few minutes. When he returned to her side, he continued, 'She must be assured and self-reliant, however. And a dash of wit might help. I do not want a wife forever hanging on my sleeve, if you must know. It would suit me well to live independent, yet joined.'

Penny was grateful when the dance separated them again, for she was deep in thought. The woman he described as the perfect English wife was precisely the life she sought, or had when she came to London. She wondered what Jonathan's concept of a wife would be.

While Lord Stephen escorted her to Lady Harford, Penny took the opportunity to ask him, 'Do you approve of a wife remaining in the country with that little world of which you spoke, content to be there and not in the gay whirl of London?' She awaited his reply with more than a little interest.

With the air of a dashing bachelor speaking to one safely beyond his reach, he replied loftily, 'Of course. No man wishes his wife to be forever looking over his shoulder, if you must know.'

'I believe you are a naughty tease,' she commented lightly before joining Lady Harford. Her fan hid the ironic twist of her mouth.

Withstanding the searching look from her sponsor, Penny watched as the people began to depart, slowly, lingeringly, chatting as they strolled down the stairs, murmuring reminders of upcoming social engagements as they drifted from the house.

Behind them servants swiftly went about removing the remnants of the party. Penny plucked a white carnation from a bouquet to twiddle it between her fingers, then sniffed the spicy fragrance with pleasure.

'I believe it was a *succés fou*, dear mother,' Jonathan said with quiet elation.

'A wild success? Is that how you view it?' Penny questioned, dangling the carnation in her hand as she also went down the staircase toward the front door and escape.

'You will see. Andrew and I shall take you and Letty home now before you fall asleep on your feet.'

'Perhaps the girls can stay here, Jonathan? I would like to speak with them in the morning, for we still have plans to make.' Lady Harford placed a staying hand on Penny's arm at the bottom of the stairs.

Knowing that morning would be somewhere around noon for them all, Penny shook her head. 'We shall come over about one in the afternoon, my lady. That way we can be in our own beds and far less bother to you.' She gave Lady Harford a quick kiss, then gathered her violet taffeta cloak from the footman who had materialized with it.

'You believe it is safe for her to be there with no protection from her aunt?' Lady Harford softly asked her son, anxious eyes on her future daughter-in-law that she had come to love.

'For tonight, I believe,' replied Jonathan, watching while Penny spoke quietly with Letty near the door. 'The Crow will take a day or two to formulate new plans, I suspect.'

'I think our strategy must be changed. You and Penny must wed immediately. No date was mentioned this evening, and even the Countess Lieven urged speed. Lord Lanscomb could arrive any day now. Who knows what the next ship will bring ashore?'

'So Penny told me. I confess I am reluctant to press her. I want no silly notions in her head that I wedded her for her money alone. She is lovely and desirable.' He studied the pretty picture she made as she chattered to Letty and Andrew Oglethorpe across the expanse of black-and-white-tiled floor. Her proud head with her beautiful blond curls in artfully tumbled charm rose regally from the violet taffeta billowing about her.

His mother smiled fondly. 'I am pleased your heart is captured. Marriage is so much more enjoyable that way.' She tilted her head in a slightly flirtatious manner and smiled broadly when he let out a hoot of laughter.

Penny wished Jonathan might have confided to her what had prompted that shout of laughter while he spoke with his mother. Was it perhaps something to do with the future and of their betrothal? Or was she being excessively sensitive about the matter?

At the house on Upper Brook Street Letty and Andrew joined Penny and Jonathan in the entry. Letty fiddled with the strings of her reticule before looking to Andrew for assistance.

'You see, the thing is, we have decided we do not wish to wait any longer,' he explained.

'Neither of us grows younger, you see,' Letty added by way of clarification.

'And you desire our help?' an astute Jonathan inquired.

'We should like very much to have you as witnesses. Tomorrow,' Andrew declared. 'Then we shall take ourselves off to the country for a bit before returning to the city.'

'I fancy it shall be a month or two,' added Letty again, looking at Andrew with starry eyes. Turning to Penny, she said, 'Although I shall be sorry to miss your wedding.'

'Of course, we shall help you,' Penny said in a soothing way. 'Do not worry about a thing. Lady Harford will doubtless be disappointed.' Penny turned concerned eyes on Jonathan.

'She will survive, and she understands the difficulty of a prolonged wait. Shall we meet, say, at eleven at the clock in the morning?'

It was decided they could all manage that time. Letty floated up the stairs after Andrew departed.

'How do you feel about not waiting, my pet?' Jonathan warily searched Penny's eyes, watching for a clue to her true feelings. He wondered what she had meant when she said she had no need for a love potion. Had she changed her mind about Stephen? He didn't like to think so. He knew what he hoped, but was he too optimistic?

'Be serious, my lord. We have only to convince the world, not each other.' She bestowed a faint smile on him, then moved toward the stairs. 'I am tired, and if we have to get up at such an ungodly hour, I must be off to my bed.'

Jonathan watched her go up the stairs, a cloud of violet and lavender. He suspected she was quite sincere in what she said. The drive to his elegant little house was a very thoughtful one. How was he to convince her that Lord Lanscomb was an unknown quantity, that he had the power to overset all her hopes and their plans? She might not think Jonathan was serious in his intent to marry her, but it made his goal no less real.

Daily the danger grew for her, for their happiness. Would that he could bring her with him before the cleric tomorrow as well!

* * *

In the morning the house on Upper Brook Street was total chaos, from the attics to the basement kitchen.

Letty, attired in a cream silk gown of simple lines and a clever little bonnet decorated with cream ribbons and peach silk roses, ignored it all. She gathered one of her many shawls, then issued an order for a few of her trunks to be packed with what she desired. When the time came to depart, she had things amazingly well in hand.

Penny trailed behind her to the carriage, marveling that her absentminded cousin could organize when she chose.

At the little church on South Audley Street the two men waited. Andrew held a posy of cream roses in one hand. His coat of deep blue contrasted nicely with his fawn trousers. He had somewhat the appearance of one who has been struck by unexpected good fortune and is not sure what to do with it.

His man had been at the church to smooth their path. All was in readiness.

Penny had eyes only for Jonathan, also attired in a dark blue coat, with biscuit trousers that strapped over his shoes and showed off a trim pair of legs. Dragging her gaze from him, she resolutely watched Letty and Andrew as they approached the front of the church.

Letty showed no signs of nervousness in the least.

'Dearly beloved,' the curate began in a richly impressive voice, 'we are gathered together in the sight of God . . . '

Penny listened and considered the portion of the ceremony that said that marriage was to bring mutual society, help, and comfort, that the one ought to have of the other, both in prosperity and adversity. It was a noble sentiment, if possible. She darted a glance at Jonathan. How would she feel to actually be exchanging these vows with him? At one time she had thought it an expedient thing. Now she wondered if she would so willingly accept that marriage of convenience. At least, to him.

The curate exhorted Letty and Andrew to love each other as they cared for themselves. Love, *not* financial arrangements, nor expediency. She simply could not bind Jonathan to anything so permanent as marriage unless there was love, that was clear. To do otherwise would be a sin.

Letty's 'I will' rang out in a defiant voice that Penny found endearing. The bridal couple signed the register, followed by Penny, Jonathan, and the curate, and the wedding was over.

After the ceremony, the four returned to the house on Upper Brook Street, where all was in readiness for a light meal. If the staff looked breathless and harried, it was not to be wondered. While the bridal party had a lovely nuncheon (Penny suspected it was deliberately drawn out), the carriage was loaded, and then the staff, along with Jonathan and Penny, waved them off.

Penny wandered up alone to her bedroom. She supposed that Mrs Flint had collapsed somewhere below.

Jonathan took himself off to see if he could find out more about Lanscomb, suspecting now was not the moment to press Penny about a wedding. She had seemed adorably confused and bewildered this morning. He hoped he hadn't made a mistake in waiting. Miss Nilsson could hold matters in hand. At least for a brief time, and by then he hoped to have Penny as wife.

* * *

When at one of the clock Penny presented herself alone at Harford House, Lady Harford took the news well.

'I daresay you were wishing you might do the same,' she said archly after patting the sofa at her side to be certain that Penny would sit close to her.

Penny perched gingerly on the striped satin sofa, drawing off her gloves, then toying with the reticule in her lap.

'Ma'am, that would be folly, would it not? Do you not recall that this betrothal is temporary, until my aunt takes herself away from London?' Penny fiddled with the handkerchief she had tugged from her reticule. Her pretty blue leather slipper absently traced a line of the pattern of the Aubusson carpet beneath her feet.

'What if she stays here until Lord Lanscomb arrives in Town?' Lady Harford inquired with a curious inflection to her voice.

'I daresay I shall contrive a way to cope with the problem. Perhaps I shall take a ship to foreign parts, where he cannot reach me?' Penny gave a lopsided grin at the lady she had come to admire. 'Never fear that I shall trap your fine son into a marriage he does not wish,' she concluded earnestly.

'You are convinced he has no desire to wed with you?' Lady Harford gave an impatient sigh. Really, these children were so silly. Why Jonathan didn't whisk Penny off to a curate was foolishness. Did he actually feel it so important that she trust in him to this degree? *Absurdité*.

They conversed awhile, discussed what Jonathan hoped to accomplish, then turned to the agreeable subject of Charis and David's wedding to come.

Lady Charis danced into the morning room, her face aglow with happiness. 'Say you will come along with us when we shop for bride clothes. I vow, there is so much to purchase and order, I scarce know where to begin.'

'Begin at the beginning,' advised Penny sagely, with a twinkle in her eyes.

'Shifts, stays, and stockings, of course,' Charis said with a bemused nod. 'Then petticoats, gowns, bonnets, and slippers in that order. Last of all a new supply of gloves and reticules to match my gowns and pelisses. I should like to buy a fur tippet for next winter, I think, Mama.'

Penny began to worry about the bills. How on earth would Jonathan begin to pay for all the pretty things Charis intended to obtain, with her mother's blessing, it seemed?

Yet she knew it was unthinkable that a young woman who is to marry the heir to a duke not be properly fitted out. As a marchioness, she would hold an elevated place in Society. Charis and David were both people who charmed, and would draw their own group about them.

'How fortunate you have time to prepare.' Penny shared a cautious glance with Lady Harford, then continued, 'Letty and Andrew were married this morning by special license. I hope you do not feel cheated that they did not wait, but he has courted her for an age and they decided not to delay another day.'

'Oh, famous!' Charis bubbled with delight. 'What fun the gossips will have with that tidbit. Shall you send in the announcement, Mama?'

'Your brother will see to it, my love. He is off this afternoon making a number of contacts. Penny refuses to believe that she is in danger of having to face her guardian before the wedding can take place. I urged Jonathan to cajole her into hurrying things along, but he has this absurd notion . . . ' Suddenly aware she had said far too much, Lady Harford closed her mouth, giving Penny an apologetic look. Really, life was most complicated.

Fearing the worst, Penny put on a brave face, returning the subject to that of the morning wedding.

'Since you stood up with Letty, you must consent to stand witness for me,' Charis cried, pleased with her clever idea. 'I feel sure that dearest David will wish Jonathan to attend him. Did Letty not seem nervous? I vow, I shall be all atwitter with anxiety that I forget something. Do you know,' she confided, 'Mama and I decided that plain white satin trimmed with white lace and tiny pearls would be just the thing?'

Penny smiled and nodded while her heart felt a peculiar twist. A longing for a mother to plan and hope with her came over her with an intensity that near ached. She was alone; she had never realized just *how* alone until now. On one side of her she had Lady Harford, who politely offered assistance. Her other side was endangered by her aunt, who seemed to become more formidable and menacing by the day, especially when supported by that entire branch of the family. The Winthrops believed in retaining their own.

Sounds from the hall preceded the entrance of the man who had been hovering in her thoughts. Lord Harford stood just inside the door, taking in the little scene. His face could not have been more grim.

Lady Harford jumped to her feet, followed by the girls. 'What has happened?'

'I just found out that Lord Lanscomb entered London late last evening with that party of Austrian diplomats. They went to the Esterhazy establishment to report. Lanscomb has set himself up at the Clarendon for the time being. I fancy it will not take long for your aunt to seek him out. I think you had better get there first.'

Penny met Jonathan's gaze quite fearlessly, then walked toward him. 'I shall go at once, and hope that he will meet with me.' She gave a peculiar little laugh. 'I do not recall ever seeing him, so I shan't know what to expect. I do hope he is not the dragon I fear. Excuse me, my lady, Charis, Jonathan.' She curtsied, then left the room, looking very alone and forlorn.

Jonathan gave an exasperated look at his mother, then followed Penny across the entry to the front door. 'I am going with you. You once admitted that my position carried some weight. Remember?' They left together, his hand firmly at her elbow. Penny found herself being inexorably guided to the curricle that stood before the house.

'My maid?' she murmured in light protest.

'Hang your maid,' he snapped back in aggravation. 'We formally announced our betrothal last night. I, for one, do not care a blasted fig for what anyone says at this point.'

'My, my,' she replied, a faint smile coming to her lips, 'we are annoyed this afternoon.'

'You seem to forget that your guardian has arrived in London.' He gave his horse the office to proceed, then spent agonizing minutes weaving through the crush of London traffic.

Penny remained silent until the carriage drew up before the Clarendon Hotel in Bond Street. She walked beside Jonathan into the building with her heart beating far too fast and her mouth as dry as day-old toast.

The request to see Lord Lanscomb was met with a curious look from the man at the desk. He merely nodded, sent a boy off with the card that Jonathan handed him, and they waited.

Penny would have liked to pace back and forth as the gentlemen did. It seemed a good thing to do while waiting. 'Pity there is not an accessible fireplace here,' she murmured, to Jonathan's confusion.

Some minutes later, the boy returned with a request they follow him. When they reached the numbered door behind which her guardian waited, Penny found her courage failing her. She turned to Jonathan, extending a trembling hand. 'I do not know if I can utter a word.'

'You'll do just fine,' he said with more hope than anything else.

The man who greeted them was not quite what Penny had expected in the many times she had thought about her guardian. He was lean and fit, as might be expected of someone who spent much of his time climbing mountains. His hair was brushed with silver, fine lines curved about his eyes and mouth, and elegant side whiskers adorned his face. He looked politely curious, nothing more.

'I am Lady Penelope Winthrop, my lord,' Penny plunged on, not waiting for Jonathan to introduce her. 'I am pleased to make your acquaintance.' She hoped her curtsy did Miss Nilsson proud.

A wry smile tilted the thin mouth beneath his veritable beak of a nose. 'Ah, so we meet at last. I must apologize, I quite forgot you should have grown up by this point.'

'There is a matter of some importance, or we would not have intruded on your first day in London,' Jonathan inserted in apology after introducing himself. He then proceeded to outline, with interjections now and again from Penny, just what had transpired and why they sought his assistance.

'I see. I shall need to discuss this with your solicitor, of course. However, Lady Winthrop has a point in her favor, it would seem.' He massaged his chin, staring off into space while he considered the matter that had been brought before him.

Penny glanced at Jonathan, then spoke. 'I shall tell you this, sir, that if anyone attempts to force me to wed the Toad, I shall flee the country. Ireland, even if cut off from all I hold dear, seems far more entrancing than being married to him.'

'The Toad?'

Narrowing her eyes with determination, Penny admitted, 'I am sorry, sir. I forgot myself. You see, we call Ernest the Toad, my Aunt is the Crow, and the girl Ernest ought to wed, the Mouse. Quite wicked of us, I know.'

The chuckle from the rather awesome stranger gave Penny heart. 'I suspect I shall meet them ere long. You wasted no time in finding me.'

'The Countess Lieven informed us of your progress,' Jonathan said. 'She urged us to wed before you arrived, to avoid any difficulty. I have gone to the Court of Chancery to obtain the necessary papers and have a special license in my pocket even now.'

'Hm.' Shaggy brows rose, while that lean hand stroked his chin once again as he surveyed the two before him. Penny imagined it must be akin to standing before a headmaster at Eton for some dire crime.

'And my coming just at this juncture complicates matters, I fear. Allow me to consult with your solicitor, my dear girl. I trust we shall be able to work this out to the satisfaction of most of us.'

'Well,' Penny said with great daring, 'I believe that to marry a girl off to an odious cousin merely to keep a pot of money in the family is perfectly dreadful.'

The two men looked over her head and smiled in mutual understanding.

'May I call upon you later, Lanscomb?' Jonathan asked, a speculative quirk to one brow.

'Indeed, I think that to be most helpful. Since you are the head of your side of the family, you stand also in line as an authority for Lady Penelope. Along with her solicitor,' he added as an afterthought. 'It might be well were you and your solicitor to join me at his law offices. I daresay you know where they are located?'

Jonathan looked to Penny, who gave the required information. Shortly, they were walking downstairs to the outside. Silently they entered the curricle for the drive back to Upper Brook Street.

'Well,' Penny said in speculation, 'I feel we made some progress. I shall await your news with anxious ears, sir.'

It was as well she did not see the annoyed look he tossed her, for it promised retribution for her formality, her intention of going off without him, and a few other matters if he could remember them all.

Inside the house on Upper Brook Street, they found a chaos of a different sort. Miss Nilsson was seated with Henri in the little morning room off the entry. He had captured her slim hands in his own, and sat gazing into her eyes with admiration rather than the exasperation usually to be observed. When Penny and Jonathan entered, he jumped up, bowing with correct formality. Miss Nilsson sat as though struck all of a heap.

'I have good news. I found my family estate in decent-enough repair, and a neighbor anxious to buy it. While there I discovered I had no liking for the place. It is no longer my home, you understand? So I sold the property and returned. I am now in the position that I may marry. Miss Nilsson has done me the honor of accepting my suit.'

He drew his dear lady to her feet. The companion still had a bemused expression on her face. 'Oh, Penny, I hope you do not mind, dear girl. But you shall be married soon, and I simply could not resist this gentleman.'

Penny felt as though her world was shattering into tiny pieces, never to be the same again. Pinning a smile on her face, she swiftly walked to her dear friend's side. 'You know I wish you every joy. I shall miss you both.'

But how would she manage without them?

15

'We intend to run a very superior sort of inn,' Miss Nilsson confided in her refined way. 'With Henri as the chef, and myself to guide the operations, we shall cater only to the most elite of people. Perhaps in Brighton, Henri?'

Henri, now that Penelope had sunk down upon a chair, joined his beloved once again on the sofa. 'I know you fancy being near the sea, and that seems a promising place.' He looked at Lord Harford for confirmation of his assessment.

'Very wise. We shall do our best to filter the word about the *ton* once you become established. Indeed, perhaps Penelope and I can pause there while on our honeymoon, if you are ready by that time. At least we shall visit.'

Penelope wished to refute his remark about their coming honeymoon. He knew very well that their so-called marriage was a subterfuge. Only, it seemed to her that everyone else was taking it quite seriously. Perhaps he needed her money and was willing to take her on without any love on his part.

Penelope now desired more than mere

expediency. Mayhap she could simply give him a sizable sum of money, then retreat to Fountains? If she might persuade her guardian and solicitor that she was quite sincere in her desire to remain unmarried, and perhaps offer to guarantee that her money and estate would revert to the Winthrops after she had gone aloft, this pressure would cease?

Of course, it would not appease Aunt Winthrop in the least, for she had it in her mind that her dolt of a son would have Penelope's fortune at his — and her — disposal immediately. As domineering as Aunt was, Penelope wondered if the old lady could be deterred in her aim.

On her part, Penelope looked forward to the completion of her new greenhouse, and the subsequent planting of herbs from around the world. She would renounce marriage to become an expert on the subject. She resolutely pushed aside the truth — that the idea brought her cold comfort.

Jonathan wondered at the subdued reaction from Penelope. Then he considered how close she had been to the two lovers on the sofa, and suspected that she felt a bit lost. First her cousin Letty had left this morning; now her companion and the man who had been a sort of father substitute to her during her growing-up years were to leave. Jonathan contemplated the effect of this on his suit and smiled with complacency.

Indeed, Penelope felt lost, but she knew that she must have courage, for it was her main resource at this point.

'We shall remain with you until your wedding, my dear,' continued Miss Nilsson. 'Henri and I can share quarters once married.'

'And then Miss Winthrop may not mind me in the house,' added Henri.

They then informed him of Letty's wedding just that morning. Penelope had the presence of mind to call for suitable wine so they might toast the coming wedding of her near-lifelong employees — and friends. The couple went off — with her kind permission — to attend to their urgent matters.

Lord Harford bowed over Penelope's hand and departed after a word with Mrs Flint.

Left alone, Penelope walked up to her room and methodically changed from her finery worn this morning to a day dress. How rapidly the world changed. Yesterday she lived with the illusion that Aunt Winthrop would take herself back to Everton, where she ruled the house and Ernest, once she saw that a betrothal had become a reality.

Today Penny's guardian had agreed to

meet with Lord Harford and the solicitors to discuss what the most suitable future for her might be. Oh, how she hated that! Why should she be denied participation? She wanted it clearly understood that she brooked no toleration of a marriage to Ernest; that another solution must be found.

She knew well that settlements could take ages to reach agreement on, particularly when an heiress was involved. But upon whom would she be settled?

Impatiently she paced back and forth before the neat fireplace in her room. She was foolish beyond permission to hope for another, more romantic conclusion to her dilemma. When had she altered? It was exceedingly gradual, her change from that of a young woman who had come to town, disbelieving in love and intent upon a marriage of convenience, to that of a young woman desiring a union based upon love and mutual respect.

Shaking off her absurd fancies, she headed down the stairs to Letty's study in the back of the house on the ground floor. Here she found paper, pens, and ink in several colors — apparently Letty liked to compose her poetry in various tones. Absently chewing on a pen, she considered what she wished to say, then began to write.

When she finished, she read over the letter of instructions to her solicitor, wondering why she hadn't thought of this long ago. Since there was no footman around, she wrapped a shawl about her shoulders, then left the house in search of a hackney.

The one she found was dirty, with bits of mud and straw on the floor and the smell of countless unsavory beings. Nevetheless, she climbed in and directed the jarvey to take her to her solicitor's office in Threadneedle Street.

Once there, she proffered the letter of instruction to Mr Parkhurst with an austere smile. 'Here, sir, since it is deemed unseemly for me to be present, I wish you to know my feelings on the matter to be discussed by my guardian and Lord Harford with you. Have they made an appointment?'

She didn't need his answer, his eyes revealed that they had set a time, and she fumed that so much could occur without her knowledge. She was totally helpless in this matter. Her fortune, her very life, was in their hands.

Would that she might appeal to them and be able to force their hands as she had done when she first approached Lord Harford. Jonathan. She murmured something vague, then left, accepting the insistence that a junior clerk at the office find her a hackney.

It was in considerably better condition, and she instructed the driver to deposit her before the fashionable Harding and Howell store. She whirled past the delights offered: silks in the gown department, furs, clocks, and furniture such as graced Carlton House.

She purchased a little coach clock she took a fancy to have. It would tick away the minutes of the rest of her life, she reflected wryly.

Then she gave some thought to wedding gifts. Miss Nilsson and Henri would need many things for their superior sort of inn and she decided to give them a draft on her bank for furniture. Letty and Andrew were far more difficult. At last, thinking of their love for reading, she settled on a particularly fine pair of Argand lamps that would burn colza oil and give excellent light, far better than candles.

As to Lady Charis and Lord Lisle, the problem of a wedding gift seemed impossible to decide. Penelope browsed through the contents of Harding and Howell's for ideas, finally electing to order a complete set of crystal for them with the family crest engraved thereupon.

With this purchase completed and the dinner hour approaching, she left the store to return the short distance to the house on Upper Brook Street. The hour grew late, but who waited for her? Unless Eva Nilsson and her Henri had returned by now.

Mrs Flint and Lord Harford met her at the door, each wearing a look of frantic concern. Mrs Flint took one glance at his lordship's face and retreated toward the back of the house.

'And where have you been?'

Penelope drew back in startled awareness of the subtle menace in his voice. 'Shopping,' she replied, all that had been accomplished with her visit to Mr Parkhurst's office safely omitted.

'Did you not think to inform Mrs Flint of your intentions?' He guided her into the morning room, then firmly drew her down upon the sofa, setting himself frightfully close to her.

'I confess I am not in the habit of telling anyone where or when I go about. Miss Nilsson is usually with me and she takes or has taken care of such in the past.' Penelope reflected that in the future she would require the services of a new companion or an abigail.

'Perhaps you have ceased to worry that your Aunt Winthrop is determined to wed you to your cousin?'

'Surely you do not believe she would use force?'

'Do you not?'

She thought a minute and reluctantly nodded her head. 'I expect you have the right of that, sir. I had my head full of other matters, I fear.'

He leaned back against the sofa, crossing his arms and studying the face turned toward his with intent eyes. She gave away a certain amount in those eyes, and he wished to know all he might. 'What matters?'

Here she was on safe ground. 'Wedding presents. I decided I would give Miss Nilsson and Henri a draft so they might buy some furnishings for their 'superior inn.' For Letty and Andrew I found some rather elegant Argand lamps of the latest style. Do you think,' she inquired with some hesitation, 'that your sister and David will like a set of crystal with the family crest on it?'

'Admirable, I am sure,' he said with exquisite politeness.

His voice nearly froze her.

'What else?'

She dropped her gaze to the reticule in her lap, fiddling with the cords with uneasy fingers. 'Nothing.'

'In other words, you do not wish me to know what you were about. When we are married, my love, I shall demand a better accounting of your days.'

'Since I doubt that will occur, I shan't worry overmuch about the matter,' she said with a light flippancy that masked the turmoil in her heart. She found her face taken firmly by his hand, and turned to him once more.

'I have decided that it is in our best interests to marry. The announcement of the betrothal will go to the papers, once I convince your solicitor and Lord Lanscomb to agree to our marriage.'

Penelope twisted her face from his grasp, jumping to her feet. With the knowledge that her wishes might actually gain her what she thought she wanted, she smiled. 'We shall see, my lord.' At the look in his eyes as he rose and advanced upon her, she retreated to the entry hall, handing him his hat as she passed the table.

'I do not trust that look in the least,' he growled at her. 'Be ready to dine in an hour. We are to have dinner with my mother, Charis and David, and the duke and duchess.'

Penelope stood stock-still by the open door, staring up at him with a fluttering heart. She could do nothing but agree for the moment. How he must detest the situation she had placed him into. 'I shall be prompt, sir.'

His annoyance spilled forth in a hiss. Then

he quickly reached for her to place a brief but fierce kiss on her mouth.

He marched down the steps, then jumped up into the waiting curricle — that she ought to have noticed when she returned to the house — and drove off in a whirl of dust. Penelope closed the door, then ran up the stairs to her room.

Since Miss Nilsson had not yet returned, Penelope had no one to assist her. She summoned one of the maids to help her dress, then arranged her own hair. In slightly less than an hour she prepared to descend, hearing the rattle of a coach on the street just outside come to a halt. Smoothing the delicate silk floral print of her gown, she floated down the stairs as he entered the house. Warmly approving eyes did much to bolster her confidence.

Jonathan inhaled the scent of tea roses as she neared him and smiled at his future wife. 'Delicious.'

She fingered one of the knots of ribbon that punctuated the lace edging at the neck of her gown. 'Good evening. How fortunate that I did not have a prior engagement tonight. You were exceedingly uncivil in the announcement of our evening, sir.'

'I apologize. It has been a rather harrowing day, my love.' He nodded to Mrs Flint, assuring her that he would bring Penelope home late but safe, then they left the house.

'You are treating me as though I am a child,' Penelope complained, once seated in the comfortable town coach.

'Not at all,' he denied complacently. 'I am concerned about you. Perhaps you ought to move in with my mother for the time being.'

She gave him a wondering look that was tinged with disbelief. In her experience the people who fussed were paid to do so. She now mistrusted her instincts. 'Miss Nilsson and Henri should return before long. She will not desert me.' Yet.

Lady Harford clearly felt that Penelope ought not be alone in the house in Upper Brook Street following Letty's departure as well, and made her feelings known.

'You are all that is kind, dear lady, but Miss Nilsson promised she would stay for a time,' Penelope said in a rather small voice, sensing a generosity of spirit that seemed to come quite often from that lady. 'I shall consider what you say. Perhaps I shall take myself off to Fountains before long, if all goes well,' she added, thinking of the settlement she had proposed to her solicitor. She turned to answer a question from the duchess, thus missed the annoyed look sent from Lady Harford to her negligent son.

* * *

The following day Penelope decided she wished to discuss a few things with Lord Harford, and not having anyone about to send, as per usual in this household, she again set off, this time alone. Miss Nilsson and Henri were off on another foray, this time to see an estate agent about a suitable building in Brighton.

Harford's elegant house no longer had the ability to intimidate her. Penelope walked past Darling, giving him her nicest smile. 'I shall wait for his lordship in the library,' she replied when informed that Lord Harford had gone out but was expected back directly. The butler's brows drew together in concern that Penelope was here unattended, but he knew better than to say a word.

Darling set about ordering up some tea for her ladyship, while Penelope strolled into the library, wondering just how soon 'directly' would be.

It truly was a lovely room, she thought once again. It exuded a warmth and homeliness that was infinitely appealing. She decided it wasn't just the shelves of varicolored tooled bindings, nor the leather chairs. The colors and textures in the room contributed as well. She would emulate that at Fountains in the small room she had turned into a library.

His desk was cluttered today. Books were tumbled about, and a letter lay open. She wondered what was written on the heavy cream paper. Too long for a business communication, she thought. And the writing looked ladylike.

Curious, unable to prudently refrain from reading another's mail — something she normally never would do — she drifted over to the desk and picked up the dainty epistle.

'My beloved, how I long for the sight of your dear face . . . ' the letter began. Feminine handwriting in exquisite copperplate disclosed the most tender expressions of love that Penelope had ever read, in spite of the volumes of poetry Letty had thrust at her. Such love shook Penelope, for it seemed so total, so very giving. As she lowered herself onto one of the leather chairs, the implication of what was in her hands sank into her mind. This beautiful declaration of love from a lady who signed the letter with a simple initial, S, was addressed to Lord Harford.

She mentally ran through the women she had met, but could think of no one with that initial who might be so terribly close to him. Yet what did that mean?

Someone had written him this vow of

eternal love, one who adored him as anyone would long to be cherished.

When Darling entered with an elegant tray of tea and biscuits, he found Lady Penelope standing by the window, gazing out at the street with an abstracted air.

Politely thanking the butler for his care, Penelope waited until he closed the door, then returned the letter to the precise place where it had been. At least she hoped that was the place.

Her hand trembled as she poured her tea. While she sipped the steaming blend, she thought furiously and hard.

What a noble and gallant gentleman Harford was. He was willing to sacrifice his happiness to save a member of his family from an admittedly horrid fate. She cared far too much about him, she confessed, to permit such a thing to happen, even if it meant losing her own joy. But what could she do? The foolish man insisted they were to be married. Nothing seemed to deter him. What a pity there was no love upon his part; exasperation appeared to be his most frequently displayed emotion when about her.

She *must* take matters into her own hands. But how? If she merely took off on her own, she sensed he would simply bring her back. She needed help. But whose?

Placing the empty teacup on the tray, she gathered her reticule and stepped from the room. At Darling's query, she only said, 'I forgot an appointment. Since I shall be seeing his lordship later on, we may discuss the matter then.'

After thanking the butler in a proper way, she left the house, walking to Upper Brook Street rather than take a hackney. The air was fresh and pleasant, far nicer than Threadneedle Street.

A phaeton dashed past her, then came to an abrupt halt. A gentleman jumped down and handed the reins to his tiger. He walked back to Penelope, his jaunty air making him instantly recognizable.

'Lord Stephen, how pleasant to see you,' Penelope said, welcoming him with an outstretched hand.

'What, pray tell, are you doing alone at this time of the morning, my lady?' He looked about as though expecting a maid to pop out from behind a pillar.

'The household is at sixes and sevens. I had a brief errand nearby, and thought it silly to pull one of the maids from her tasks merely to walk along behind me.' Penelope knew she should be in disgrace by her ill-advised actions. It was one thing to drive to the village for a paper of pins or to saunter along the village walks by oneself. It was quite another to venture beyond the front door of a London residence without a maid or footman in attendance.

'Suppose I offer you my carriage for the rest of the way? Since you are engaged, I expect you will escape censure.' He slanted a grin at her, a rather charming one.

The very reflection on that so-called engagement to a man who so passionately loved another chilled her. She studied Lord Stephen as he assisted her, and her face grew thoughtful.

'Problems?' Lord Stephen said as he joined her in the phaeton. 'You look as though your day has not been all you could wish so far.'

'I do need help rather badly, as it happens.' She gave him an assessing look, wondering if he would be willing to dare the possible lash of Society tongues should his help be revealed if he assisted her in what she planned.

'Why do we not take a little drive through the park while we discuss this. You do not think Harford will mind?'

Touched at his obvious concern, she shook her head. Recalling that tender letter of love, she seriously doubted that Lord Harford cared a jot. He most likely wished her to Jericho. That letter explained his unloverlike proposal and abrupt kiss quite well.

They jogged along at a fine pace through the Stanhope Gate and along the wooded lanes of Hyde Park. It was thin of company at the moment, for this hour of the day saw most women at home tending to household matters, or sleeping off the rigors of the previous evening. A few riders could be seen cantering beneath the trees along Rotten Row.

When they reached an area where few people were around, he drew the carriage to a halt. 'Why do we not take a stroll, Lady Penelope?'

She thought his excessive politeness amusing, yet she sensed his respect for her had grown since her betrothal to Lord Harford. How lowering to realize your esteem was so dependent upon another, in spite of wealth.

Leaving the carriage and horses in the care of his tiger, they set out along a pretty path. Stately oaks and elms, tall beech trees, new plantings being nurtured for the future, grew about them. Thick green grass had yet to feel the heat of summer. Sparrows chirped in the shrubbery and around the base of an elm.

'So, suppose you tell Uncle Stephen all about it, hm?' he said with a hint of joviality.

'Uncle Stephen, indeed. Are all men intent upon making me feel like a little child?' She knew she sounded petulant, but she felt strongly ill-used at the moment.

His gaze was warm as he shook his head. 'Hardly that, Penny, my dear, to use Harford's pet name for you. Rather, I believe that you are a woman that men instinctively feel protective toward.'

Why hadn't Lord Harford said something like that to her rather than give her such a wigging?

'I see. How kind of you to think that way.'

'So?' He slowed their steps until they stopped. While he studied her face, Penelope searched for the right words to use.

'I must return to Fountains immediately. I want to keep it a secret from Jonathan. He mustn't know where I am, at least for several days.' She found it extremely difficult to say this much, for she sensed Lord Stephen would press for more answers.

'Why? What could possibly have happened that you could not tell your future husband?'

Inspiration struck. 'It is a wedding surprise. I am having something built for him at Fountains, and I wish to see how it goes. I have lent my coach to Miss Nilsson and Henri so they might travel to Brighton. They are to set up a very superior inn there and need to inspect some property. I cannot take a stage and don't know a thing about arranging for a post chaise. Could you see it in your heart to help me? I shall be happy to pay for everything, you know.'

She fished about in her reticule and pulled out a staggering sum in banknotes, flourishing them before Lord Stephen.

He eyed the notes, then motioned her to put them away. 'What a shocking girl you are, to be carrying such an amount about with you. I shall make the needed arrangements for you.'

Narrowing her gaze at him, she said, 'I suspect your silly pride will be offended if I insist on handing you this money, but I shall anyway. I always pay my way, you see.'

The warmth had left his eyes as they turned to go back to his carriage. 'Have you never been taught that one must learn to accept a gift graciously? After all, if it is more blessed to give than to receive, it stands to reason that a number of us must be the recipients of all that giving.'

Embarrassed, Penelope bent her head, looking with sightless eyes at the path they trod. 'I have found myself in the other position most often. When one is unaccustomed to receiving gifts, it is difficult to learn the ability to graciously accept.' Deciding to explain, she added, 'My parents did come a few times at Christmas to bring me presents. I was very little then. Later they were too busy with parties and such. Then they were killed. Solicitors and guardians do not send gifts, you know.'

'Miss Nilsson? Your cousins and aunt?'

'My employees are very loyal, for which they are well paid. As to my aunt and relatives, I fancy they wished to forget I existed until there was a danger my fortune might slip out of the Winthrop hands.'

He shook his head. 'Dashed rotten business, if you ask me. I'll help you.'

On the ride back to Upper Brook Street, he explained what would be necessary and admitted to the costs. She outlined what she wished arranged in greater detail. They were passing Everton House when Penelope espied a clearly overset Aunt Winthrop.

'Whatever can be the matter? It is quite unlike my aunt to be dithering about in front of the house in that manner.'

Lord Stephen brought the carriage to a halt and Penelope leaned over to inquire, 'Is there some trouble, Aunt?'

'Trouble?' she snapped back. 'I should say so. Ernest has gone. Disappeared. I mean to find him at once, and he has taken our carriage!'

'Perhaps he merely went for a ride?'

'His valet is gone as well, and the wardrobe is near empty of clothes. He has decamped! I am undone. I shall have a spasm.' She fanned herself with a handkerchief of black-bordered linen.

Anyone less likely to collapse with a case of nerves, Penelope couldn't imagine. Recalling the words of caution from Lord Harford, Penelope was reluctant to offer her assistance. Yet she felt sorry for the old woman, standing there with her elaborate lace cap askew and wringing her hands with apparently sincere worry.

Signaling Lord Stephen that she wished to get down, she added, 'Please wait for me if you can. I do not trust my aunt. It is possible this is a trap set for me.'

Looking astounded at this, Lord Stephen nodded, assisting Penelope from the phaeton with courtesy, then remaining at her side while she approached her aunt.

'You ought to return to the house, Aunt Winthrop. It is unseemly that you remain out here,' gently prompted Penelope.

'What? Oh, of course. Well, then, I shall find out the truth of the matter somehow.' She was about to march up the few steps to the house when a footman neared.

The trio paused while he approached Lady Winthrop with a missive in hand.

Curtly dismissing the man, she broke open the seal and rudely began to read. Penelope was about to retrace her footsteps to the carriage when she observed her aunt's face turn ashen. The older woman groped for the iron railing to one side of the steps, looking about ready to collapse.

Tossing an alarmed glance at Lord Stephen, Penelope ran forward to help Lady Winthrop. 'Unpleasant news, ma'am?' she gently inquired.

'He could not serve me so. I cannot believe this.' Her voice was cracked and weak. All power and force seemed to have seeped from her upon reading the letter. Thrusting it at Penelope, she commanded, 'Read it for yourself.'

Penelope scanned the contents with growing amazement. She glanced up at Lord Stephen, hardly knowing how to phrase her words. At last she said, 'Lord Everton has eloped with Miss Dunston. He politely informs his mother that she may remove herself to the dower house at Everton. She is not to be here when they return from their wedding trip.' Turning to her aunt she added, 'At least he gives you a month.'

'A mere month, and I must be removed. Cast aside! I do not know how to bear this insult.' She turned and hobbled back into the house.

Penelope watched her leave. It seemed her aunt wanted no comfort from her niece, for before the door closed she could be heard calling for her abigail.

Turning to Lord Stephen, Penelope tried to keep a straight face and failed. She grinned as she entered the phaeton. Glancing down at him, she said, ‘The Mouse has turned into a fearsome tiger. One never knows, does one?’

And then Penelope realized that her menace was gone. All need to marry had vanished. She was free, and so was Jonathan.

16

After bidding Lord Stephen good-bye in the entry, Penelope ran lightly up the stairs, nearly bumping into Mrs Flint as she rounded the corner on the first floor.

'Forgive me, my lady,' the flustered housekeeper said, looking most curiously at Penelope's laughing face.

Bubbling with relief, for Ernest's elopement had removed her greatest fears, Penelope said happily, 'Can you credit that my cousin Ernest has eloped, Mrs Flint? He marries Miss Dunston. And he has ordered my aunt to the country. She will hate the dower house, for it is small and not at all what she had planned for her future.'

Penelope continued, deciding to rush ahead with her plans, 'Mrs Flint, I shall need someone to take Miss Nilsson's place, now that lady is to be married.'

'You will wish to request one of the agencies to send you suitable applicants, my lady. Shall I notify the establishment Miss Letty uses?'

'Please,' Penelope replied with relief. She hurried into her room, hoping she had turned the housekeeper's thoughts to something else other than what Penelope intended to do once the new abigail appeared.

Within an hour a young woman presented herself for Penelope's inspection. Named Betsy, she appeared to be neat and modest, claiming skill at dressing hair and offering good references. She was hired on the spot.

Upon discovering that the abigail could commence work immediately, Penelope motioned her to follow up the stairs.

Once inside her room, Penelope pointed to the trunks she had ordered brought down from the attic. 'I wish to have all my things packed. I find it necessary to return to the country. I trust you have no aversion to a pleasant stay in a rather nice country house?'

Betsy cautiously smiled. 'No, my lady. I've never been to the country, being a city girl. But I'm willin'.'

That was all Penelope required. Watching a few moments, she observed the girl worked quickly and neatly in her packing of Penelope's things. Once she realized that effort was well in hand, Penelope walked down to Letty's little study.

She owed Jonathan an explanation. After thinking about what Lord Stephen had said respecting gifts, she knew it was rude and ungrateful of her to simply disappear from

London without a word to the man with whom she had been so intimately involved the past weeks. After all, for a dashing bachelor to offer marriage was no small thing.

She couldn't tell him she had stooped to reading his mail; that would be disgraceful. Embarrassing as well, she admitted. She had never done such a thing in her life, but she was glad she had now, she fiercely insisted. A man so devotedly, tenderly loved ought not marry anyone else. It was plain that the unknown woman had felt loved in return, sure of total regard. Oh, to be adored, loved so totally. Penelope sighed and turned to her difficult task.

At last she managed to pen a few lines. The letter was inadequate at best, for how could she reveal to him that she had come to love him, that he had taught her how to trust in others? It was an impossibility. But she thought it conveyed her polite regard, her sincere recognition of his willingness to sacrifice on her behalf.

Next she penned a heartfelt letter of appreciation to Lady Harford. She wrote that the threat of marriage to Ernest had now disappeared, what with the elopement of the Toad and the Mouse, who really was a tiger in disguise, and now Lord Harford was free. She added a line regarding the removal of

Aunt Winthrop to the dower house at Everton Hall. Lady Harford would have a fair idea how ill the Crow would receive such instructions.

Penelope smiled wistfully as she then wrote an additional message to Lady Charis, explaining that with the peril of marriage to Ernest gone, she would return to Fountains. While there might possibly be another Winthrop cousin that Penelope had never heard about, she felt confident her solicitor and guardian would not compel her to marry if she chose to remain single. The instructions regarding the future disposal of her estate ought to cover everything. She begged Lady Charis to ask Letty to attend her, for the honeymooners should be home by then.

The task completed, Penelope returned to her room. It had been stripped bare of all her belongings. How swiftly Betsy had worked.

Glancing at her timepiece, Penelope noted that she had another hour before the post chaise arrived.

The potboy and a lad from the house next door carried her trunks to the entryway. Penelope decided to explain to Mrs Flint that she had elected to be married from her home chapel. She felt quite certain that the good housekeeper would think it romantic and nothing unusual.

When the chaise arrived, she handed the three letters, carefully folded and sealed with some of Letty's colorful wax, to Mrs Flint. 'Please see that these are delivered for me. There is no rush; tomorrow would be ample time.'

Being of the opinion that any mail ought to be promptly on its way, Mrs Flint merely nodded, then waved farewell to the young lady she quite liked. Wiping a tear from her eye, she commanded Rose to deliver the letters immediately to the houses not far away.

Rose took a pleased breath and, pausing long enough to grab a cloak from a peg in the back hall, dashed off in the proper direction.

⋆ ⋆ ⋆

Penelope found the post chaise acceptable, although she thought that changing carriages at each posting stage to be an annoyance. Had she a coach of her own, this would have been avoided. Still, it was far more acceptable than to travel by the stage or the mail coach.

Betsy sat on the far side, watching out the window with rounded eyes as the miles whizzed by at the great speed of seven miles per hour. Penelope leaned back against the squabs, wondering if the new greenhouse and herbs could possibly begin to compensate for what she had lost.

Some miles out of London they paused for a change of horses. Penelope decided to walk about, sending Betsy off for some buns and lemonade. The bright yellow post chaise stood out among the more sedate vehicles at the posting inn. Penelope didn't claim to be an expert, but she thought the yellow chaise ill-designed, not as well-balanced as the others around it. But then, she was no authority.

Betsy returned with refreshments about the time the driver informed her they were ready to be off again. She directed Betsy to cork the bottle of lemonade and take it with them. Rather than delay eating, she took her bun and returned to the chaise. She wished to arrive at Fountains as soon as possible.

They were well along the Deptford Road when she became aware of an approaching vehicle. There was nothing untoward about this, for there had been any number of coaches on the road today. A glance out of the window revealed a tollgate neared, so Penelope called out to the driver to let the other vehicle pass. She wanted no chance of an accident.

Her driver had ideas of his own, unfortunately. The coming carriage challenged his skills, and he took umbrage at the very thought he might be bested. The horses were lightly touched with the flick of his whip, and they surged forward.

Penelope fell back into the corner, grabbing for the strap, darting an alarmed look at Betsy. The abigail seemed about to swoon. Concern for this possibility flew out the window when the post chaise began to wobble most frightfully.

'Oh, my lady,' Betsy moaned. 'I fear we are going to tip over.'

Penelope thought to assure her it was most unlikely, when the chaise bounced, tilted badly, then crashed to the ground with a horrible splintering of wood and frightened neighing of horses, mixed with the cries of anxious men. Betsy's screams were quite lost in the melee.

Penelope lay still for several minutes, assessing her personal injuries, which, thank the good Lord, appeared to be few. Her abigail had sustained a nasty wound on her forehead. She had collapsed in a heap, and now lay huddled against the side of the chaise, quite fainted away.

Looking up, Penelope could see bits of blue with scraps of clouds scudding by. She wondered when and if someone would come to her rescue, when a head appeared at the window.

'Penny, dash it all, if you aren't the most totty-headed female I ever knew!' Exasperation rang from every syllable.

She tried to move, and cried out in pain. Her chest, the ribs, most likely, hurt like the very devil. A moan escaped her as she sank back, unable to rise and thus be pulled to freedom. The blue sky faded as the world disappeared from her consciousness. For the second time in her life, she fainted away.

Sometime later she awoke, feeling disoriented. She could hear the ripple of a stream somewhere nearby, and she thought she must be settled beneath a tree, for over her head leafy boughs tossed in the breeze. The lilting song of a number of birds serenaded her. Far away she could hear angry voices and horses in distress. She moved her head and spotted Betsy not too far away, close by another tree, still unconscious.

Of her rescuer there was no sight.

Penelope closed her eyes, furious at the upset in her plans, and wondering what that man was doing chasing after her in such a nonsensical manner. How had he known she was gone? Hearing a rustle in the grasses, she raised her eyelids to find him scrunching down at her side. Attack seemed the best defense.

'Precisely what are you doing here, sir?' she

said, surprised her voice seemed to be oddly weak instead of snapping.

'Fetching you back to London. I suppose I could have sued you for breach of promise, but I would rather have you.'

Knowing that to be all a hum, she merely shook her head. 'Rubbish.'

'Touching.' Then in a strained voice he added, 'How do you feel?' His hand reached out to stroke a wayward curl from her forehead.

'I am alive, but I ache in every muscle and a few bones as well,' Penelope replied, trying for a bit of humor. She shifted, and winced at the pain in her chest.

'I dare not take you back until you are somewhat better,' he mused aloud.

'You shan't take me back. I am on my way to Fountains.'

'Ah, no: *were* on your way to Fountains. My dear girl, have you maggots in your head? There is to be a wedding. In spite of that stupid letter you brought to your solicitor, it has been agreed that you and I are to proceed with our marriage.'

'But we cannot,' she cried in anguish. 'I refuse to let you sacrifice yourself. Unless,' she said, a sudden thought popping into her head, 'you are so far in Dun territory that you desperately need the money. In which case I will gladly give you all you require.'

A look of sheer exasperation crossed his face; then he bent over her prone form, his look intent.

'Listen to me very carefully, my love. I do not need your money.' At her sigh of relief, he smiled a trifle grimly. 'In matter of fact, I have never needed your money. As near as I can piece it together, you overheard something to do with a bet I had lost, but it was a mere trifle, an exchange of money between Stephen and me that occurs all too frequently. I next won a sizable amount from him, thanks to you. But my loss had scarcely put a dent in the Harford estate funds. I do not wager unless I can easily afford to lose the sum.'

She struggled to sit, and sank back against the ground in pain, her face a frozen mask.

'Nevertheless,' she said through gritted teeth, 'there is no point to our marriage. Ernest eloped with Carola Dunston, who has turned into a tiger.'

'I know,' he said in an effort to stop her from talking. 'However, my little heart, there is still the matter of our betrothal.'

'No need,' she muttered, fading rapidly, her lashes fluttering down to rest, utterly exhausted.

He watched, frustrated, as she slipped into unconsciousness once again. He turned with thankfulness at the sight of a doctor making his way along the road, then across to the grassy spot where Harford had carried Penelope.

Although reluctant at first, once he was assured that Harford and the injured woman were married, the doctor proceeded without shooing Harford away. He needed assistance, and the abigail was no help. Penelope's traveling pelisse was hastily slipped off and the doctor examined her as best he could, given the primitive conditions.

'Good thing she had a gown that buttoned in front and her stays left off for comfort while she traveled,' he muttered. 'Those ribs needed to be bound up, and make no mistake, she'll be as sore as can be for a few days, at the very least.'

Harford was still trying to come to terms with the sight of his beloved arrayed in nothing from the waist up. Never had he seen such exquisite white skin, petal soft and begging to be caressed. He assisted the doctor, lifting Penny so he might wrap her up. The feel of her slight body would ever remain with him. He fully intended to have the right of access, and not before too long.

'Will I be able to return her to London?'

'Reckon she can travel that far, like as not,' declared the blunt-spoken countryman. 'Slip her a bit of sleeping potion and she'll not know a thing until you get her into bed.'

The words brought a most agreeable image to Harford's mind and he struggled with those rather improper thoughts while transporting Penny to his carriage. Once the abigail was seen to, the baggage transferred, and the post chaise paid off, the Harford traveling carriage headed for London.

The bottle of lemonade produced by the injured Betsy enabled him to offer Penny a generous sip, well-doctored, the next time she came to. She grimaced at the horrid taste, but was far too thirsty to quibble about it. Within minutes she had sunk into a blessedly drugged sleep, unmindful of the jarring along the road or the transfer from coach to Harford House once they reached London.

She had nestled in Harford's arms while he studied her face, memorizing every line, the way her long lashes fanned over her pale cheeks, the tiny mole he discovered near one ear. Never again would she travel without his presence.

Betsy was taken away by the housekeeper.

Lady Harford fluttered about as Jonathan carried Penny up the stairs, horrified by the sight of her torn gown, her ashen face, and the grim set of Jonathan's mouth.

'I knew you were making a mistake not to

tell her everything,' she scolded softly.

'Mother,' he ground out, his patience at the utter limit by this point.

'Well, and so I did, dear boy.' She watched as he gently placed Penelope on the bed in the best guest chamber. Then she shooed him out the door while she directed her abigail in undressing Penny and getting her beneath the covers.

Jonathan stood in the hall for a moment, wondering what his mother would say if she but knew all the circumstances of the accident. It had been partly his fault. Had he not been so blasted intent on catching up with her, that fool driver of her post chaise might not have had the stupid notion to race him to the next gate.

Weighed down with this knowledge, not to mention the vision of her slim body before it was bound tightly in a bandage, he made his way to the drawing room. He suspected that his mother would return here once she had seen to Penny.

He had worn a path in the carpet when he heard the sound of footsteps in the hall.

His mother entered, her face concerned but not overly worried. 'I believe she will do well enough. Blaine says she has seen worse. Indeed, other than those bruised ribs you mentioned, there seem to be no further serious injuries. A few scratches and black-and-blue marks. Poor darling.'

Since Blaine had attended every injury and illness in the family in addition to being his mother's competent abigail for many years, Harford felt he might relax a trifle.

He leaned against the fireplace mantel, his face a study in reflective thought. 'I wish I could understand why she thought it so necessary to leave London. Or for that matter, why she is so insistent we not wed. She muttered something about my not making such a sacrifice. What gave her such a fool idea as that?'

The wry look from his mother was followed by her assessment. 'I do believe you made a hash of the affair.'

'She seemed very receptive.'

'What happened, then?'

'I admit I hadn't had a chance to tell her about the money, but that didn't seem to bother her nearly as much as I thought. She insisted that if I needed the blunt, she'd give me what I require. Dashed odd thing to do if she was angry with me.'

The countess settled on her favorite chair while inspecting her dearest son. For all that he was the head of the Harford family and had accepted his responsibilities at an early age, there was at times an endearingly boyish air about him. Behind that fashionable and dashing facade, that whimsical sense of humor, existed the trustworthy gentleman, the rock-solid honorable person she knew deserved the woman he loved.

'Did you tell her that you loved her?' she probed.

It was the sort of question mothers were not supposed to ask, and he gave it the expected masculine response.

'She knew.'

'Lovely. By your kind words and gestures, I fancy. You disappoint me, dear boy. I trust you will not make a second mistake.' She rose and slipped from the room to consult with the cook regarding a diet for the invalid when she eventually regained consciousness.

Jonathan decided he had best return to his house to clean up, then come back later on, when it was more likely that Penny would be awake. They needed to talk, something she did all too well — without revealing a thing.

Darling clucked with sympathy when he heard of the disaster. 'Those post chaises are a poor design, my lord,' he declared. 'Too tippy by half.'

Jonathan absently agreed with him as he ducked into the library to check his desk for the letter he had discovered in a book that had been one of his father's favorites. He thought his mother might be pleased to know how much it had meant to her husband, for he had tucked it in a book of poetry, never parting with it.

The letter was where he had left it. He took it along with him while he went up to change his clothes. In record time he came pounding down the stairs, then out to where his carriage awaited him. Darling saw him off, standing at the door with worried eyes as his master tore off down the street.

At Harford House Jonathan encountered a most unearthly silence. Before the house, straw had been placed on the cobbles to cut the noise from passing carriages, a thing normally done in serious illness or childbirth. Rushing up the stairs, he charged into the drawing room, his eyes frantic with worry.

Charis and David looked up to greet him from where they sat on a sofa across the room, discussing their plans.

'Any change?' Jonathan barked, not bothering to explain, and fearing the worst.

'Mother said she seems to be coming to now.' Charis gave her brother a look of concern. In all her life she could not recall seeing him so wild-eyed.

'Good.' He whirled about and dashed up the next flight of stairs and down to the best guest chamber, where he rapped on the door before entering.

Penelope gave him a narrow look, looking pale and delicate in the vast bed. 'You might have waited for a reply.' Her voice, though faint, held its normal asperity.

'I might. Hardly need to at this point. We shall be married shortly and then I shall have the right to enter as I please.' He slowly grinned as he studied her face, taking note of the faint flush of color in her cheeks.

'I said there is no need for that.' She gave a fretful look about the pretty room, taking note of the pink-and-white-striped silk draping the tester on her bed, the same used for window draperies, and pink silk moire hung on the walls. An exquisite gilt looking glass hung over a cherrywood chest. It might be a beautiful room, but she didn't wish to be in it. 'You ought not be in here,' she reminded him.

'We need to talk, and I wished to see how you are.'

'Well, I have no wish to natter with you,' she sniped in a peevish tone, suspecting she sounded a trifle childish in her complaint.

'Why do you persist in saying we won't be married? I said it is the best thing to do. It has been announced,' he reminded her.

'Unannounce it,' she said, then sniffed back

a threatened tear. 'I fully intend to com-compensate you for all you have done for me since I came to London. If I had realized how painful it would be for you,' not to mention me, she added mentally, 'I'd have stayed at home. At least Ernest is no longer a threat to my peace. I believe I have you to thank for that, sir,' she admitted in all honesty, 'one way or another.'

'Penny,' he warned, moving closer until he stood at the side of her bed.

'I'll not have you making so great a sacrifice for me,' she said, tears at last creeping from beneath tightly closed lids. She turned her face away from him, hating him to see her weakness.

He longed to crush her in his arms, so he might reassure her of his love. He flexed his hands in frustration. 'Why do you say it is a sacrifice, my love? I look forward to our marriage with great eagerness.'

'Stop those lies,' she cried, outraged he could joke when she had read that letter, she *knew* of his true love.

He frowned at her words, then sat on the edge of her bed, heedless of any discomfort he might give her. 'Just what brought this on?' he demanded in that voice his servants knew would brook no refusal.

Penelope had no resistance to that tone in

her weakened state. She opened her eyes, tears clinging to her lashes as she glared at him. 'I did a most unladylike thing this morning. While I waited for you, I read a letter that was on your desk . . . a letter from one who obviously adores you and one you love in return.' She gave a woeful shake of her head. 'I could not stand between you and such a wonderful love, Jonathan. Please understand, I wish you only the best. Leave me. Go to the one you love.'

The eyes she tightly shut now flashed open at his shout of outrage.

Ignoring her bruised ribs, Jonathan as gently as possible placed an arm on either side of her, then stared intently into the bluest, truest eyes he had ever seen. 'That letter was to my father, who was at the time the earl, if you stop to think about it. It was written by my mother. I found it in a book of poetry in which I had foolishly hoped to find a love poem to quote to you. I have the letter with me, for I thought my mother would like to keep it.'

'Oh,' Penny said in a whispery voice, not daring to meet those blazing black eyes staring down at her. Which was a pity, for those eyes were filled with an infinite love and great tenderness. However, she couldn't evade the loving kiss that shortly touched her lips.

When at last he allowed her to catch a breath, one he needed as well, he inquired in a deceptively gentle tone, 'Is that all you have to say, wife-to-be?'

'I am sorry . . . for everything, the trouble, the trip, all — ' Her words were cut off when he continued where he left off.

A scandalized gasp halted what might have been a painful seduction, given the state of her poor ribs.

Jonathan lifted himself from his captive sweetheart to meet his mother's eyes. Reaching into his pocket, he pulled out the letter, handing it to her with a half-smile. 'Read it.'

'Goodness, wherever did you find this?' she exclaimed, forgetting all about the scolding she had intended. She skimmed the page, looking up to give them a misty smile.

Jonathan watched her drift from the guest chamber, then turned again to his love. 'As I was saying . . . ' and he bent his head to draw closer, fully intending to make the most of his opportunity.

'Stop! This does not mean we need to marry.'

'Oh, I believe it does. My mother might well broadcast our indiscretion to all the world and his wife, or at least to London.'

'Be serious.' She punched him lightly on

the arm, a feather-weight touch.

'I am, my sweet. I suspect it is you who have had a change of heart.'

'True,' she admitted. When she saw the look of pain in his eyes, she explained, 'I cannot marry for an estate, for money, for any reason save love.'

'Could you learn to love me, given time?' He anxiously surveyed her precious face, his inventive mind searching for all the possible ways he might use to convince her of his love, and to love him in return.

Quite confused, for this was not at all how the scene was supposed to go, she blurted out, 'But I do! Love you. Quite desperately, in fact.' Then she blushed a rosy pink and snapped her eyes closed again, utterly mortified at her boldness.

'Fine,' he said with satisfaction. 'For I believe I fell in love with you the day you barged into my home demanding that I help you. I suspect my heart has been yours from that day on.'

Blue eyes instantly looked back at him, a wondering look creeping across her face as she considered his words. Ignoring the discomfort, she shyly wove her arms about his neck, bringing his dear face close to hers.

'Show me.'

We do hope that you have enjoyed reading this large print book.

Did you know that all of our titles are available for purchase?

We publish a wide range of high quality large print books including:
Romances, Mysteries, Classics
General Fiction
Non Fiction and Westerns

Special interest titles available in large print are:
The Little Oxford Dictionary
Music Book
Song Book
Hymn Book
Service Book

Also available from us courtesy of Oxford University Press:
Young Readers' Dictionary
(large print edition)
Young Readers' Thesaurus
(large print edition)

For further information or a free brochure, please contact us at:

Other titles published by
The House of Ulverscroft:

DOUBLE DECEIT

Emily Hendrickson

Miss Caroline Beauchamp had accepted a very tricky task. She must seduce Hugh, Lord Stanhope, the handsome husband of her dearest friend, Mary. This was in order to break the hold that an infamous beauty had on the vulnerable viscount. But she also faced an even greater challenge — she had to bedazzle the most renowned rake in the realm, Lord Rutledge, to keep him from making Mary his latest conquest! Caroline knew as she began her juggling act of deception that letting down her guard would mean disaster. And falling in love would be even worse . . .

QUEEN OF THE MAY

Emily Hendrickson

Young Lady Samantha Mayne had no desire to be a proper lady. Let her cousin Emma dress in fashionable gowns and hunt a mate in the marriage mart; Samantha preferred to help with her brother's scientific experiments, and ride horses astride, not side-saddle. Then Samantha met Lord Charles Laverstock. Samantha had never imagined that there could be a man as handsome, and charming. Lord Charles also clearly could never be interested in a girl who broke every rule and scorned femininity. For Samantha, becoming a lady would be the hardest task — even if it was a labour of love.

THE GALLANT LORD IVES

Emily Hendrickson

Shy country girl Alissa Ffolkes prefers the company of her peregrine falcon and the comfort of sculpting to handsome London lords. With a failed Season behind her, Alissa remains at home, leaving her sisters Henrietta and Elizabeth to dazzle and charm the local beaux. Yet Alissa yearns for true love, and as she tends her herbs, she longs for a potion to help her impress her father's guest Christopher, Lord Ives. In Wiltshire to study Alissa's father's sheep, he has found far more. Drawn to Alissa's gentle beauty, can his love work a miracle to make Alissa bloom?

LADY SARA'S SCHEME

Emily Hendrickson

Lady Sara Harland was as sensible as she was beautiful. Since she had to have a husband, she decided to take her pick from a list of the choicest lords available. One name, however, she crossed off her list. Why even consider Myles Fenwick, the Earl of St Quinton, when other eligible lords were neither so arrogant, nor so shockingly libertine? Sara was sure she would easily ensnare a perfect mate whilst avoiding the infamous charm and insidious attractiveness of the earl. But though this level-headed young heiress had her mind made up, her heart had ideas of its own . . .

HIDDEN INHERITANCE

Emily Hendrickson

Beautiful Vanessa Tarleton accepts a position repairing tapestries for the Earl of Stone, knowing full well his reputation as a handsome rake. She had heard gossip about him during her London season, but when her father gambles everything away, she knows the offer is too good to reject. Nicholas, Lord Stone, faces his own dilemma. He must wed an heiress to restore his nearly bankrupt property and to keep a promise made to his grandfather — but is the beautiful and wealthy Mrs Hewit the right choice? Although forewarned about the dangerously attractive earl, is Vanessa forearmed to resist his charm?

501 502 503 504 505 506 507 508 509 510 511 512 513 514 515
516 517 518 519 520 521 522 523 524 525 526 527 528 529 530
531 532 533 534 535 536 537 538 539 540 541 542 543 544 545
546 547 548 549 550 551 552 553 554 555 556 557 558 559 560
561 562 563 564 565 566 567 568 569 570 571 572 573 574 575
576 577 578 579 580 581 582 583 584 585 586 587 588 589 590
591 592 593 594 595 596 597 598 599 600

601 602 603 604 605 606 607 608 609 610 611 612 613 614 615
616 617 618 619 620 621 622 623 624 625 626 627 628 629 630
631 632 633 634 635 636 637 638 639 640 641 642 643 644 645
646 647 648 649 650 651 652 653 654 655 656 657 658 659 660
661 662 663 664 665 666 667 668 669 670 671 672 673 674 675
676 677 678 679 680 681 682 683 684 685 686 687 688 689 690
691 692 693 694 695 696 697 698 699 700

701 702 703 704 705 706 707 708 709 710 711 712 713 714 715
716 717 718 719 720 721 722 723 724 725 726 727 728 729 730
731 732 733 734 735 736 737 738 739 740 741 742 743 744 745
746 747 748 749 750 751 752 753 754 755 756 757 758 759 760
761 762 763 764 765 766 767 768 769 770 771 772 773 774 775
776 777 778 779 780 781 782 783 784 785 786 787 788 789 790
791 792 793 794 795 796 797 798 799 800

801 802 803 804 805 806 807 808 809 810 811 812 813 814 815
816 817 818 819 820 821 822 823 824 825 826 827 828 829 830
831 832 833 834 835 836 837 838 839 840 841 842 843 844 845
846 847 848 849 850 851 852 853 854 855 856 857 858 859 860
861 862 863 864 865 866 867 868 869 870 871 872 873 874 875
876 877 878 879 880 881 882 883 884 885 886 887 888 889 890
891 892 893 894 895 896 897 898 899 900

901 902 903 904 905 906 907 908 909 910 911 912 913 914 915
916 917 918 919 920 921 922 923 924 925 926 927 928 929 930
931 932 933 934 935 936 937 938 939 940 941 942 943 944 945
946 947 948 949 950 951 952 953 954 955 956 957 958 959 960
961 962 963 964 965 966 967 968 969 970 971 972 973 974 975
976 977 978 979 980 981 982 983 984 985 986 987 988 989 990
991 992 993 994 995 996 997 998 999 1000